**Step into the sparkling wo**

'Lovely books filled with warm and likeable characters'
**Jill Mansell**

'Escapist and uplifting'
***Woman & Home***

'Deliciously entertaining'
**Liz Fenwick**

'The ultimate summer reading escape!'
***Yours Magazine***

'Enjoyable and uplifting'
**Jo Thomas**

'A feel-good read for summer'
***The Sun***

'Warm and funny and feel-good. The best sort of holiday read'
**Katie Fforde**

'Romantic and life-affirming'
***Woman's Weekly***

'Will make you laugh and cry'
**Miranda Dickinson**

**Phillipa Ashley** writes warm, funny romantic fiction for a variety of world-famous international publishers.

After studying English at Oxford, she worked as a copywriter and journalist. Her first novel, *Decent Exposure*, won the RNA New Writers Award and was made into a TV movie called *12 Men of Christmas* starring Kristin Chenoweth and Josh Hopkins. As Pippa Croft, she also wrote the Oxford Blue series – *The First Time We Met*, *The Second Time I Saw You* and *Third Time Lucky*.

Phillipa lives in a Staffordshire village and has an engineer husband and scientist daughter who indulge her arty whims. She runs a holiday-let business in the Lake District, but a big part of her heart belongs to Cornwall. She visits the county several times a year for 'research purposes', an arduous task that involves sampling cream teas, swimming in wild Cornish coves and following actors around film shoots in a campervan. Her hobbies include watching *Poldark*, Earl Grey tea, Prosecco-tasting and falling off surfboards in front of the RNLI lifeguards.

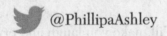 @PhillipaAshley

# *It Should Have Been Me*

## Phillipa Ashley

**REVIEW**

First published in 2009 by Little Black Dress
An imprint of HEADLINE PUBLISHING GROUP

This paperback edition published in 2022 by Headline Review
An imprint of HEADLINE PUBLISHING GROUP

Cataloguing in Publication Data is available from the British Library

Paperback ISBN 978 1 0354 0139 0

Typeset in Transitional 511 BT by Avon DataSet Ltd, Alcester,
Warwickshire

Printed and bound in Great Britain by Clays Ltd, Elcograf S.p.A.

HEADLINE PUBLISHING GROUP
An Hachette UK Company
Carmelite House
50 Victoria Embankment
London EC4Y 0DZ

www.headline.co.uk
www.hachette.co.uk

For Barbara, Charles and Smudge

# Acknowledgements

I had a fantastic time doing research for this book, even if only some of it made it into the final version. So to the doctors, medical students, RAF SAR personnel, camper van owners, actors, farmers, teachers and others who answered my questions: thank you. Any mistakes are definitely all mine!

In particular I have to mention Dr Tim Sowton, Dr-to-be Alex Brooks-Moizer, Moira Briggs, Sgt Matt Weetman, Sally Lawton, Anna (Jancis), Christine Cawson, Adrian Barber and Pete O'Connor from O'Connors Campers. Taking the amazing 'Bill' to North Devon in a chilly Easter was an experience I'll never forget. I'd also like to thank Janice Hume, Nell Dixon, Rosy Thornton, Julie Haggar and my friends at C19 for their support.

Mega thanks to Claire, Cat and Sara at LBD for keeping me on the straight and narrow and to Broo Doherty for keeping me writing, come what may.

Finally to Mum, Dad, John and Charlotte who gave me tea, sympathy and advice on fights in nightclubs. ILY.

# Chapter One

Carrie Brownhill was standing outside the stage door of the Starlight Theatre wondering how to respond to her friend's outrageous comment.

'So. What would you actually do if Huw had an affair?' Rowena asked again.

Carrie paused longer than she should have done before answering, partly because her teeth were chattering with the cold but also because the prospect of her fiancé, Huw, shagging another woman was something she'd never even dreamed of. 'You mean if I actually *caught* him with someone else?' she said.

'Well, I don't mean in the act, with his pants round his ankles,' said Rowena, in between puffs on her cigarette. 'I just wondered what you'd do if you found out he was dipping his wick on the other side of the fence.'

'Oh, blimey. I don't know,' said Carrie, stamping her feet to keep warm. It wasn't surprising she was freezing, because (a) it was February, and (b) she and Rowena were dressed like fifties tarts. They were taking a break from a dress rehearsal for the local drama society's production of *Grease*. One of the Pink Ladies had set fire to her wig which had triggered the smoke alarms and sent the director into a hissy fit. It had also given Rowena the chance for a sneaky fag.

'Now come on, honey. Would you be calm and dignified or turn into the vengeful bitch from hell?' drawled Rowena, getting into the part of her character, Rizzo, but managing to sound more like Marge Simpson.

'Oh, calm and dignified, of course,' simpered Carrie, pretending to be Sandy.

Rowena took a long, slow drag on her ciggie, then blew out a smoke ring. 'Bull *shit*, honey.'

'Okay. Maybe you're right. If I caught Huw with another woman, I'd probably go totally berserk and wreak vengeance on him.'

'What? Pour paint stripper over his car?' said Rowena, flicking her ash into a tub of winter pansies.

Carrie feigned horror. 'The Range Rover? My God, no. I love that car. It's my baby. I couldn't hurt it.'

'Cut up all his clothes, then?'

Carrie thought for a moment, then felt her mouth stretch in a smile of glee. 'No. Way too clichéd. I'd make the punishment fit the crime. Hit him where it really hurts.'

'You don't mean you'd do a Bobbitt?' gasped Rowena.

'Oh, much worse. I'd pour sugar in the fuel tank of his Massey Ferguson.'

'His *what*?'

'His Massey Ferguson. It's his new tractor. He adores it. He said he'd like to shag me in it.'

'You farming types are all pervs,' declared Rowena, throwing her fag end on to the flagstones and grinding it out with her foot. 'Ow. Buggering hell. I've just burnt my bloody foot! These ballet pumps are as old as the hills.'

Carrie laughed as Rowena hopped about cursing cheerfully. The two of them had been friends since uni, where they'd both studied English and Drama. Now they were stalwarts of the local drama society in Packley, the Oxfordshire village where they both lived. Carrie had met Huw at university too, and they'd been together ever since. She'd once dreamed of appearing in the West End but had ended up helping him run his farm business instead. It was a full-time job just keeping up with all the admin while he managed the dairy herd and small business units at the farm. But if she ever had a pang of regret about not making it in professional theatre, she felt the rest of her life more than made up for it. She knew she'd never have to sabotage Huw Brigstocke's beloved tractor, slash his clothes or wreak vengeance on him. In two weeks' time, she and Huw were getting married at Packley church. Everyone was coming. The drama society, the Young Farmers, their university friends, at least half the village – it felt like half the county in fact, because Huw's mother knew absolutely *everyone*.

'Carrie? Rowena?' A vision in pink peeped nervously round the door of the theatre.

'Out here, Hayley,' said Carrie.

'I just came to warn you that we're ready to start again and Gina's been looking for you. She's already ballistic that I set off the fire alarm,' said Hayley, shivering in her Pink Ladies outfit.

'Gina is the love child of Simon Cowell and Attila the Hun,' declared Carrie, picturing the show's director searching the theatre for her and Rowena like a headmistress looking for girls smoking in the bogs. 'Can't a leading lady have some privileges? Tell her I'm just

taking a call from Hollywood. Tell her,' she said dramatically, 'that George Clooney has asked me to play the part
of Scarlett O'Hara in his new remake of *Gone with the
Wind*.'

Rowena let out a giggle.

'It's okay, Hayley. I'm coming,' said Carrie, finally
taking pity on Hayley, who was so naïve she might
actually tell Gina what Carrie had said.

'I expect Gina will be on the warpath for the rest of the
night now because we've sloped off,' grumbled Rowena.

Carrie flounced towards the door, flinging back her
hair like Scarlett would have done. 'Frankly, darling, I
don't give a toss!'

A week later, Carrie was belting out the show's finale to a
packed theatre.

'*You're the one that I want . . .*'

'More! More! More!' chanted the audience.

Carrie went for the big one. '*The one that I waa-nnt!*'

The audience leapt to their feet, stamping the floor
and almost shaking the roof off the theatre.

'Listen to that,' hissed Rowena as they made their
bows. 'Don't you just bloody love it!'

Carrie felt like a giant pink bubblegum about to pop
with joy. Every night had been a sell-out and a roaring
success, and if her voice was on its last legs, she didn't
care. They might not be in the West End, they might only
be amateurs, but they were bloody good ones. The
curtain dropped and the girls chattered excitedly as they
dashed off stage.

'Let's get changed and get to the bar. I need an
urgent dose of spritzer and Huw can pay for it. I tried to

spot him in the audience but he must have been right at the back.'

'Knowing Huw, I'll bet he's waiting now, with one of those totally clichéd bouquets he's always sending you,' said Rowena.

Carrie sighed dramatically. 'I just hope he's bought red roses this time. Yellow ones are so-ooo passé, darling.'

She wouldn't really mind if they were yellow roses, or even a bunch of dandelions. All she wanted was to see Huw, who had promised to be at her final performance even if it did mean calling in en route from his stag weekend. In fact, she wouldn't mind if he turned up half naked with a ball and chain round his ankle, just as long as he'd made the show somehow. This had been her final performance as Carrie Brownhill; the next programme would have her new name in it: Carrie Brigstocke. Tonight was special in so many ways; she couldn't wait to hear what he'd thought of her performance.

'I hope *Oxfordshire Life* send a reporter to the wedding,' she said.

Rowena mumbled a reply through a face full of cleansing cream. 'I should think it will be picked up by the nationals. You might end up in *Hello!*.'

'Now you're taking the piss, Rowena,' laughed Carrie.

'Would I?'

'Yes, you would.'

Ten minutes later, Rowena was handing over a drink as Carrie scanned the packed bar for Huw's unmistakable profile. He was normally easy to spot, even in a crowded room. Six foot five in his stockinged feet, a shock of thick sandy hair and shoulders like Hercules. Stooping slightly because he was self-conscious, of course.

That was what she'd first fancied about him when they'd met at their university freshers' disco: that combination of capable shoulders and self-deprecation. She never could resist a man who didn't know how sexy he was. Flashy blokes turned her right off, but Huw, who'd braved the laughter of the entire rugby club to ask her to dance, had won her heart straightaway. She still remembered their first shag in his tiny student room, the ancient water pipes creaking and the sound of the rugby club belting out 'Roll Me Over in the Clover' from the students' union.

Over by the bar, she caught sight of Rowena batting her eyelashes at a strange man with a fake tan and an outrageous toupee. Pulling her mobile from her handbag, Carrie checked the screen. No message from Huw. Yet he'd promised faithfully to be here tonight. He always managed to make her last nights, had never missed one except for the time Millicent had had a Caesarean and he'd had to stay with the vet. Carrie hadn't really minded; the herd came first, and anyway she'd been crap that evening.

Rowena returned. 'Who's your friend Wiggy?'

'Oh, just one of my many fans. He said he thought I'd put in a performance of poignancy and vitality, a combination he'd rarely seen in amateur theatre.'

'Bloody hell. Does he want to get your knickers off?'

Rowena frowned, seemed almost offended but then grinned and declared, 'Doesn't everyone, darling? Has Lover Boy phoned yet?'

Carrie was puzzled at the sudden change of subject but dismissed it. Everyone was tired and overemotional. She shook her head. 'No. Not even a text.'

'Maybe he's decided to stop off at the Red Lion for a nightcap on his way home from London.'

'He promised he'd be here for the play. I wouldn't mind but he's already had a two-night bender in London with his mates. How long should a stag party last?'

'Depends who he's met,' said Rowena.

Carrie snorted. 'How can he have met anyone?'

'Well, I know the concept is hard to grasp, but you never know, he could have decided to grab his last chance to escape and run off with a Serbian lap dancer.' Rowena's eyes glinted wickedly.

Carrie laughed. 'Well, if he has run away, I hope she likes his cold feet in bed.'

All around them hugging and kissing was breaking out like the plague, a sure sign that the after-show party was breaking up.

'Look, Huw's obviously not coming, so I'm going home,' sighed Carrie, fishing for her car keys from the depths of her bag. 'You don't think anything could have happened to him, do you? He is with that bunch of Young Farmers and some of his rugby club mates. He could have been stripped naked and chained to a statue.'

Rowena rolled her eyes skywards. 'There is no way that Huw has got involved in anything like that. He's far too responsible. I'm sure he'll be waiting and desperate to make it up to you, if you know what I mean.'

Rowena was right, thought Carrie. After ten years together, she ought to know Huw well enough. In fact, she thought, as she drove home from the theatre towards Packley Farm, she had a pretty good idea exactly what he'd be doing right now. He'd be sitting by the fire with a large bunch of flowers and an apology. All of which she would graciously accept – after she'd made him suffer just enough.

Relief swept through her as she saw his Range Rover parked in its usual place in the farmyard. At least he'd made it home. There were no lights on in the farmhouse; maybe he'd gone straight up and was waiting for her in bed. Pushing open the front door with her bottom, she fumbled for the light switch.

'Oh!'

Fur brushed her legs. She sighed in relief as the farm cat wound his way round her ankles.

'Hello, Macavity,' she laughed as the cat rubbed his warm body against her calves with a welcoming *miaow*.

Then Huw's voice cut through the gloom. 'Carrie? Is that you?'

'That's a very clever trick, Macavity. You sound just like my fiancé,' Carrie joked before flicking the light switch. Huw was sitting by the hearth, one arm hanging over the edge of the chair, the other clutching a tumbler of whisky. 'Hello. Have we had a power cut?' she said, depositing her stuff on the tiled floor.

'No.'

'Then why were you sitting in the dark?'

He downed the rest of his whisky before answering. 'Dunno. Guess I just felt like it.'

'You just *felt* like it?'

Carrie crossed the kitchen. Her skin prickled when she saw him close up. There were dark shadows under his eyes, which also had a glazed look in them. He stank of whisky too; she could see the almost empty bottle at the side of his chair.

'I was upset that you missed the play, but there's no

need to hit the bottle,' she said lightly. 'I'm not going to start hurling china at you. You missed a treat. I was great, you know. Everyone said so . . .'

'I'm sure you were. You always are,' he said. Picking up the bottle, he sloshed whisky into the glass, spilling half of it on his trousers. He was completely plastered. She swallowed down a rising feeling of unease. 'How much have you had?' she asked.

'Enough. So what? It was my stag weekend.'

She flinched. It wasn't like him to be whiny either. She put it down to too much booze and too little sleep.

'Sounds like you've had quite a time, but I was expecting you at the play. Where've you been?'

He shrugged. 'Just driving about.'

Carrie frowned. Huw did not drink and drive. Huw didn't even break the speed limit. Huw played by the rules, unless it was on the rugby pitch. 'You were driving about pissed?' she said, unable to believe it.

He took a slug of the whisky and wiped his mouth with his hand. 'No. I drove first. Then I got pissed. Do you have a problem with that?'

The edge of sarcasm in his voice made her hackles rise. This wasn't the man she'd known for the past ten years, and it definitely wasn't the one she was looking forward to marrying in two weeks' time. This wasn't her Huw. She tried to stay calm, hoping he'd cool down and sober up.

'I don't have a problem with you drinking on your stag weekend, but I do have a problem with you acting like this. I don't deserve it.'

He raised his glass and tilted it, peering at the liquid as if he didn't want to meet her eye. Then he shrugged as if to say he didn't care what she thought or deserved. Carrie began to simmer. She'd had enough.

'Look, Huw. If you've had a row with some of your mates over bloody rugby or a poker match or something – or you've just got pissed off with each other – I don't mind. But I won't have you thundering home in this state and taking things out on me. I'm not sure how much whisky you've had, but I think it's enough—'

'Can't you just *shut up*?'

Her mouth fell open. This wasn't the gentle, placid giant she loved, but an angry bull of a man. She was shaking but she stood her ground, wound her five foot two frame up and said, 'Shut up? I asked you a perfectly reasonable question. Just because you've fallen out with the tribe, don't blame me.'

His knuckles whitened round his glass. He glared at her. She was angry herself and determined to face him down, because what he was doing was so unfair. Missing her last night, coming home pissed and behaving like a total shit.

'I just won't be treated like this, Huw. I won't . . .'

'Can't you see how hard this is for me?' he said softly.

Her heart started ricocheting madly. She knew something was very wrong. 'Hard for you? What do you mean?'

He was staring down at his glass again, swirling the whisky round in circles. 'I've been sitting here for hours wondering how I was going to do this, but it's no good,' he said.

She felt a cold sweat breaking out on the small of her back. 'Huw, what are you talking about? I don't understand you.'

'I don't really understand myself, Carrie, but I do know there's something I need to tell you.'

'Like what? Has your mother ordered the wrong flowers? Has the cake company gone bust?' She tried one last stab at humour, pretending that he was only joking, that he wasn't going to say something terrible, but he shook his head.

'It's been tearing me up for weeks, Carrie. I thought the stag weekend would help – make me realise that this was what I wanted, that I'd be fine once all this wedding shit was over, but it's no good. I can't do this to me, and certainly not to you, love. God knows I've tried, but I just can't do it. Carrie, I can't marry you.'

# Chapter Two

Four months later, the sun was hot on Matt Landor's back as he glared down at his boss's face. The two of them were standing on the wooden veranda of the medical station, sheltering from the mid-morning sun. Dr Shelly Cabot was glaring back at him, arms folded, and Matt was trying desperately hard not to smile. If he did, she might think he wasn't serious, and he'd never been more serious about anything in his life.

'It's not that bad, Matt. You'll be back here before you know it,' she said, in the voice she often used before inflicting major pain on one of their patients.

'It would be so much better if I didn't go at all,' he said, shifting position so she had to blink against the sun to answer him.

'We've talked about this. You need to get out of Tuman and go home to England. Drink tea. Play cricket . . .' she said.

'Nice try, Shelly, but there's a problem with that. I don't drink bloody tea and cricket bores the crap out of me.'

Shelly let out an exasperated gasp. 'Matt, you know damn well what I mean. Go and do whatever the hell you Brits do. Get pissed and wreck a bar if you like. Just take a break. A *proper* break. For God's sake, you could even try talking to someone.'

That last piece of advice had Matt snorting in derision, but Shelly's smile faded and her eyes hardened. 'You've been here nearly a year and you're overdue some decent leave. Even if you hadn't been involved in the accident I'd still have expected you to go back home for a few weeks. After what's happened it's an order, and if you don't do as I say, so help me, I won't have you back at all.'

Ah, the accident. He'd known she'd bring that up sooner or later. It had been four weeks since it happened and he admitted he'd been shaken up by it . . . *more than shaken, mate*, a voice whispered in his head. He balled his hands into fists as he felt the tremor invade them, but finally let a smile touch his lips.

'Shelly, has anyone told you how sexy you look when you're pissed off?'

Her mouth opened in an 'o'. 'You cheeky sexist basta—'

'Shhh. The children are listening.'

On cue, a gaggle of kids burst out of the entrance to the medical station, swarming around them and dancing in excitement.

'Dr Matt! Are you going?' a boy shouted.

'When are you coming back?'

A small girl slipped her hand in his, curling her warm fingers around his. 'Why are you going away?' she said, gazing up into his face.

Matt held his breath. He couldn't use a child to score points over Shelly, no matter how wrong he thought she was in sending him back to the UK; no matter how much doctors were needed in the remote South Pacific jungle community or how much he wanted to stay. He smiled down at the little girl, who was now twisting the hem of her skirt round and round in her hands.

'Do you have to go away?' she said.

He squatted down on the veranda so he could be at her level. 'For a little while, but I'll be back very soon,' he answered, laying emphasis on the *soon*, knowing Shelly was listening to his every word and would understand him perfectly.

'Good,' said the girl. Satisfied, she let go of his hand and skipped off down the steps towards the stilted houses fringing the river.

'Kids, can you let me say goodbye to Matt properly, please?' called Shelly.

Laughing, the children raced off, leaving Matt and Shelly alone again. He could feel the sweat pouring down his back, his shirt sticking to him. Above them the sun, white and blinding, beat down like a furnace but the fierce heat felt kind on his skin. It was natural. It reminded him of where he belonged.

Leaning on the veranda rail, he looked out over the clearing, the village and the river to the lush jungle that stretched endlessly all around.

'If you care about them, go home and take a break,' said Shelly as the children piled into canoes at the water's edge, laughing and squealing with glee.

'That's emotional blackmail.'

'That you didn't use on me when you had the chance just then. And that's because you're not the stubborn bastard you like us to think.'

Matt kept his eyes forward. 'Well, thanks for your support, Dr Cabot.'

'And thank you for your cooperation, Dr Landor. Now, your carriage awaits.'

She nodded at the rusty Jeep idling on the muddy red track that led from the medical centre to the tiny airstrip twenty miles away. It was the only way out of the village, other than by canoe or on foot; the only route to reach patients in the outlying communities and the only way home.

'You know this is ridiculous. You're desperate for medics and you send one of your most experienced back home,' he said as they walked down the steps to the track.

Standing on tiptoe, Shelly brushed his cheek with her lips. 'We can manage without you for a while, and despite what you think, you're not the only shit-hot doctor in Tuman.'

'I never said I was,' he growled.

'Really? You could have fooled me, the way you've been behaving, as if you want to take on the world single handed. Jeez, you almost killed yourself.'

'I'm fine. It wasn't me that got hurt, remember?' he said, trying to banish the memory of the accident, the smell of burning rubber, of spilled diesel, the panic that had threatened to overwhelm him, the sight of his friend Aidan bleeding and unconscious in the wreckage.

'Are you okay, Matt?'

Shelly touched his arm and Matt flinched.

'You know damn well I am.'

Shaking her head, she called to the driver of the Jeep, 'Dr Landor is ready to leave now.' She turned back to Matt. 'Have a good trip. I'll see you in the autumn, *if* you behave back in England,' she said, kissing him briefly. Then she was walking back towards the wooden veranda

of the medical station, and he was turning his back and
trudging towards the Jeep with all the enthusiasm of a
man heading for the tumbril that would take him to the
guillotine. Ahead of him lay a two-hour road trip to
the airstrip, a hop on a Cessna to the island's main airport
and a long, tedious flight to London.

Stretching out like a sluggish brown river lay four
months of enforced rest and recuperation in England.
Four months if he was lucky and could convince the
powers-that-be at the medical charity that he was fit to
come back and practise again. But there was one
consolation, if you could call it that. He'd get home just in
time for the wedding. An old university friend had invited
him to be an usher; not that Matt liked weddings –
usually he found catching malaria more fun – but it would
be good to meet up with an old mate after all these years.

Throwing his bags into the back of the Jeep, Matt
climbed in beside the driver and grunted a hello. The
engine started and he glanced round. Shelly was standing
outside the medical centre, her hand raised in farewell.
The kids were dancing round her, waving wildly. Then
the wooden huts became smaller, the river glittered one
last time and he was swallowed up by the jungle.

# Chapter Three

It was June, and the tiny spare bedroom at Rowena's cottage in Packley Village, Oxfordshire was sweltering. Through the floor Carrie could hear the juicer whirring in the kitchen, and behind it, a CD was belting out the soundtrack to *Ten Things I Hate About You*. Closing her eyes, Carrie tried her magic trick again: the one, where, if she wished very hard, the past four months vanished like a puff of smoke.

In some ways, she'd been lucky. That was what she'd tried to tell herself in the darkest moments, when she hadn't been howling with pain, or sitting piggy eyed with crying, using up tissues as though she was trying to kill off what was left of the world's forests. She'd been lucky because she had her shocked parents to cancel all the wedding arrangements and explain the situation to their relatives and friends. She'd been even luckier to have Rowena, who had offered her spare room the same night that Huw had left her. Two o'clock in the morning it had been when she'd finally finished rowing and shouting and pleading and crying with him.

Rowena had turned up at the farm in a taxi and taken Carrie to the cottage she owned in the village high street.

She had sat up all night with her, handing over vodka and tissues and unrelenting sympathy. She had been one of the few people who hadn't said: *'You'll get over it. You just need time.'* Or even: *'There are plenty more fish in the sea.'* Instead she had called Huw every name under the sun – and a few Carrie had never heard of – and offered to help her sabotage his tractor.

For a few weeks, a couple of months if they were feeling generous, people had expected Carrie to wallow in self-pity, to indulge her grief; but then, quicker than she could ever have imagined – not that she *had* ever imagined – they'd expected her to get over it and move on. So she'd become an expert at nodding in agreement when they offered their condolences, smiling bravely and tactfully changing the subject. Everyone agreed how well she'd coped. 'You've been so brave,' they said. 'You deserve a medal.' Because that was what the world expected her to do: be dignified, stoical and calm.

But they'd forgotten how good an actress she was.

The other Carrie – the one she wanted to be – had been a vengeful bitch from hell. In her dreams, that Carrie had maxed out Huw's credit card on male escorts, outrageous handbags and a full-page ad in the *Farming Times* calling him a heartless spineless shit. In her dreams, Huw was strapped naked in the stocks, while every woman in the world who'd ever had her heart split in two pelted him with rotten eggs and rancid diet shakes.

She opened her eyes to find a red-faced Rowena standing over her with a large wooden spoon. 'My God, what are you doing?'

'We are going into town,' Rowena declared solemnly.

'Okay, but what do you need the spoon for?'

'We're having a cooked brekkie first.'

'That would be the royal "we", then, would it?' asked Carrie over the top of the duvet.

'Don't be a plonker. Not just me. You're coming too.'

'And resistance is futile, I suppose?'

'Utterly,' said Rowena, before sweeping out of the bedroom like Queen Victoria.

Throwing off the duvet, Carrie shoved her feet into flip-flops and shuffled downstairs. In the kitchen, a pan of bacon and eggs was sizzling on the hob while Rowena filled two glasses with a gloop of indeterminate colour somewhere between puce and sludge.

'It's a smoothie. Acai berries, wheatgrass and pomegranate. Very healthy,' she said as Carrie leaned against the door frame, rubbing her eyes.

'But you smoke twenty a day, Rowena,' said Carrie, eyeing the smoothie with distaste.

'And this will redress the balance. All those antioxidants will cancel out my free radicals.' She handed over the gloop, smiling. 'Go on. Close your eyes and taste.'

Not wanting to upset her landlady, Carrie swallowed, hoping she wouldn't gag. She hadn't slept that well; she'd been lying awake wondering whether she dared visit Huw at the farm to sort out their entangled financial situation. 'Bloody hell!' she spluttered.

'Good, isn't it?' said Rowena proudly.

'Is that Jack Daniels I can taste?'

'I thought it would help it slip down.'

'At nine thirty?'

'Yes. Any objections?'

Carrie slurped again; this time it tasted even better. 'No. It's delicious. They should hand it out on prescription.'

20

Rowena grabbed her own glass and grinned broadly. 'That was the first part of your therapy.'

'And part two?' asked Carrie suspiciously, wondering if the smoothie was a sweetener for some nasty medicine. But Rowena just smiled and said: 'We're going shopping with Hayley, and then we're going for lunch at the Turf. Nelson's driving, so we can have a drink and you, my girl, are going to enjoy yourself if it kills you.'

# Chapter Four

Twenty miles from Packley in the centre of Oxford, Matt was lying in a strange bed in a strange room. Snoring gently beside him was a chartered accountant called Natasha Redmond whom Matt had known since his sixth-form days when they'd been at boarding school together. He'd bumped into her in one of the city centre pubs the previous evening.

After getting home from Tuman, he'd unpacked, showered, and then headed to the Lamb and Flag for something to eat. He'd sat at an outside table, nursing a pint of Morrells and pretending to read a biography of Nelson Mandela so he could avoid getting into conversation with anyone. However, for Natasha, he'd made an exception.

'Minty darling, is that you?' she'd shrieked, making him spill his pint and drop his book on the cobbles. He knew it was her without even looking; she'd used the bloody stupid nickname he'd had at school for a start. She was also purring; she did a lot of purring – that was what had attracted him to her in the first place when he'd met her many years before. Since then they'd got together occasionally when their paths had crossed.

So when he'd seen her in the beer garden, with a girlfriend who'd discreetly disappeared after half an hour, he'd known where the night – and morning – would end.

'Good morning, Dr Landor, are you feeling any better?' she asked throatily.

Matt ran his hand down the length of her thigh, feeling it smooth and warm beneath his fingers.

'What do you think?' he said, stroking her and feeling her satisfyingly wet.

Natasha gave a sigh of pleasure before closing her fingers around his. 'This is all very tempting, Minty, but I'm going to have to pass on this one. I have to get up. I have a wedding to go to, as do you, remember?'

Slipping out of bed, she padded towards the shower room, stark naked. He'd seen it all before, but he was still very impressed. Even at school, his teenage hormones had almost exploded at the sight of her in a skirt so short it broke every rule. But best of all, at no point had Natasha ever gone soppy on him or he on her. They were two of a kind, he'd always thought. A good-time boy and girl, both desperate to throw off the shackles of education and get to university and the real world.

Above the sound of the water, he could hear cars swooshing past the flat on their way into Oxford city centre. He'd rented the place from an ex-colleague, a strait-laced anaesthetist who'd probably have had a heart attack if he knew what had been going on in his bed. He fumbled on the bedside tabletop for his watch. When he couldn't find it, he pulled back his share of the duvet and edged out of bed. Natasha emerged from the bathroom, half wearing a hand towel.

'So you're alive then, darling?' she said.

He rubbed sleep from his eyes as she stared meaning-fully at his crotch. 'I could be more alive if you'd come back to bed, woman. Failing that, I guess I'll take a shower.'

Natasha groaned. 'I feel so awful about this, but I think I've just used the last of the hot water.'

'Don't worry. I'll manage.'

Natasha pulled a face. 'Oh gosh. I suppose we should have shared.'

'Maybe a cold shower would be best, unless you do want to be here all day,' he said gruffly.

Half an hour later, his skin tingling in the cool summer morning despite a shirt, sweater and jeans, he found her at the cooker making pancakes. She was wearing one of his T-shirts from Tuman. He didn't tell her that the last time he'd worn it, he'd been syringing out a patient's ears.

'Natasha . . .'

'Hmm,' she said, licking batter off her fingers in an almost pornographic way.

'Are you around Oxford over the next couple of weeks?'

She poured a cup of batter into the pan and swirled it round. 'I might be,' she said.

'And are you . . .'

'Shagging anybody else?' said Natasha.

'Well. Yes,' said Matt. 'Because you know how much I enjoy your company, but I don't want to come between you and some bond trader from Dulwich Village.'

Sliding a pancake on to a plate, she handed it over and tutted. 'Dear Matt. You always did have a conscience, didn't you? I'm between bond traders at the moment, so if you want to find some relief from the dreary world every now and then, I can help you out.'

'That's good,' he said, watching her top up two mugs with coffee from the cafetière. He wondered why she wasn't married or living with anyone yet. She was thirty-two, the same age as he was, give or take a few weeks. God knows, she must have had plenty of offers. She sat down at the table, sipping her coffee as he ate a second pancake. 'Aren't you going to have any?' he asked.

'Yuck. All that fat and cholesterol. I'd rather eat a deep-fried spider,' she said.

Matt laughed. 'Believe me you wouldn't.'

'You don't mean . . . My God, Matt. That is absolutely disgusting.'

'But very nutritious. It's a cultural thing, Natasha. No different to a langoustine or a nice piece of steak.'

She put her feet on the table next to his plate, wrinkling her pretty little toes. The fact that they were slightly grubby curiously turned him on even more.

Half an hour later, she'd cleared away the plates and he was washing up while she dried.

'Right. That's me done, I'm afraid,' she said, wiping her hands on his top. 'So. Shall I see you later this week? I don't suppose I'll get you to myself at the reception this evening so that won't really count as a date.'

'Can I give you a call?'

'Whatever,' she said, but he knew her too well not to hear the edge of disappointment in her voice.

'Maybe Tuesday night? We could go to see a film and then for a meal?'

She brightened. 'Mmm. I think I can fit you in on Tuesday. Shall I meet you here?'

'We could meet in town. I'm sure you can suggest somewhere.'

'The Duke of Cambridge then. They do gorgeous champagne cocktails and the bar staff are completely divine.'

Matt had to laugh. 'Fine. If you get bored of me, you can pick one of them up.'

While she dressed, Matt took a couple of paracetamol to stave off the effects of his hangover and jet lag. He decided to take a walk to liven himself up and then get ready for the wedding. Natasha was back, stuffing her purse into her handbag. Matt collected her wrap from the sofa and placed it round her shoulders. As he did he said casually, 'Natasha, you do know I'm only on leave for four months, maybe less. I have to be back in Tuman in October. I wouldn't be here at all but they asked me to come home and sort a few things out.'

He hadn't told her about the accident and there was no way she could have heard. Even his own family only knew sketchy details of what had happened. She shook her head as if he was very dim indeed and tutted loudly.

'Matt. I'm disappointed in you. You don't need to warn me off. I know the score. We're two peas in a pod, you and I. You want a little light relief and I want to shag your very gorgeous arse off.'

Matt smiled. Good old Tasha. Maybe he might actually enjoy his few weeks in England.

'See you Tuesday then. By the way, I love your hair long, and as for the tattoos . . . Oh my word,' she said.

She clattered off down the stairs and Matt lay back on the sofa. He had a few hours before the wedding. Maybe he'd manage to read a few newspapers, find out what was going on, catch up with how Arsenal were doing and who was running the country. Maybe he should slink off to that little coffee bar round the corner. Get a few gallons of caffeine down him. Kill or cure . . . But first he needed his wallet. How much did they sting you for an espresso these days? he wondered. A pound? Two quid? Ten? Thirty . . .

He came to on the sofa some time later with a crick in his neck and a dead leg. He'd fallen asleep again and had no idea of the time. Eventually he found his watch in the bedroom under last night's boxer shorts. It seemed to have stopped sometime during the night; most likely, he guessed, when he and Natasha had fallen into a taxi when the club had closed. And yet . . . maybe not, because the second hand was still moving. If his watch was correct, that meant . . .

He unearthed his mobile phone and looked at the time on the screen. Then he closed his eyes, hoping that the jet lag and drugs were making him hallucinate. When it was obvious that he wasn't dreaming and this nightmare was actually happening to him, he crossed to the walk-in closet and opened the door. The things were still there, hanging from the rail in all their ghastly glory.

Oh fuck, he was going to be late for the wedding.

# Chapter Five

Rowena's plan for Carrie had involved a triple whammy of therapy: alcohol, shopping and Nelson driving them. They were now at the Turf, a medieval pub shoehorned into a space between two of the colleges. As, apparently, was half of Oxford, students, shoppers and tourists all squashed cheek by jowl in the little courtyard. It was a hot June Saturday towards the end of the exam season and the place reeked of the cheap cider the students sprayed over each other to celebrate finishing.

'And what can I get you, madam?'

Carrie shook her head as the barman shouted into her ear. 'God. Yes. Sorry. Three halves of Old Rosy and a pint of Coke.'

She bumped her way through the drinkers in the beer garden towards Rowena, Hayley, and Nelson, who was Rowena's on-off boyfriend. They were huddled together on a spare patch of wall by the gents' toilets. Hayley waved madly. Too madly. She'd been hyper all morning, like Tigger on speed.

'Carrie! Oh thank you. I'm sooo thirsty and I shouldn't have kept you all that time in Monsoon. But I have managed to get a pashmina exactly the same shade as my shoes and if I can just see a handbag to tone with it I'll be done and dusted.'

Carrie smiled, handing Hayley a glass of cider. They'd spent two hours looking for the pashmina and she'd almost lost the will to live.

Rowena helped herself to a glass too, but not before she'd checked her watch again.

'Got to get back for something?' said Carrie.

'Me? No. No rush.'

'Aren't you glad we decided to come into town today? I mean, isn't Oxford just gorgeous in the sun?'

'Lovely,' said Carrie as a bow-tied student knocked into her, splashing her top with lager. A party popper exploded next to them. Nelson stared into his pint of Coke, looking as though he'd been invited to his own funeral.

'Nelson's missing out on a Vintage Volkswagen Festival for this,' said Rowena, stroking the back of his neck as if he were a favourite pet. 'I won't forget this, babe. I promise I'll make it up to you.'

'Exactly how much longer do we have to stay here?' he grunted. Nelson had only two loves in his life: one was his collection of vintage VW camper vans; the other was Rowena. The trouble was, while he worshipped the ground she walked on, Rowena simply trampled all over him.

'Oh Nelson, it's not that bad,' she said.

'You do know I was hoping to check out a new splitty at the festival, and now I won't be able to get into the place for poseurs and surfers,' he moaned.

Carrie couldn't resist. 'What's a splitty? It sounds faintly pervy.'

Nelson sounded disgusted at her ignorance. 'A splitty,

for your information, is a VW camper van with a split screen. There's an orange one I've got my eye on. I was thinking of making an offer, if it was in any kind of condition . . .' he said, glaring sullenly at Rowena.

Carrie felt sorry for him. Poor long-suffering Nelson. He'd been pursuing Rowena, in his own plodding way, for several years now. Occasionally, usually when she was half-cut, Rowena would throw him a bone and let him stay the night. But she had no intention of letting him move into the cottage. Carrie didn't really know how Nelson put up with it.

'Look, Nelson, we're nearly done. Hayley's finished her shopping and it's roasting here in the city. Let's drink up and you can take us home, then maybe you can still make the festival,' she soothed.

'Nelson's fine,' said Rowena sharply.

Carrie ignored her. 'Nelson? You do want to go home, don't you?'

'I'm going for a slash,' he said, looking as if he'd been offered a choice of hanging or electrocution.

After he'd scuttled off into the gents', Hayley started to regale them about the new range of edible lingerie from Sweet Nothings, the adult shop she worked for. 'We've just launched a special hen night collection. It's made of rice paper and tastes like chicken. You can suck it or swallow. It's perfect for hen nights, wedding nights, honeymoons . . .' Her hand flew to her mouth. 'Oh, sorry. I'd forgotten. I didn't mean anything . . .'

Rowena blew a smoke ring. 'Keep digging, Hayley.'

'It's fine. You don't have to treat me like an invalid. I don't go around stalking bridegrooms, hoping to kidnap one and keep him for my very own,' said Carrie.

Rowena sniffed. 'What's that smell?'

Carrie wrinkled her nose. 'Probably me. Some Hooray Henry spilled his pint over me. I'll try and get some of it out in the loo.'

Inside the toilets it was musty and quiet. She soaked a paper towel in cold water and patted the beery spot on her top before slipping into the cubicle and locking the door. She sucked in a breath, wondering what would it take to convince her friends she didn't have to be treated with kid gloves any more.

'Fack!'

The cubicle door rattled loudly.

'Hell-oo, is there anyone in there?'

Carrie unlocked the door and came face to face with two girls wriggling into silk dresses. The tall blonde looked like a horsey version of Joely Richardson, while the other one reminded her of a young Nigella Lawson.

Nigella's hand flew to her mouth as Carrie stepped out of the cubicle. 'Oops! Sor-ry. We really didn't know you were in there.'

'Thought the lock had broken,' boomed Joely. 'We're off to a wedding and we needed to get changed.'

Nigella picked up a hat from the washbasin. 'We thought we'd have a little shop and a little drink, you see, before we set off.'

'And now we're a little late and a little drunk. Bloody late, actually. Are you from round here, by any chance? Do you know any short-cuts to Steeple Fritton, darling?'

Carrie knew the place slightly, having acted in a few productions in the village hall. 'Hmm. That's north of here. I suppose if you take the B-roads you might do it in about forty minutes, unless you get held up by a tractor.'

'Fack,' said Joely, stabbing herself in the eye with a mascara wand.

'What time's the wedding?' asked Carrie.

'Half past three,' said Nigella.

'And what time is it now?'

Joely picked up her mobile. 'Almost three.'

'Then I think you're going to be late.'

Joely sighed. 'Do you think they'd mind very much if we missed the actual ceremony and just dropped in for the Pimm's and canapés?'

'Depends how well you know them,' said Carrie, desperate to make her escape. She'd decided that Nelson had been tortured long enough.

'Not very, actually,' said Joely conspiratorially. 'In fact, between you and me, we hardly know her and we've never met him.'

'She's our boss,' hissed Nigella, as if the bride could somehow hear them. 'And we feel obliged to go.'

Joely adjusted the angle of a flying-saucer hat. 'We must sound like such bitches!'

Carrie just smiled to herself and held her hands under the icy water from the tap, weirdly enjoying the sensation of her fingers turning numb. 'You'd better set off now if you do want to try and make the ceremony. You never know, you might get there in time. Brides are supposed to be late . . .' she said, thinking how she had never made it at all.

Nigella's snort echoed round the toilets. 'Late! You have to be joking. Fenella Harding would be early for her own funeral.'

Carrie was taken aback. 'Fenella Harding?'

'Yah. Do you know her?'

She shook her head and turned off the tap. 'No. I don't.'

'You looked as if you recognised the name,' said Nigella suspiciously.

Carrie flashed them a smile. She did know Fenella slightly – she ran the firm of accountants who looked after the farm's business affairs – but the last thing she wanted was to prolong the conversation. Her friends would be thinking she'd disappeared down the loo or something.

'No, I can't say I've heard of her,' she said.

Nigella let out a sigh. 'Lucky you. Just between us, she's an absolute cow. How she ever found someone to marry her, I have simply no idea.'

Joely wrinkled her nose. 'Drugs probably, or a cattle prod. She's roped some rustic farmer person.'

Carrie caught sight of herself in the mirror and wondered whether she could be bothered to get her eyebrows waxed. 'Really?'

'Yah. Weird, eh? You'd have thought someone like Fenella would have sunk her claws into a stockbroker or a lawyer. Still, this guy's absolutely dripping with family money apparently, even if it is in fields and cows,' said Nigella.

'She's been boasting about pinching him on the rebound from some poor girl he'd been living with for absolutely aeons,' said Joely, applying a Juicy Tube to her lips. 'Though everyone thinks she was shagging the guy before they even split up.'

'Still, the woman's always the last to know. Monty Morrison spotted Fenella in Le Quat' Saisons with some hulking great bloke in cords and a Tattersall shirt. Well, that had to be him, didn't it? They got into a brand-new

Range Rover, Monty says, and headed for Wytham Woods for a quickie,' Nigella went on.

Carrie's heart stopped momentarily. Her face stared back at her in the cracked glass of the mirror. 'What colour?' she murmured.

'Sorry?'

She spoke louder. 'What colour was the Range Rover your friend saw?'

Nigella sighed. 'Oh, I don't know, darling, but he said they headed off for the woods in it.'

Carrie reached for a paper towel, her hands shaking. 'How awful for his girlfriend,' she said, feeling sick.

'God, yes. Total bummer. Still, if he was bonking a witch like Fenella, he wasn't worth having, now was he?' Joely was saying.

'What was his name, Joely?' said Nigella. 'Sounded rustic to me.'

'It's got a funny spelling. Foreign, I think. I remember it from the invitation.'

'It's Huw Brigstocke,' said Carrie.

The girls turned to her and trilled in unison, 'Sor-ry?'

'It's Huw with a "w". It's Welsh,' she said to their astonished faces.

'Oh. Gosh. Do you know him? Is he really rustic? Do you know his ex? Do you . . .' Their eyes widened, then they both opened their mouths at precisely the same time. 'Oh fack.'

Sunlight and noise spilled into the toilets as Hayley walked in.

'Carrie? We were wondering where you'd got to. Nelson really doesn't mind missing the VW festival, so there's no need to rush off.'

She might as well have been invisible. Carrie pushed past her, knocking her against the toilet door. Outside in the courtyard, the clock on New College tower was striking the hour. Its chimes drowned out all the chatter, the laughter, the clatter of glasses.

One, two, three . . .

'Carrie. Whatever's the matter?' Hayley's voice was behind her but it was coming from another planet.

'Nothing. Just a headache. Tell Nelson and Rowena I'm off to get some aspirin,' she said.

At first she walked slowly out of the beer garden and along the cobbled alley, numbed by shock. By the time she reached the traffic lights that led into Broad Street, she was running. Her heart thumped as she pounded past the colleges and shops, heading for the taxi rank in St Giles. She nearly knocked over a cyclist, who wobbled past her, ringing his bell and shouting angrily.

The numbness had gone, replaced by a stabbing pain that felt like rage and hurt all rolled into one. How could Huw have done this to her? It had been bad enough bearing the pain of him jilting her a fortnight before their own wedding, but now he'd pledged his undying bloody love to another woman barely four months later. God, they'd probably been having an affair while she'd still been sharing his bed. And why Fenella Harding? The sour-faced, holier-than-thou, iron-knickered *cow*!

When she reached the taxi rank, a cab was just pulling in. A large woman with about ten shopping bags was first in the queue.

'Sorry. Emergency!' shouted Carrie.

'How dare you! This is my cab!'

Carrie pushed past the furious woman. 'It's a matter of life and death.'

'I don't care. Give me back my cab. I'm going to be late for my train.'

'I don't want no druggies in 'ere,' said the driver.

'I'm not on drugs and I'll pay you double the fare if you take me where I want to go.'

He still looked dubious and she didn't blame him. He must think she was a nutter, which was true. She just wasn't a drugged-up nutter.

'Triple the fare?' she offered, hoping Rowena could do without rent that week.

'Okay. Done.'

The cab roared away from the kerb, shooting her backwards against the seat. As they queued at the lights on St Giles, the driver called back through the grille, 'Where exactly are we going that's so important?'

She gripped her seat and said it out loud so there could be absolutely no mistake.

'St Mark's church, Steeple Fritton. I'm late for a wedding.'

# Chapter Six

The one thing Carrie had clung to after Huw had called off their wedding was the fact that at least there wasn't another woman involved. It had been the first thing she'd asked that terrible night – and the first thing he'd denied. After the initial aggression, he'd seemed so horrified, so hurt, that even in the midst of her pain and rage, she'd believed him. Something in the saner recesses of her mind had told her that if he'd had the courage to call off the wedding, he'd have had the courage to tell her the real reason why.

The shock had literally knocked her off her feet. She was overwhelmed with disbelief at what had happened. Then came the grief, laced with anger at what he'd done to her. She never wanted to see him again; she'd give anything to have him back. He'd change his mind; she wouldn't see him again if he was the last man on earth.

The night he'd told her they were splitting up, she kept asking herself why. She'd kept screaming the word at him over and over but got a hundred versions of the same answer. He felt trapped. He felt suffocated. They'd never known any other life. The fact that it was Huw who'd begged her to marry him made no difference. Nothing could change the way he felt and that was that. Goodbye and thanks very much. He'd told her she could stay at the farmhouse, but she'd rather have walked over red-hot coals.

That was when Rowena had arrived.

Two weeks later, Carrie had finally found the courage to text him and arrange to collect her stuff from the farm – on the condition that Huw stayed out of the house until she'd finished.

Even on a raw March day, Packley Farm had held a strange kind of beauty. The farmhouse was largely Victorian, though parts of it were much older. It straggled across the yard with odd wings protruding here and there as generations of Brigstockes had added their own mark. Inside, the rooms were just as unconventional, shooting off landings unexpectedly, some reached by little half-flights of stairs. She'd adored it from the first day that Huw had taken her home.

As usual, the farmhouse door hadn't been locked, and as she pushed her way inside, feeling as though she was burgling her own home, something furry brushed against her legs.

'Macavity.'

Tilting his face up, the farm cat turned his green gaze on her before strolling to the food cupboard and twitching his tail hopefully. Fighting back the tears, she ran her hand along his coat and whispered, 'I'd love to take you with me, but Rowena's allergic to cats, and to be honest, Mac, I think you'd be allergic to Rowena.'

Macavity wasn't the kind of cat you could scoop up

and cuddle, so she filled his bowl with fishy biscuits and straightened up, knowing she was only putting off the next task: clearing out the bedroom.

Grabbing her cardboard box, she trudged up the stairs, hearing every familiar creak. The beamed door to their bedroom had been padded with foam to save the heads of several generations of Brigstocke men. The latch door was wide open and she noticed that the pillows were plumped and there was a new duvet on the bed she'd never seen. It was one she wouldn't have tolerated on any bed of hers; all chintzy flowers and Laura Ashley tweeness.

She wondered if Huw had decided to change the bed linen along with her, but that was just being dramatic. It was more likely that his mother or her 'little woman' had come over and changed it. Either that or he couldn't bear sleeping in the same sheets they'd shared. Maybe he wanted to move on . . . or was there a chance he was regretting what had happened?

She tossed a few paperbacks and trinkets into the box, then set to work on the wardrobes. Her jewellery casket was the only other thing left. She knew what she'd see if she opened the lid, so she just stuffed the casket on top of the box. Finally she took her carrier bag and went into the sitting room. It was silent but for the sombre ticking of the clock on the mantelpiece. Carrie had never liked the clock; it was an ugly old thing, shaped like Napoleon's hat, but it had been in the sitting room for ever so she hadn't had the heart to get rid of it. There was only one thing she really wanted: a photograph from the sideboard. It showed her and Huw goofing around in mortarboards and gowns on graduation day.

'Carrie.'

Her heart beat faster at Huw's deep voice but she didn't turn round.

'You promised to stay out of the way,' she whispered.

'I know I said that. I stayed out as long as I could, but we had a problem with one of the cows.'

'Which one?'

'Millicent. She's got mastitis. I've just left the vet with her.'

It never ceased to amaze Carrie that Huw, unromantic and businesslike in every other respect, knew each of his four-hundred-strong herd by name. She had to fight the urge to sympathise with him; her emotions were so raw that their shared concern over the cow might well set her off.

'She'll be fine, though?'

'Of course.' Finally she faced him. He was taller than she'd remembered, even in his socks. She knew that his wellies, caked in mud, would be abandoned outside the door. His thick straw-coloured hair hadn't seen a comb and there were darkish blue shadows under his eyes, almost the same shade as the overalls he always wore for farm work. He also had cow muck spattered across his face, which for some strange reason made her heart lurch with a perverse longing for him.

'I know I said I wouldn't bother you, but I had to come in and see how you were.'

Her heartbeat quickened. Could he be trying to holding out an olive branch? Then she saw his grim expression and knew there was no hope. She clutched the photo frame tighter. 'Oh, I'm fine. Never been better. There was a bit of a wobble recently after my fiancé broke off our engagement, but apart from that, you know, life's hunky-dory.'

'I suppose I deserved that, but you know I do care about you. I didn't just make this decision on a whim.'

'Didn't you? Oh, silly me. Here I've been thinking you just rolled home after your stag night and told me to piss off out of your life. I hadn't thought it might be a whim.'

She could see he was trying desperately to be patient with her, which infuriated her even more.

'I know you're upset, Carrie, but this isn't helping either of us.'

'Upset? I'm not upset. See, I'm already over it.' She hoisted up the carrier bag. 'I've collected my things and moved out of your life, just like you wanted. You don't mind me taking a few bits and pieces, do you?' she added sarcastically.

Huw shook his head. He looked like a great big shaggy hound who'd peed on the carpet. Guilt and shame dripped from every pore. She so badly wanted to hate him, but it was no good. It wasn't hate making her heart thud so hard it was hurting her chest.

'Of course I don't mind. Take what you want,' he said wearily.

'Do you really mean that?'

'You know I do.'

'No, I don't,' she said, alarmed at the way her voice had risen higher.

'I meant that you should take everything you need.'

'Everything? You want me to have *everything*? Like the cowshed? The chickens? Your tractor?'

'You know exactly what I mean. You may as well have what you want. We'll have to sort things out sometime.'

'What exactly do you mean by sorting things out?'

'I mean financially. You're entitled to your share of the house and business,' he said gruffly. 'That's only fair.'

Had it come this already? Barely two weeks after they'd split up, he was already making her part of his balance sheet?

'Isn't it a bit soon to be thinking about that?'

The sun, suddenly shining through the old panes on to his face, showed his true feelings. His expression wasn't unkind, but she felt a chill run through her. She'd seen that set of his jaw before, when his mind was made up.

'Sooner or later we have to sort things out financially. I want to be fair to you after all the work you've put in over the years.'

'You mean you're feeling as bloody guilty as hell!'

'Carrie, please don't be like this again.'

'Don't be like what? You've *jilted* me, Huw. You asked me to marry you. I didn't ask for the bloody royal wedding. You and your mother wanted it.'

'And you didn't?' he said angrily, then rolled his eyes to the ceiling. 'Look, I won't be drawn into another shouting match. There's nothing more I can say. I'm sorry for what happened between us and I wish things could have been different but they're not. The only thing we can do now is get on with our lives. I want you to be happy, Carrie, and I know now that you could never have been happy with me.'

'Well, thank you so much, Huw, for that string of platitudes.'

'If you're expecting some kind of deep emotional response, you're going to be disappointed. You know me by now. I've got to get back to the milking parlour.'

He was going. He was leaving again and the panic was almost suffocating her. She'd known she should keep her mouth shut and maintain some pride and dignity but she couldn't. She'd known what she was going to say next and had even guessed what the answer would be, but she had to go ahead like a moth drawn to the flame.

'Do you – do you even *love* me any more?'

'I'm . . .' he stammered. 'I'm . . . very fond of you . . .'

She was glad that no one had come with her to the farm, because that meant no one else had to witness what happened next. Suddenly the photo frame was flying through the air. Huw must have ducked or her aim was wildly off target because the frame smashed into the clock with an enormous crack. Shards of glass and mechanism exploded into the room.

'Jesus Christ, Carrie!'

As he cowered by the hearth, she snatched up her plastic bag of belongings and screamed, 'You know, I've always hated that bloody clock!'

She hadn't seen Huw since that day, three months ago now, and despite what he'd said, nothing had been sorted out between them. But that was the last thing on her mind now as she hurtled towards Steeple Fritton in the taxi. What cowards Fenella and Huw were – choosing a church twenty miles away from Packley!

It was obvious now, of course. It was so she wouldn't find out about the wedding. In fact, she didn't know how she hadn't heard about it before on the Packley grapevine. Someone *must* have known, but if so, why hadn't they told her? For now, that could wait. She had a job to do first. She might not be able to prevent Huw and

Fenella becoming man and wife, but she could manage one thing. She could make sure that everyone in that church – and for miles around – would remember the bride and groom's special day for the rest of their lives. They would just remember it for all the wrong reasons.

# Chapter Seven

The cab screeched to a halt. Throwing money at the driver, Carrie jumped out, hurtled up the path to the church and almost crashed into the barrel-shaped usher blocking the way to the doors. His embroidered frock coat made him look like an extra from a camp Dickens musical, but she wasn't the least bit surprised. Trust that bitch Fenella Harding to have no taste whatsoever.

'Have they started yet?' she demanded.

The fat usher mopped his brow. 'Er . . . well I'm not sure, 'cos I just stepped out here for a breath of fresh air. Maybe. I think they might have just got going.'

'*Exactly* how long ago?'

'Well, it was all supposed to kick off at three thirty, but Her Highness kept Huw waiting a good ten minutes, so I reckon they can't have got very far through the service. Must have wanted to give him time to ask for any last requests, I reckon, though I'd have taken the chance to leg it myself.'

'Well, could I possibly still come in? I've had rather a rush to get here.'

His eyes roved over her cami top and miniskirt. 'I can see that, my love. Alarm clock didn't go off, eh?'

'It's such a hot day, I thought I'd ditch the silk two-piece and just go for comfort,' she said sweetly.

'You do look very comfortable, I must say,' he said lecherously.

She smiled the smile of a crocodile before it swallows up a fat and fluffy duck. 'I am. So can I go inside?'

'Wouldn't want you to miss the execution, would I? Not every day a man signs his life away for ever.'

He pushed open the heavy door to the church vestibule and Carrie almost punched the air in relief. She'd thought she might have to wrestle him to the ground if he hadn't let her past soon.

'Bride or groom's side, love?' he asked.

'Oh, the groom, definitely.'

'In that case, strictly speaking, you should sit on the right, but it's packed in there so I'd just plonk down anywhere you can find. I'm sure a trim little thing like you will be able to squash in somewhere. Personally, I'm going to have a sneaky fag before the photographs start.'

The vestibule smelled of disinfectant and musty vestments. The door to the nave was open a crack and Carrie could hear the vicar's voice booming through the gap. As she crept to the doorway, her heart was pounding so loudly she was sure one of the guests would hear her and turn round.

Carrie couldn't believe what she saw. The church was a sea of big hair-do's and enormous hats. Naturally, the bride's side was by far the worst. It reminded her of one of those cheap bouquets you could pick up in the market: a clash of horrible colours like cerise, turquoise and acid lime. The groom's side was more muted. Huw's family and friends were farming stock, mostly old county and very conservative. They'd gone for taupe, olive and the occasional daring beige. And the flowers . . . The whole place looked like an explosion in a florist's shop and stank like a tart's boudoir.

Fenella was wearing a long beaded dress in dazzling white with a stand-up collar that made her look like the Wicked Queen in *Snow White*. As for Huw, even with his back to her, in his camp frock coat, he was imposing and handsome.

'*Marriage was ordained for the procreation of children. . .*' declared the vicar.

Carrie balled her hands into fists, anger beginning to replace shock.

'*Secondly, it was ordained for a remedy against sin, and to avoid fornication; that such persons as have not the gift of continency might marry . . .*'

As if on cue, Fenella clasped Huw's hand. Carrie gave a tiny snort. A remedy against sin and fornication? Too bloody late for that!

'*Thirdly, it was ordained for the mutual society, help, and comfort, that the one ought to have of the other, both in prosperity and adversity, and therefore if any man can show just cause why they may not lawfully be joined together . . .*'

She opened the gap in the door a little wider.

'*. . . let him now speak, or else hereafter for ever hold his peace.*'

This was the point at which she could have stepped out into the aisle and made herself known. The point at which everyone would have turned round in horror and gasped as she stood in the middle of the aisle and said loudly, for everyone to hear, 'My fiancé is a spineless bastard and Fenella is a husband-stealing witch!'

The vicar's voice would falter. The congregation would gasp. Huw's jaw would drop to the floor and Fenella's face would turn even whiter than her horrible frock. The vicar would peer at Carrie and say, 'Well, this is most irregular, but I'm afraid I have to hear what this person has to say. Do you have an objection to this marriage, young woman?'

Every eye in the house would be glued to her, every ear straining to hear what she had to say. It would have been a leading lady's dream.

But the moment passed by and she hadn't said a word. Even though she was knotted up inside with fury and the injustice of it all, she had her pride. She was a good actress, and a good actress knew when to hide her feelings; knew how to pretend to be calm and dignified when every instinct made her want to scream out. She closed her eyes as she heard Huw promising to love and be faithful to Fenella and she knew she'd had enough. She closed the door, hardly caring about the *thunk* it made in the hushed church.

She'd come here to see with her own eyes what Huw had done, because she hadn't quite been able to believe it. He'd broken off their engagement just a few months ago and now here he was actually standing at the altar with another woman.

She walked down the steps and out of the church. Next to the door stood a totally over-the-top flower arrangement. From the corner of her eye Carrie saw a hose snaking along the ground. She glanced around, but there was no sign of the fat guy who'd let her into the church. In fact, there was no sign of anyone, only the sound of a hymn being sung from inside.

She knew that what she was going to do was childish, but she just couldn't resist it. Calmly but purposefully she headed for the tap and turned it on full. The hose filled with water instantly, the end whipping up like a demented snake, spraying water everywhere. She picked it up and was just about to aim it at the flower arrangement when one of the ushers came out of the church. It wasn't the fat guy, but a much taller man with a ponytail and a beard.

'Don't even think about it,' he said, as Carrie stood with the hose in her hand. 'Believe me, you really don't want to do this.'

'Yes I do,' she declared, raising the hose so that the stream of water spurted on to the ground a few feet from the flowers. Droplets splashed the usher's shoes.

He folded his arms. 'What good will this do you?'

*What good?* He was talking as if he knew who she was, yet she didn't recognise him. At least, she thought she didn't. She stared hard at him. He did seem vaguely familiar.

'Why don't you calm down?'

'Why don't you mind your own business and get out of my way, unless you want a soaking.'

She edged the stream a little nearer, but her aim was off and she ended up wetting the bottoms of his trousers.

'Look, I don't give a flying fuck if you drown me, but trashing these flowers won't help you one bit.'

'You have no right to interfere like this.'

'It's for your own good,' he said.

'Like hell it is. It's for Fenella and Huw's good. You

just don't want me wrecking their perfect wedding day.'

He regarded her coldly. 'True, but I also don't want you making an even bigger fool of yourself.'

'Then you've wasted your time, because I don't care about making a fool of myself.'

Suddenly he stepped in front of the arrangement, like a bodyguard. Carrie jerked the hose, soaking his shoes. 'Bloody hell.'

'Well, I did warn you,' said Carrie.

'Look. I know you don't care now, but tomorrow, believe me, you'll care. You'll care very much indeed. Now, why don't you put down the hose and just go home. You're obviously very distressed.'

'Distressed? Me? Distressed? Oh no! I'm completely, deliriously happy. See, listen to me. Ha ha ha! That's how over-the-fucking-moon I am that my fiancé chucked me before our wedding and then went and married the Wicked Queen.'

'Have you finished?'

'I think so.'

'Then why don't you wipe your face? It's wet.' He pulled a handkerchief from his top pocket and held it out to her.

Carrie touched her face. It *was* wet but she didn't remember shedding any tears. She couldn't have been. And there was no way on the planet she was going to use one of Fenella's vile lilac handkerchiefs.

She shook her head. 'Keep back.'

A cloud crossed the sun and a gust of wind blew across the churchyard, whipping up confetti, dry leaves and sweet wrappers.

'You're shivering, which is probably down to all the

adrenaline. I'm going to call you a cab and make sure you get home,' he said with infuriating calmness.

'What for? A nice cup of hot sweet tea?'

'I should think a stiff whisky might work better, but that depends what your poison is.' He gestured to her miniskirt. 'More clothing might help, too. I'd give you my coat, but I need it.'

'Well, hey, I might have dressed a tad more formally if I'd had time, but you see, I didn't actually plan on attending this particular function. In fact I wasn't aware it was taking place until about, oh, forty minutes ago when I overheard two of the guests discussing it in a pub toilet.'

His bushy eyebrows knitted together in concentration. She frowned. There *was* something very familiar about him but she couldn't put her finger on it. With the hair and the beard he looked like Robinson bloody Crusoe.

'Carrie!'

Twisting round, she saw Rowena clambering out of Nelson's van, Nelson following behind.

A look of relief flooded the usher's face. 'There're your friends. I think you ought to go with them,' he said.

'I've decided it's not worth the effort,' she said, dropping the hose as Rowena thudded up the path.

'Good. Now I've got a wedding to get back to.'

As he turned his back, Carrie called after him, 'And you can tell that cow Fenella you all look as camp as a whole field of tents!'

He'd gone by the time Rowena arrived, face red as a beetroot. 'Carrie, I tried to tell you. I tried to stop you but we didn't know where you'd gone. I'm really sorry you had to find out like that.'

Carrie's glare froze Nelson in his tracks and Rowena held up her hand to him.

'Carrie's a bit overwrought right now, sweetie. Do you want to wait in the van? We'll be along in a minute.'

Nelson trudged away. Carrie didn't think she'd ever seen her friend look so worried, but she didn't care, because all she could see was Rowena obsessing over the time in the pub garden, Hayley coming to check up on her in the toilets . . .

'Are you okay? I'll never forgive myself for this. This is exactly what we didn't want to happen. I really—'

'How long have you known?' she demanded.

Rowena opened her mouth.

'Don't lie!'

'Okay, I won't. A few weeks.'

A few weeks? Her best friend had known about Huw and Fenella's wedding for *weeks* and still hadn't told her?

'Hon, I was as horrified as you were when Hayley told me.'

Carrie was almost too stunned by this revelation to reply. 'Hayley told you?'

'It was Hayley who found out about the wedding. She goes to the same nail technician as Fenella.'

'That bitch!'

'That total bitch Fenella,' repeated Rowena loyally. 'The nail technician was gossiping about this big wedding she was doing and Hayley realised just who she was talking about but didn't know what to do about it. She didn't want you to be hurt, you see. And so we – Hayley and Nelson and me – decided to ask your mum and dad what they thought.'

'You mean Mum and Dad knew about this too? You all

knew that Huw was getting married again and you kept it from me. You lied to me for weeks, knowing what was happening. Why? Why didn't you tell me?'

'Because of this, hon, because we were afraid of exactly this. We've been so worried about you,' said Rowena, beginning to steer her in the direction of Nelson, who was waiting by the van. 'I'm just glad we got here in time. I saw you talking to Matt Landor.'

'Matt Landor? That – that ape was him?'

'Yes. He was at uni with us.'

'Oh God. So it was *him*.'

'He definitely recognised you,' said Rowena. 'But what were you up to with the hose? You weren't thinking of doing anything silly, were you?' she said anxiously.

Carrie felt herself simmering again. Why did people think she was deranged? 'What the hell do you mean, something silly? I'm not some bunny-boiling madwoman. I just wanted to see it for myself. Just see if it was true about Huw and . . . and her . . .' she said.

Rowena didn't seem convinced, but she touched Carrie's arm and said, 'Come on, I'll take you home. Nelson, we're going. Carrie?'

'I suppose so,' said Carrie reluctantly.

'Your feet are getting wet. Shall I turn off the water?'

'No. I'll do it.'

'Fine. We'll wait for you in the van.'

As Rowena walked off, Carrie picked up the hose. She was halfway to the tap when the church bells began to ring, ding-dong, pealing out for Huw and bloody Fenella. They clanged as if they were reminding her of the injustice of what had happened.

It took a split second for her to decide. Gripping

the hose with both hands, she aimed it like a gun right at the heart of the arrangement. Instantly the flowers exploded, petals flying through the air. The metal stand teetered and clattered to the ground.

'Sod the pair of you. You're welcome to each other!'

Then, picking her way between the stems and blooms, she calmly turned off the tap and walked down the drive to Rowena, just as Huw and Fenella emerged from the church.

# *Chapter Eight*

Matt, his mother and his brother Rob were sitting round the dinner table at their family home the day after the wedding. Even after their father had died when Matt was fourteen and Rob barely seventeen, they'd kept up the family tradition of a proper Sunday lunch. Their father had been a stickler for family meals, and for their mum's sake, the boys had always tried to be there as often as they could. For the past year, Rob, with his busy schedule, had done his best to turn up, but Matt had been on the other side of the world. He felt guilty, so he gave his mother a smile as she handed him the vegetable tureen.

'I hear there was some fuss at Fenella Harding's wedding yesterday,' she said, returning his smile in a faintly worried way.

A dark-haired girl in her early twenties brought in a tray with a plate of roast beef and a jug of steaming gravy. She was wearing shorts, a T-shirt and an old-fashioned apron. Much to Matt's relief, the conversation stopped as she served their lunch.

'Hello, Niki,' said Robert. The girl smiled, her eyes glinting.

'Matt, this is Niki. She's been helping Mum with the house. Niki, this is my reprobate brother Matthew, but you can call him King Kong.'

'Hi, Niki,' said Matt.

'Hi.'

She wasted all of a nanosecond on him before turning her attention back to Robert. The look that flashed between them was almost imperceptible but enough to tell Matt that Rob was shagging her. He didn't blame him. Niki was cute and pretty, and a couple of years ago he might have seen it as a challenge to wrest her from Robert's clutches and shag her himself.

'Thank you, Niki. When you've washed up, you can go home,' said his mother firmly. When the girl had gone, she turned to Matt. 'So, what about the wedding? What happened?'

'Some flowers got knocked over,' said Matt, ladling sprouts and carrots on to his plate. 'It really was no big deal, Mum.'

'Hmm. That's not what I heard. Marion Thompson telephoned me this morning. She was at the wedding. Did you know she's Fenella's godmother? She says that someone deliberately destroyed a very expensive flower arrangement. Marion was furious – the flower club had spent all morning on that arrangement and the roses had cost an absolute fortune. She says that Fenella thinks it might have been Huw's ex-girlfriend. Caroline somebody-or-other, isn't it?'

'I've no idea,' said Matt evenly. 'I expect it was just kids messing about.'

'Really? Are you sure you didn't see her? Fenella thought she'd spotted her getting into some bizarre orange van as they came out of church. She must have been very upset when Huw left her for Fenella.'

'Mum, I've been eight thousand miles away for the past year. I've no idea what's been going on in deepest Packley or who's left who.'

'Whom, dear.'

'Whatever. I didn't even know if I could go to the wedding until a few weeks ago.'

'Hmm,' said his mother, reaching for the salt cellar.

In his mind, Matt saw Carrie again, her mass of chestnut hair trailing in the breeze, holding the hose like a deadly weapon. He allowed himself a secret smile. With her blood up like that, he wouldn't have liked to face her in the boxing ring. She might have flattened him, pint-sized as she was. Then he remembered the tears on her cheeks and he stopped smiling. Life stank sometimes and love didn't just hurt, it twisted the knife for good measure.

From the head of the table, Rob Landor started laughing. 'That's my little brother. Always there when there's trouble. Matt, can't you go anywhere without getting involved in some kind of drama?'

'I wasn't involved in a drama.'

'Whoever did it – and I'm with dear old Marion on the crazed ex-girlfriend theory – was probably high on drugs,' said Rob.

'Oh. Do you think she was? You don't think she's dangerous, do you?' said their mother.

Rob was grinning wickedly, clearly enjoying winding her up. Matt wished he was within kicking distance but instead said pleasantly, 'Rob, you are completely full of shit.'

His mother rapped his hand with the serving spoon. 'Do you mind not using words like that at the dinner table? Pass the roast potatoes, please.'

'And the red wine,' said Robert. 'Matt'll have orange squash.'

'I'm glad you could make it,' said his mother, as they sat in the sitting room after lunch.

'Would you like a glass of port?'

'No thanks, Mum.'

'Matt's gone teetotal,' said Robert, taking a glass and settling into their father's old chair.

'That wouldn't do you any harm, Robert.' His mother raised her glass to Matt. 'Well done, you.'

'It's really been incredibly tough, but worth all the self-denial,' said Matt.

His mother narrowed her eyes. 'Don't overdo it, Matthew. Now, tell me all about what you've been up to. I want to know everything about this accident. All I got was a phone message and some kind of nonsense from your brother. I know he wasn't giving me the full story.'

So here it was, thought Matt. He had no choice but to go through the whole thing again, but that didn't mean he had to go into the gory details. He sketched over the worst part of what had happened that night in Tuman as best he could, making light of his role in the events to spare his mother. When he'd finished she seemed satisfied, but Robert was watching him closely.

'Oh, thank goodness for that,' said his mother, and Matt hoped she was satisfied. He was also hoping she wouldn't want him talking about misery and medical matters over the port and cheese, and would rather hear about the wedding.

Later, as Matt made coffee in the kitchen, Robert grabbed his arm. He was swaying slightly and his eyes were glazed.

'How are you really then, Landor Minor, apart from the terminal hair?'

Matt was disappointed. His hair was tied back in a ponytail with an elastic band, just the way it had been for the wedding. He'd thought he looked pretty smart. He'd kept the beard; he often didn't have time to shave when he was working in Tuman and now felt naked without it.

'I'm fine,' he said.

Robert raised his eyebrows. 'Really? I heard you got into a spot of bother out there. You idiot, when are you going to settle down and get a proper job?'

As ever, his brother had moved on to his favourite theme. Matt used to get annoyed when Robert goaded him, launching into elaborate justifications of why he was working with a medical charity rather than climbing his way up the surgical ladder like Rob. While Robert had become one of the youngest orthopaedic surgeons of his generation, Matt had 'farted about royally'; as Rob put it. He'd followed up his five-year medical training with a year in a hospital, four years' GP training and then a stint in tropical medicine. He'd finally found his niche and spent the past four years working in a variety of places for the charity, a jack-of-all-trades, according to Robert. He smiled to himself. You had to be, in his line of work, treating someone for TB or HIV one minute and carrying out a Caesarean the next. Via Africa, the Balkans and the Far East, he'd now ended up in Tuman. He'd been shot at, had malaria and once spent a night in prison after being mistakenly arrested by the military junta. Then there was his latest escapade in Tuman.

'Any chance of you coming to your senses and coming back home to stay?' Robert said, opening cupboards. 'Jesus, is there no decent whisky in this bloody place? I know damn well there's a bottle of Laphroaig in here somewhere. Mum keeps it for when her fancy man comes round.'

'You've already drunk all Mum's sherry, wine and port,' said Matt, spotting the whisky in full view on the worktop.

'Yeah, and now I need a proper drink. You're a bloody fool, Matt, always getting involved. You should keep out of stuff that doesn't concern you.'

'I'll do what I want,' growled Matt.

Robert glared at him. 'Now don't get touchy. You can't blame me for worrying about you. I mean, rushing off like that in Tuman, trying to act the bloody hero. You might have been killed. As it is, I hear you've been sent home to lick your wounds.'

They were eye to eye now, squaring up.

'I know all about it, you see,' Rob went on. 'News travels fast in our world, which, despite what you think, is actually a very small one. I notice things, Matt. Always have. I know you fed Mum a load of bullshit back there. You were involved in that accident up to your neck. I know you pulled that guy out while the fucking Jeep was on fire. In fact, from what I hear, two more seconds and you'd have been toast. And it's shaken you up good and proper this time, hasn't it?'

Matt smiled, even though he was boiling inside. If he

lashed out, Robert would have exactly what he wanted. Since they'd been boys, he'd always tried everything he could to provoke him, and Matt never really understood why.

'You're misinformed, Rob. It was more like ten minutes before the Jeep exploded, and if I had been toast, you'd have been able to buy another new suit for my funeral.'

Robert shook his head, his eyes murderous. 'You think I don't give a shit, do you? You think I'm a selfish bastard only out to make a million. Which I already have, by the way.' His eyes gleamed. 'But you're wrong. I don't want to be left here picking up what's left of our mother when you get sent home in a coffin.'

'Rob, stop worrying about me. I'm a big boy now and I can look after myself.'

'I don't worry about you. Well, hoo-fucking-ray. Here's the whisky.'

Pulling out the stopper, Rob sloshed whisky into a glass, took a slug and leaned back against the worktop with a sigh of satisfaction. Matt watched him.

'Are you sleeping with Niki?'

'Of course, among others. Unlike you, I actually have a life,' he said, topping up his glass.

Matt reached into his jeans pocket and pulled out a business card. 'How d'you know I haven't already got plans? Don't you think that after what's happened to me, I'm not going to make the most of every second back here?'

'Who is she?'

Robert snatched the card from his hand, which was exactly what Matt wanted. This was a motivation he knew his brother would understand – unlike Matt's apparent lack of self-preservation instinct. His face cracked into a grin as he saw the name on the card.

'You cunning git. Natasha Redmond. Whew. Saw her the other day in a club. Legs up to her arse and a rack like a porn star. Well, I hope she gives you plenty of therapy.'

# Chapter Nine

Carrie woke up the morning after the wedding drenched in sweat. Seconds after opening her eyes, the memories rolled over her like a great wave, cold and grey.

She was lying in bed at her parents' house under her old Take That duvet cover, the one from when they'd been famous the first time round. That duvet had always hidden her when life got tough. She'd languished beneath it when she'd had glandular fever in the sixth form and cried beneath it when she'd flunked her A levels and thought she'd miss her place at uni. That duvet had always represented comfort, safety, an 'it'll be all right in the end' feeling. But not any more.

The question of who had known about the wedding and for how long had paled into insignificance beside another mystery: exactly how long had Huw been involved with Fenella if he'd had time to organise a wedding just four months after he'd jilted Carrie?

Rowena had carried on denying all knowledge of anything beyond discovering that the ceremony had been taking place. She and Nelson had driven her not back to the cottage, but to her parents' semi in Packley Heath.

Carrie hadn't protested. By that stage she was slumped in the passenger seat like a road accident casualty.

Back home, she had vague memories of rushing up the stairs to her bedroom and shutting the door on her mum and Rowena. With the help of two sleeping tablets left over from the night Huw had dumped her, she'd finally fallen into unconsciousness. Now the bedroom door opened and her mother came in.

'Carrie?'

She closed her eyes and lay back on the pillows, willing herself to pass out again.

'I've brought you a cup of tea. Are you awake, love?'

'No.'

There was a pause. 'Okay. I'll leave your drink on the bedside table in case you wake up.'

'Thanks.'

She could feel her mum standing there holding out the cup, even if she couldn't see her. Her mum left the door open, as Carrie knew she would. She'd never known if it was a hint or a habit left over from her teenage days when the only way to get her arse to school had been to plug the radio in outside on the landing and play the Terry Wogan show at full volume. That had *always* worked.

This morning, back in the bedroom she hadn't slept in since her last university vacation, the smell of frying bacon was drifting upstairs from the kitchen and she was sure she could hear some crap sixties tune even now. It was just as if the last ten years hadn't happened. As if she'd never met Huw, never made a life with him, never agreed to marry him. Huw and Carrie, Carrie and Huw . . . almost from the moment when Huw had lumbered over to her at the freshers' disco ten years before, the two of them had been inseparable. From then on it was one Christmas card, one invitation, one engagement card, of course. One of almost everything because slowly, without realising it, she and Huw had almost become the same person.

But there would be no joint cards ever again and definitely no presents. They'd be lying abandoned in people's wardrobes or returned to Argos and John Lewis, not piled up on a table at Grantley Manor so everyone could see how popular she and Huw were.

Eventually she threw back the cover, realising she must have fallen asleep again, because she didn't remember the curtains being open when her mum had last come in. This must be how Dracula felt at sunrise – except he had the power to consign his victims to the living dead with one bite.

'You've let your tea get cold. Shall I make another?' Her mum was standing in the doorway of her room, having retrieved the mug, and trying not to sound the least bit exasperated but failing.

'I don't know.'

'I really think you should get up and come down and have some breakfast.'

'You mean I should pull myself together.'

'I mean you should put some proper clothes on and get up. Rowena's here. Do you know, she stayed until nearly midnight last night to make sure you were okay? And she phoned at half past six this morning. We thought someone had died.'

Half past six? Rowena was awake at half past six? Things must really be terminal. 'I can't talk to her.'

'Okay, don't, but it's no use lying around in here like a sack of potatoes, is it? You're going to have to face the world sometime, and your best friend must be a good place to start.'

'I suppose I'd better come down,' said Carrie, pushing herself up the pillow. Gary Barlow stared back at her from the duvet, faded and stained with something purple that might have been vodka and Ribena. She used to sneak it upstairs when she was in the sixth form.

'I'd appreciate it if you did come down,' said her mum. 'Dad and I want to go to IKEA for a new wardrobe and I don't really want to leave you on your own.'

So, even her parents thought she was deranged. 'I'm not going to do something silly, you know,' she said.

'I know that, Carrie,' said her mother, picking up the waste bin, which was overflowing with tissues. Carrie leaned back against the pillow and closed her eyes.

'Is it okay to hate someone you once loved?' she said out loud.

But when she opened her eyes, her mother had gone.

When Carrie shuffled into the lounge, dressed in an old pair of jeans from her uni days and her dad's old Marks and Spencer sweater, Rowena was sitting on the sofa, cradling a mug of coffee in one hand and a chocolate finger in the other. Her eyes were like saucers as Carrie appeared.

'Oh my God,' said Rowena.

'That bad?'

'You look terrible.'

'I know.'

'I tried calling you earlier but your mum said you were asleep. The girls at am dram have been phoning about you. Even Emily Macintyre has been asking. I am so sorry about what's happened.'

Carrie watched Rowena lick the chocolate off her biscuit. 'Are they laughing at me?' she asked.

'No, of course they're not laughing at you! They all think Huw's a Grade A shit too.'

Carrie gave a little snort. She didn't believe Rowena for a moment. She knew at least two members of Packley Drama Society who'd have given a kidney to marry Huw Brigstocke, including Emily, who owned a stud farm and, appropriately, looked like a stallion.

Rowena's fingers hovered over the plate of biscuits on the table.

'You're twitching,' said Carrie, unable to stop herself from smiling.

'That's because I'm dying for a ciggie. It's either that or I eat the whole plate of these.'

'Come on,' said Carrie, sliding open the patio doors to the garden. 'Dad will stake you out on the lawn and feed you to the crows if he smells fag smoke in the house.'

Outside, the sun was quite strong, despite the breeze, and they could hardly move for tubs full of geraniums. They sat down on Carrie's mum's new teak patio furniture next to her dad's latest toy: a stone statue of a mermaid spitting into the pond.

Rowena lit up, took a drag and sighed with something approaching ecstasy. 'Matt Landor phoned,' she said at last.

'What the hell for?'

'He wanted to know how you were. Did you know he's a doctor?'

'It explains his patronising attitude,' Carrie said, feeling mutinous.

'Well, you knew he was a medic at uni,' said Rowena, flicking her ash over the geraniums. 'He was nearly chucked out for sticking a skeleton on top of the bell tower.'

'He was always pratting about. Huw thought the sun shone out of his bum.'

Carrie thought back, trying to picture Matt as a normal person rather than a Neanderthal. She felt herself smiling, but not because she'd found Matt Landor's antics funny. She remembered the event only because it was the morning after the night Huw had first told her he loved her. It was near the end of her first year. After he'd said the 'L' word, they'd spent a glorious night making love and been woken by a noise outside her room. She could see Huw now, leaning out in his boxers, pointing and cheering and whooping. Matt and a couple of his mates were half naked outside their halls of residence, showing off a haul of traffic signs in a stolen supermarket trolley. It was obviously a rugby club prank and she'd suspected Huw was involved on the fringes somewhere, but he'd denied all knowledge of it . . . He had such a lovely bum. She'd reached forward and pinched it before he'd had a chance to put his trousers on.

'The hair and beard threw me, and let's face it, I was hardly in the mood for polite conversation yesterday. He was a total nutter.'

'Aren't all medics? Maybe he turned over a new leaf. He's been working abroad with a medical charity, apparently.' A smirk spread across Rowena's face.

'What's so funny?'

'There were some really filthy things written about him in the SU toilets.'

'Were there? He always seemed a bit full of himself to me, though I know Huw liked him,' said Carrie, still basking in the glow of memories about her university days with Huw.

'I wouldn't have kicked him out of bed,' said Rowena wistfully. 'But I'm not so sure now. It's the beard. Nelson tried to grow one, but I had to put a stop to it. They tickle too much.'

'That's too much information, Row.'

'But you are smiling, hon, and that has to be good.'

Unfortunately, Rowena had just refocused Carrie's mind on the current situation. 'Have you heard anything about *them*?' she said.

Rowena shifted in her seat. 'Well, Hayley says that Huw's cousin told her they've gone to Mauritius for two weeks. Sounds crap. All those beaches, waving palms and cocktails. Fancy sharing it with Miss Farty Pants.'

'Serves him right,' said Carrie, but inside she felt cut in two. Huw and Fenella were in Mauritius. She hadn't been able to persuade Huw to leave the farm for more than a week, not even for a honeymoon, and even then he'd only agreed to Paris in case he needed to come back urgently. The fact that he had sacrificed two weeks away from his precious farm for Fenella hurt even more than the lifetime he'd promised her.

Rowena leaned back in her chair. 'I wouldn't mind a fortnight in Mauritius. I've got a month or two before my course starts, but it's the cash that's the problem. I haven't got a couple of thousand to spare right now, not with giving up my job.'

Still trying to recover from the shock of Huw having agreed to a proper holiday, Carrie only caught the tail end of this. 'You've given up your job?'

Rowena grinned broadly. 'Yes. I was going to tell you all when we got back from shopping yesterday but I never got the chance, and then it didn't seem the right time, but yes, I am no longer an employee of Bartlett's Bank plc. I've had a bit of good luck. Well, bad luck really. Great-Auntie Madge – the one from Penrith – popped her clogs a few months ago and she's left me some cash. I always loved Auntie Madge. I was the only one of us kids who'd kiss her, even if she did have a moustache and smell of mothballs. She'd been to RADA, you know . . .'

'Wow. Rowena. You mean . . .'

'Yup. I've signed up at drama school. I'm going to give it a proper go. I don't care if it all goes pear shaped. Well, aren't you going to say something?'

'I'm gobsmacked. That's wonderful, Rowena. I'm really happy for you, it's fabulous.'

'Then why are you crying?'

'Because I'm a silly bugger. I'm so thrilled for you, Rowena. It's great news, and . . .'

Rowena leaned forward. 'And? Spit it out, Carrie. We've known each other too long to have secrets.'

'I'm thrilled for you.'

'You've said that, babe. Any more gushing and your dad won't need the fountain.'

At one time all they'd talked about was getting a job in the theatre, but all that had evaporated when Carrie had moved into the farm. It was a full-time job managing the Brigstocke empire, and her acting ambitions had become confined to the village drama society. Rowena had taken a 'temporary' job with Bartlett's and was still there ten years later, a junior manager at the regional office. Their dreams had been put on the back burner and eventually boiled themselves dry. Or so she'd thought.

Because Rowena, bless her, had finally had the courage to go for her dream. Carrie felt guilty at feeling so . . . There was no other word for it. So bloody envious! She swallowed hard. They knew each other too well to lie.

'You know what hurts the most?' she said, staring out over the garden. 'It's all the time I've wasted.'

'You haven't wasted time, hon.'

'I have. I've wasted so much time, and what for?'

She thought of the decade she'd spent with Huw, ten years during which she'd been fiercely faithful, despite temptation and opportunity. Those years could have been spent doing what she'd wanted. While their other friends had split up, they'd stayed together. She'd honestly thought she and Huw would be different. How could she have deceived herself? How could any one person be enough for another?

'I am happy for you, Rowena,' she said. 'But I won't lie. I'm green with envy too.'

'Don't be. I've only just got enough from Auntie Madge to fund the course. I'll be relying on the rent from you to help out, and I'll have to get a bar job or something as well.'

'D'you know what I'd really like to do?' said Carrie.

'Fly off to Mauritius and crash Huw's honeymoon?'

'Wow . . . what a great idea.' Rowena's face was a picture. 'Don't worry. I'm having you on, Row. There's no way I ever want to see Huw and Fenella again. They can go to hell for all I care. From now on I'm going to make the most of being young, free and single. I'm going to make up for all the days I spent cooking him fry-ups, cleaning his sodding overalls and sorting out his bloody VAT. She can do the lot now and I hope she enjoys it.'

Carrie felt a new fire stealing through her veins. She wasn't sure whether it was rage or sheer bloody-mindedness, but it felt so much better than the misery she'd endured for months that she didn't care. 'When did you say your course starts?'

'Middle of September. I was planning on drinking a lot of vodka and smoking a lot of fags, but if you're saying you're up for an adventure . . .'

'Oh, I'm up for it all right.'

'Then we'd better start now.'

'But how? Where? What with? We're both broke.'

Rowena stubbed her fag out in the geraniums. 'I think I've got an idea.'

# Chapter Ten

'Well, it's certainly an idea.'

Carrie stood with her hands on her hips outside the cottage, fighting a battle between laughter and disappointment. Parked at the kerb was a vehicle that should have been more at home in *Scooby Doo* than Packley village.

'It's very . . . interesting,' she said, as the sun bounced off the bright orange paintwork. 'Very . . . different.'

Rowena let out a giggle.

'Right. I'm off. I knew you'd be like this. People who don't understand always are. You either get it or you don't, and you two don't,' said Nelson in disgust.

'No. No, don't get upset, sweetie. Not everyone has your discerning eye. It's gorgeous. Really.'

Carrie stared at the windscreen of the van, which was divided into two panes like the windows of a house. It was cool, in a surf-bum kind of way, but it was also tiny. How on earth would she and Rowena fit into that space? Her make-up would fill the storage cupboard on its own, and as for her shoes . . . Yet Nelson looked bereft, so she tried to look interested.

'Is that . . . is that a splitty?' she asked.

Nelson hesitated, unsure whether to stay or go. 'Yeah,' he grunted at last.

'I wondered what it meant. It's the windscreen, isn't it?'

'Yeah, but . . .' he said, sliding back the door with great reverence, 'this isn't just any old splitty. This is a 1967 split-screen VW camper van with, I might add, the original Canterbury Pitt conversion. I had a right job persuading the bloke to let her go and she cost me a fortune. But she was worth it. Dolly is one of the finest vehicles of her type in the whole of the south of England.'

*Dolly?* Carrie couldn't believe he'd given the van a name. She tried to ignore the fact that Dolly was worth a fortune.

'Of course she's a fine example. In fact, she's a genuine babe,' said Rowena, sidling up to Nelson and patting his bottom. Nelson ignored her, clearly far more taken with the charms of Dolly. He caressed her orange paintwork lovingly. Carrie thought he might actually lean forward and kiss her.

'Why have you called it – sorry, her – Dolly?'

'After Dolly Parton, of course,' said Nelson, giving her a look as if she was mad to think there was any other Dolly in the world.

'Of course.'

'These old VW campers are very hip,' cut in Rowena as Carrie stood there, still slightly gobsmacked by the form her adventure was going to take. 'And the best thing of all is that Nelson's insured it for us to go abroad.'

'I must need my head examining,' he said gloomily.

Carrie poked her head inside. 'Where abroad?' she said suspiciously.

'Oh ... Europe, I suppose. I thought we could go through the Channel Tunnel into France, on to Paris, Venice, maybe Rome. We can go anywhere we like, really. Just take off, no cares, no worries. Like Thelma and Louise. Or Cliff Richard in *Summer Holiday*.'

'Cliff Richard buggered off in a London bus, not a lovingly restored vintage vehicle,' said Nelson.

'Okay. Like Thelma and Louise, then.'

He shook his head. 'They drove off a cliff.'

'But *we* won't. We'll have a fabulosa time, and if we're very lucky we might meet our very own gigolo in the shape of Brad Pitt. I mean, you might meet Brad Pitt, Carrie.' Rowena started to backpedal, seeing Nelson's thunderous face. 'I shall just take the opportunity to see the sights, learn the language, and try out the local cuisine.'

'I'm not sure this is such a good idea. I don't know if I can hand Dolly over to novices. This is a vintage vehicle. She needs careful handling.'

'Nelson, worry not, it – she – *will* get careful handling. No one handles a vehicle more lovingly than me or Carrie.'

Carrie could see he was totally unconvinced and she didn't blame him.

'Can I see inside?' she asked.

'Help yourself.'

She climbed in through the side door and was instantly transported back twenty years. When she'd been a little girl, she'd loved going on caravan holidays with her parents. The tiny scale of the fittings had fascinated her: all those hidden cupboards, pull-down beds, pint-sized cookers and minuscule fridges. She'd loved the way they'd moved on each morning to a different site, sometimes on a cliff by the sea or alongside a stream where she could catch fish with her net. It was all a big adventure to a six year old. The problem was that Dolly was a lot pokier than her parents' caravan and Carrie was about to hit thirty.

'Be nice about Dolly. Nelson loves her to bits and she is gorgeous, isn't she?' said Rowena, joining her inside the van and carrying on with the typical Rowena sales pitch. They sat down opposite each other. The seats matched the curtains: fetching shades of orange and brown, adorned with huge yellow sunflowers. Carrie ran her hand over the material. 'The upholstery's lovely. Very retro kitsch,' she said loudly enough for Nelson to hear.

'It's a work of art. There's a fridge for beer and a cooker, see,' said Rowena, lifting up a lid to show a neat gas stove, its chrome burners gleaming. 'Not that we'll be doing a lot of haute cuisine. I'm planning to sustain myself entirely on the local wine.'

'You'd better not be drinking and driving,' warned Nelson, popping his head round the door.

Rowena rolled her eyes.

'Do you really think we can get round Europe in this?' said Carrie doubtfully. 'Where are the beds?'

'A double rock-and-roll inside and another double in the roof. But you'll probably want to sleep out in the awning as it's summer,' said Nelson.

'I know it's a bit compact.' Rowena lowered her voice as Nelson lifted up the rear bonnet to check the engine. 'But I had a terrible job persuading him to let us have it. You won't believe what I had to do.'

'Doesn't he want to come along too?' said Carrie hastily.

'With two mad women? God, no. He's got to work at the garage, and besides, it's the VW festival season. He'll be happy as a pig in muck as long as we look after Dolly.'

'Looking after Dolly is what worries me . . .'

'Rubbish. All we have to do is drive the van, park it on a site and go out on the lash. What can possibly go wrong?'

She winked, then they both jumped as the engine spluttered into life. Nelson was sitting in the front seat, revving it for all he was worth. The stench of diesel filled the van.

'Listen to that,' he called enthusiastically. 'It's like a bloody symphony!'

# *Chapter Eleven*

In his Oxford flat, Matt was lying on the sofa flicking through a textbook while trying not to shout 'Bollocks!' at a TV movie, which was the only thing on the telly at two thirty in the afternoon. After two weeks in the flat, he was already climbing the walls with frustration and boredom.

Have a rest, Shelly had told him as he'd left Tuman. A total rest. No work, no reading. He was going slowly insane and already wondering if he should phone her and see if he could go back earlier. All he could think of was how they would manage with all the clinics and workload with one fewer doctor. It seemed ridiculous that he was here, sitting on his arse doing nothing. His mobile rang and he pressed the button that muted the TV sound. He recognised the number immediately.

'Matt, it's Rob.'

'Rob who?' said Matt, sounding puzzled.

'You know damn well who, you idiot.'

'Oh. That Rob. What can I do for you?'

'I'm calling to let you know about Friday. I'll be on the six thirty-five from Paddington. Meet me at Oxford station.'

'Yes, Rob,' said Matt, pulling a face at the screen in disbelief. The TV doctor seemed about to perform an emergency tracheotomy on some guy lying on the floor of a fast-food restaurant.

'You have booked a table for Friday night, haven't you?' Rob barked into his ear.

'Yes, Rob.' Matt was shaking his head in disbelief. He'd done an emergency tracheotomy himself once. It had been on a little girl who was choking on a toy soldier, but he'd been in A&E at the time with full medical back-up. 'You can't do it with a bloody steak knife and a cocktail straw,' he muttered.

'What did you say?' said Rob.

'Nothing.'

'Good. Now shut up and listen to me. I want to impress Natasha and her friend Bryony, maybe both together if you know what I mean.'

Matt knew exactly what he meant but said, 'You'll be lucky.'

Ignoring him, Rob carried on issuing orders. 'It's twenty minutes to Packley from the station so we'll have time to stop off for a drink at that nice little pub down the road from Grantley Manor. I think it's called the Trout. I want to make the most of the fact that you're driving . . .'

'Sorry?' said Matt as the TV patient miraculously recovered.

'For fuck's sake, are you even listening to me? Tell me what I just said.'

'Six thirty-five. Station. Trout,' repeated Matt mechanically. 'Rob, have you ever performed a tracheotomy with a steak knife?'

'Have I what? Christ, I give up with you,' cried Rob in

exasperation. 'Look, be there or else. I want this to go well. Natasha and Bryony don't come cheap and I'll blame you if I don't get a shag,' he shouted, before slamming down the phone.

Matt pushed himself off the sofa and stabbed the button on the TV. He felt he'd go mad if he didn't get out of the flat soon. He needed something to do, but *what*? As he straightened, he caught sight of himself in the mirror and leaned closer.

He'd shaved off his beard and had his hair cut that morning, partly because he was bored and also because he looked like Grizzly Adams. After an hour of shampooing and conditioning, cutting and blow-drying, a stranger had stared back at him from the salon mirror. 'You look like a modern-day Mr Darcy,' the stylist had teased, while running her fingers through his hair. When he'd got outside, he found she'd written her phone number in a heart on the back of an appointment card. He shook his head and smiled wryly. Mr Darcy his arse. She couldn't have fancied him that much: she'd still charged him thirty-five quid.

# Chapter Twelve

My God, this trip was going to be *fantastic*.

Carrie was lounging on the sofa of the cottage, her freshly painted toes propped up on a stool, drying in the breeze from the French windows. She had the *Rough Guide to Europe* in one hand and a glass of sangria in the other. She could hardly believe they were taking off on their tour in a few days' time. By next Saturday they could be standing on top of the Eiffel Tower or strutting their stuff on the beach in St Tropez, sipping a cappuccino in Venice, eyeing up the talent from the back of a scooter in Madrid . . .

Okay. She knew it might be pushing it to get round the whole of Europe in one month, especially in a vehicle so old it ought to be listed, but so what? With the sun on their faces and the wind in their hair (because Dolly had no air-con and they'd have to have the windows down or fry), she and Rowena were ready to take on the world.

It was *exactly* what she needed to take her mind off the past few months.

'*Summer niii-gh-hts!*' she heard Rowena warble from the bathroom. Then a screech. 'Bugger! Carrie!'

'Yes!' shouted Carrie.

'Can you find me some more shampoo? We've run out. I'd get it myself but I'm dripping wet.'

Carrie almost skipped up the stairs, then stopped at the top, realising that the strange sensation pulsing through her veins was happiness. Or if not happiness, something very like it.

It wasn't just the trip making her feel as if the sun had come out after a long winter. Since Rowena had announced her intention of starting a drama course, Carrie had been thinking about the future too. She'd hoped to get a place on a teacher training course, been convinced she was too late then phoned up anyway. Five of the six training colleges she'd contacted had almost laughed her off the phone, but that afternoon the sixth had come up trumps.

She couldn't wait to tell Rowena her news over a drink at their local.

Scrubbed and buffed, the girls made their way into the beer garden of the village pub. The Trout was an ancient thatched inn that hugged a bend in the river. It had been thundering during the day and was now a middling kind of summer evening. Insects buzzed round their heads as they bagged a table among the early evening drinkers.

'I don't want to get bitten,' said Rowena, batting away a gnat. 'I've just had my legs waxed.'

Carrie nodded. 'I popped into Tan Tastic courtesy of Huw's latest guilt payment. You don't think it's too . . .'

'What?'

'Well. Too *orange*?'

Rowena shook her head. 'You can never be too thin, too rich or too orange. Look at Paris Hilton.'

'Good. Because I thought I deserved a little treat. Just to celebrate, you know.'

'Celebrate? What are we celebrating? Has Huw gone bankrupt?'

'No. Not that good. I've heard back from the college in town. They said I'd left it too late for the primary teaching course but they could offer me a secondary place. I'm going to specialise in English and drama.'

'Wow! That sounds great, hon,' said Rowena.

Carrie felt a warm glow of pride. 'Well, it's not as glam as going to drama school, but it's a job and I'm looking forward to it. I can't live off my salary from Huw much longer, however much I want to.'

The truth was, the thought of going to Huw – and Fenella – to sort out their joint finances was still way beyond her comfort zone. She still occasionally harboured thoughts of sabotaging his tractor.

'I think it's a bloody brilliant idea. You know, I think you've done really well to get over him so quickly. I'm proud of the way you've put the bastard behind you,' said Rowena.

'What's the point in lying here rotting away? He'll have won then, won't he? I'm sure Huw's not hiding in his bedroom, using up the entire world supply of tissues, is he?' said Carrie.

'Well, no.'

'I expect he's out working the land, preparing it for future Brigstockes to enjoy one day.'

Rowena hesitated, then took a long drag on her cigarette. 'I wasn't going to tell you this, but seeing as you're so over him . . .'

'What?'

'Rumour has it that Fenella's up the duff. Hayley saw them at the Dirty Duck the other night. She said she was sure Fenella had put on weight and she was drinking mineral water even though Huw was driving.'

'In the Duck?' Carrie repeated, as if it was the location not the information that had shocked her. Fenella pregnant . . . She couldn't be. They'd only been together a few months.

'They were in the lounge. Maybe I shouldn't have told you but I thought you ought to know. Are you okay?' Rowena said anxiously.

'Of course. Why wouldn't I be? I don't want a baby. In fact, I can't think of anything worse,' said Carrie brightly. Which wasn't strictly true. She and Huw had never exactly discussed the idea, but now she realised the prospect had still been there, unspoken between them. One day, she'd assumed, there would be children, their children, running around the farm, chasing the chickens and helping to milk the cows. Perhaps that had been the problem: she and Huw had assumed too much about their relationship. They'd grown too comfortable. But it still didn't justify what he'd done to her. No way.

Rowena stubbed her cigarette out in the ashtray and patted Carrie's hand. 'The more I come to think of it, the more I realise what a lucky escape you had. Shall we have another drink?'

'I'll get them this time,' said Carrie, determined to push Huw and Fenella from her mind and focus on the future. She stood up and gathered up the empty glasses, feeling her palms slick against the cool glass. A trip across the garden to the bar would give her a chance to take in this latest news. But she hadn't taken a step when she froze.

'Oh no. Not here.'

'What's up?' said Rowena, craning her neck to try to follow Carrie's gaze. Heading over towards their table from the pub's rear entrance were two men, both tall and dark. One was wearing Ray-Bans and what was obviously part of a business suit, except he'd ditched the tie and had his sleeves rolled up. The other one was Matt Landor.

'Don't look.'

Rowena pulled a face. 'Why not? Is it Huw? Is *she* with him?'

'It's not Huw. It's Matt Landor. At least I think it is. He looks different.'

She longed for the ground to open up or a meteorite to hit the pub. Anything rather than have to face the man who'd practically thrown her out of St Mark's church.

Rowena's head whipped round, and she waved.

'I don't want to speak to him,' said Carrie.

'Don't be silly. Now's your chance to show him you're normal. After all, he is a doctor. I'm sure he'll understand you weren't in your right mind at the church, and he did call you to see how you were.'

The man with Matt waved back, but Matt didn't. He just kept on heading for them.

Carrie closed her eyes briefly, hoping that she could be beamed up out of the pub garden to just about anywhere else in the universe. Rowena was wrong. She wasn't sure she *hadn't* been in her right mind.

Close up, it was obvious the other man was Matt's brother – a slightly older, stockier, much paler version – apart from the florid cheeks.

'Hello,' said Matt, his mouth twitching in a smile as they reached the table. 'This is my brother Rob.'

'Well, good evening, ladies!' said Rob, holding out his free hand. He had a whisky in the other.

'Pleased to meet you,' said Rowena in the voice she usually kept for serious roles.

'Hi,' said Carrie, unable to stop staring at Matt, who stood with a bottle of Coke in his hand. She hardly recognised him. The beard and ponytail had gone. His dark, almost black hair was now only long-ish and swept back from his face, revealing sharply defined cheekbones and dark, brooding eyes that seemed to be assessing her, unselfconsciously, from head to toe.

'You've cut your hair,' she said.

His lips twitched in a smile. 'I got fed up with buying scrunchies.'

Carrie wondered if Matt had already told his brother who she was. Had they been talking about her before deciding to come over? But Rob dispelled that by perching his whisky on the table slats and saying, 'Matt, for God's sake stop flirting and introduce me properly.'

'This is Rowena Kincaid and Caroline Brownhill. We were at university together,' said Matt.

*Caroline?* Carrie hadn't heard anyone call her that for years. It always made her sound like a Tory Party candidate. Carrie was so much more *Sex and the City*.

Rob's eyes glittered. 'Really? You've never mentioned either of them before, and I can see why. Keeping them to yourself.'

'We didn't see much of each other,' Carrie replied. 'Different subjects.'

Rowena was visibly fluttering. 'And what do you do for a living, Robert?'

'Oh, this and that, you know,' he replied, squeezing

himself into the vacant bench space next to Rowena.

'Rob's an orthopaedic surgeon,' said Matt.

Rob smiled. 'Matt doesn't approve of me being in private practice. He's a saint, you see.'

'You'll have to excuse my brother. He's pissed,' growled Matt.

Rob curled a lip. 'And Matt's a sanctimonious git, but in the morning I'll be sober.'

The atmosphere between them was so charged that Carrie half expected them to start duelling in the pub garden, but Rowena, relishing the scent of so much testosterone, was melting in a puddle of lust.

'Do you come here often?' she squeaked.

Matt threw a smile at her and Rowena turned to mush. 'I would do if I was in the country, but I've been working abroad and I'm only back here for a few months.'

'He's going to save the world if he lives that long. He attracts trouble like a cow-pat attracts flies,' laughed Rob. 'D'you mind if I have one of your cigarettes?'

'Not at all,' twittered Rowena.

'Where are you staying?' Carrie asked Matt.

'I've rented a friend's flat in Oxford.'

'Oh. That's handy. Where is it?' said Carrie, glad of a safe topic. She managed to spend five minutes talking about the merits of Oxford versus living in Packley village. She'd have gladly talked about train timetables or paint charts rather than the circumstances in which they'd last met. She just hoped that he and his brother would go away very, very soon, but fate wasn't on her side.

'You ladies look like you could do with a top-up,' said Rob.

'That's very kind,' Rowena trilled. 'I'll have a gin and tonic.'

'Coke,' said Carrie, knowing they had no chance of escape now.

Matt shook his head, holding up his half-full bottle.

Rowena pouted seductively at Rob. 'Do you need a hand?'

He raised his eyebrows and held out his arm for her to take. 'Always.'

'So how are you?' Matt asked Carrie when the others had gone to the bar.

'I'm fine, thanks,' she said tightly, heart sinking as she realised what was going to happen.

He studied her for a moment as if she was an interesting specimen. 'Hmm.'

'What's that supposed to mean?'

'Just that in my experience, "I'm fine" is probably the number one lie on the planet,' he said taking a swig from his Coke. His Adam's apple bobbed beneath the stubbled skin of his throat.

'It also happens to be true,' she said defiantly.

His eyes narrowed. 'Perhaps,' he said.

The seconds ticked by. A group of girls in the corner of the beer garden started singing 'Happy Birthday' before Matt broke the silence. 'Nice weather we're having for the time of year,' he said.

'Unseasonably warm,' Carrie shot back. 'Though I think it might rain later in the evening.'

'I think we could have a real storm if we're unlucky,' said Matt.

'And what's the temperature like here compared to where you've been working? Are you finding it cold?'

He gazed down at her, giving nothing away, then said, 'It's fairly frosty from where I'm standing.'

'Then I advise you to head for somewhere warmer. Somewhere you can be more comfortable,' she said.

He laughed out loud. 'Carrie. You don't know me very well. I never run away from a challenge. Even when it seems like a lost cause, I keep on going until I get what I want.'

Carrie dropped her eyes from his face. Annoyingly, she couldn't think of a smart reply, but fortunately Rob and Rowena returned, carrying a tray of drinks.

'Has my brother told you about his claim to fame yet?' said Rob, splashing Coke on Carrie's dress as he put down the tray none too gently. He didn't seem to notice and Carrie wasn't going to draw attention to it, but Matt was tight lipped.

'Oh! What claim to fame?' cried Rowena.

'My brother's a hero,' said Rob, sitting down.

'Piss off, Rob.' Matt said the words lightly enough but Carrie could hear the static crackling between them.

'I heard you'd been working in the jungle,' she said, wondering why she felt the need to help him out by changing the subject.

He nodded. 'I've been in Tuman, working for a medical charity,' he said, but stopped short of elaborating, almost as if he was shy, though she hardly thought that possible.

'You won't get any more out of him than that,' said Rob. 'So when are you ladies going on this road trip Rowena's been telling me about? It sounds like a blast, bumming round Europe in a camper van. Wish I'd taken a year off and done something like it but I've never had the time. Now Matt, of course, is at a loose end until he goes back to his job saving the world. And you know what they say. The devil makes work for idle hands.'

'I do hope so,' said Matt. 'Where are you planning on going?'

'Paris, Provence, northern Italy, maybe Switzerland too,' said Rowena.

Rob tutted loudly. 'Stop angling for an invitation, Matt.'

Carrie was horrified. 'Oh, there wouldn't be room. It's only a very small van and we've got piles of stuff.'

Rob unwrapped a cigar he'd bought from the bar. 'You see, Matt, the ladies can't squeeze you in.'

'Even if they wanted to,' said Matt, keeping his eyes on Carrie.

Rowena held out her lighter. 'Let me help you with that, Rob.'

Carrie picked up her Coke and took several large gulps. Matt pushed back his shirt cuff and checked his watch, frowning.

'Expecting someone?' said Carrie.

He glanced back at her, reading her full meaning. 'As a matter of fact, yes.'

And on cue, his lips parted slightly as he spotted someone behind her, his eyes crinkling at the corners in pleasure and recognition. It was as if, Carrie thought, the sun had suddenly burst out through the clouds on a grey and rainy day.

# *Chapter Thirteen*

They all turned to see two girls pushing their way through the drinkers and diners. One was a willowy blonde in a catsuit, the other a curvaceous brunette whose ample bosom was spilling out of a pale blue silk dress. There was no mistaking Nigella and Joely, and there was also no escape. They'd seen her in the pub toilets, they'd seen her outside the church and they must have lapped up every last juicy detail about her performance from the other guests. When they reached the table, their eyes lit up in confusion, then disbelief.

'Natasha, Bryony. This is Rowena and Carrie,' said Matt.

Nigella and Joely hadn't been that far off then, thought Carrie.

'We've already met,' said Natasha.

'In the toilets at the Turf,' added Bryony.

Natasha lowered her voice and bowed her head towards Carrie's ear. 'How are you doing? Bloody Fenella! Has to steal someone else's man instead of getting her own. Still, what do you expect from an accountant. It must have been so awful for you.'

Rob tore his eyes from Natasha's cleavage and pricked

up his ears. 'What must have been awful?' he said, then took a puff of his cigar and said meaningfully, 'Ah.'

'Actually, we were just leaving,' said Carrie, unable to bear the torture any longer.

'Oh, don't go on our account. I'm sure we've time for another drink before we have to set off for Grantley Manor. Minty booked a table to celebrate him being safely back home,' said Natasha, stroking Matt's arm. 'Has he told you about his adventures in the jungle?'

*Minty?* Carrie bit back a smile as Matt squirmed. She spoke very politely. 'Not yet, and it's very kind of you and, er, Minty to ask us to stay, but Rowena and I have got a date with Dolly. We're off on holiday next week and we need to check our route.'

'Dolly?' said Bryony, slipping on to the bench next to Rob. He kissed her on the cheek.

'She's a vintage camper van,' said Rowena, glaring her displeasure at having to leave.

Natasha beamed. 'How retro. Where are you off to?'

'Oh, somewhere on the continent. We're not sure yet. We're just going to set off and see where life takes us,' Carrie replied airily.

'Gosh. Sounds like bliss. How lovely to have no ties or responsibilities. I'd absolutely love to simply take off. It's so boring to have to work. You've got an amazing tan there. That must have taken days of lying about in the back garden,' said Natasha.

'Weeks actually,' said Carrie, smiling until her jaw hurt. 'But it was worth it. I'd hate to be on the treadmill. It must be so tedious.'

'Well, I'd do the same if I were you, Carrie darling. God knows, you deserve a little bit of happiness after what you've been through. Matt's told me what a horrible ordeal you've endured with Huw.'

'Quite,' said Carrie, adding Natasha to her list of people to put in the stocks with Huw. 'But I'm afraid we do have to leave you. Goodbye, Rob, Natasha, Bryony. Nice meeting you.'

'Have a great time. Don't do anything I wouldn't,' said Rob.

Carrie steamed off towards the car park, leaving Rowena trailing in her wake.

'Wait a minute. I can't keep up in these shoes! And I need the loo!' she protested.

'I'll wait for you in the car,' called Carrie. She couldn't stand it a moment longer. The humiliation of bumping into Natasha and Bryony was just too much to bear. It had been by far the worst moment since the church thing. She'd had to endure some funny looks in the village shop for a few days afterwards, but thankfully she hadn't achieved the notoriety she'd expected. Village gossip moved on fast and Carrie's escapade had soon been eclipsed by the vicar's son, who was living with a trans-gender asylum-seeker. No, village tittle-tattle was nothing to receiving the dubious sympathy of two strangers in front of Matt and his brother. When she reached the car park, though, she realised she'd left her bag behind in the beer garden. Now she'd have to go back for it, which would be excruciating. 'Shit.'

'Is this what you're looking for?'

Matt was alongside her, holding out her handbag, looking as sheepish as any man did when forced to hold a green sparkly clutch.

'It won't go off in your hand,' she said.

'Yes, but the colour doesn't suit my eyes,' he said.

But your eyes are twinkling, thought Carrie with a smile, because you feel awkward at following me out of a pub with a bag, and I'm enjoying you squirming.

'What's so funny?' he said, folding his arms.

'Nothing. Thanks for bringing my bag,' she said, then murmured, '*Twinkle*,' and started marching towards the car.

'Caroline, wait.'

'That's not my name,' she said, stopping and daring him to repeat it.

He folded his arms, looked down at her and said with perfect seriousness, 'And mine's not Twinkle.'

Carrie smiled sweetly back. 'Or Minty?'

His lips twisted. 'I know this isn't any of my business, but I can understand it was a shock for you, what happened with Huw.'

The breath stopped in her throat and she felt her cheeks flaming with shame.

'You're right. It isn't any of your business and I don't think you can understand.' Her words came out harsher than she'd meant but she didn't want his sympathy.

He shook his head. 'How do you know I can't understand? You're the only one on the planet who's ever suffered, are you? The only person who's had to deal with rejection and guilt?'

'Guilt? What have I got to feel guilty about? As for being rejected . . .' No, she mustn't get into a conversation with him. That was probably what he wanted, to draw her out. 'Matt, thanks for bringing my bag but I don't need your help. All I need is a good holiday away from Packley. I'm a big girl, Dr Landor. I can fight my own battles.'

94

He smiled. 'I'm sure you can. I've seen you do it, remember?'

She turned back towards the car.

'Have a good trip,' he called after her.

'Yeah, I will,' she murmured. Closing the driver's door firmly, she took a deep breath and laid her hot cheek against the cool leather of the seat. Rowena was walking out of the pub door. Carrie brushed her hand over her eyes and wished they would stop stinging. Matt had brought those tears to her eyes and she didn't know why, but she hated herself for her weakness and hated him for making her feel vulnerable.

Rowena opened the passenger door and popped her head in. 'Was that Matt I saw talking to you? What did he want?'

'I left my handbag behind,' said Carrie, hoping Rowena wouldn't hear the catch in her voice.

Rowena rolled her eyes. 'Oh bugger. Is that all? He's absolutely gorgeous, isn't he? Both of them are. Sort of dangerous and smouldering.'

'What? Like a bonfire?'

'Oh. You are touchy. I just thought that maybe . . .'

'No. Last man on earth and all that,' said Carrie, turning the key in the ignition with unnecessary force. 'Rowena?'

'Yes, hon?'

'How early can you be ready to set off for the ferry next Saturday? I can't get out of Packley soon enough.'

# Chapter Fourteen

Later that evening, Matt wound down the window of his ancient Mini to let in the cool night air. After leaving the pub, the four of them had enjoyed a very good, if extortionately priced meal at Grantley Manor. Robert had paid, which had made the food taste even better, but Matt had still felt uncomfortable. Spending so much on feeding just four people felt wrong, but it wasn't only his social conscience that was bothering him. Natasha had been regaling him with gossip about the Carrie-Huw-Fenella thing for most of the evening.

'Of course, this was where Huw had booked the reception for his wedding to that girl,' she'd said as soon as they'd set foot in the oak-panelled foyer of Grantley Manor.

'Really?' Matt gritted his teeth but it had taken him some time to steer the girls off the subject.

He'd wondered, too many times, whether he should have interfered that day at the church. After all, Carrie was entitled to do what she wanted; he wasn't her keeper. He admired her feistiness, her spark and her guts and he didn't blame her for being mad with Huw either.

She hated him now, and he could understand that.

He'd hate someone who had seen him in that state: raw and upset. Slightly deranged too, he thought with a smile. No wonder she was angry and awkward with him. That was why he hadn't stood up for her in the beer garden; why he'd kept his mouth shut this time and let her fight her own battles.

By the time the waiters had brought the first course, Matt had been determined to force any thoughts of Carrie from his mind, despite the fact that Natasha gossiped about her for most of the evening, and by the end of the night, he'd actually found he was rather enjoying himself. He'd dropped Robert and Bryony off at his brother's house in Summertown and then surprised Natasha by sailing past the flat and heading towards the city.

He had the perfect antidote to his guilty conscience about Carrie.

'Oh, are we going clubbing? Or for a cocktail at Quod?' asked Natasha.

'That isn't quite what I had in mind. Close your eyes and don't open them until I tell you.'

'Can I look yet?' she begged from the passenger seat. 'I can't wait much longer.'

'Absolutely not,' said Matt, flicking the indicator to turn left off the main road.

'Oh please.'

'Not long now.'

The Mini trundled happily between the parked cars and bicycles that lined either side of the quiet north Oxford street. It was midnight but it was also midsummer and not properly dark. The orange glow of streetlights combined with the moon shining down from an almost cloudless sky lent the houses and trees a strange gilded quality. Matt was glad of the twilight because he couldn't have done what he was planning if it had been pitch dark.

'Matt,' pleaded Natasha, almost bouncing up and down in her seat.

He grinned. 'Patience.'

Seeing the gates of the boathouse ahead, he managed to squeeze the Mini into a space between a scooter and some yellow lines, then got out and opened the door for Natasha. 'Okay. You can look now.'

She took her hands from her face and seemed puzzled. 'Oh.'

'I thought we'd take a stroll in the moonlight,' said Matt.

'A stroll?'

'Yes. What did you think we were going to do?'

He almost laughed at her disappointment but took her hand and led her between the stone pillars and into the grounds. The river glittered in the distance. It had been years since he'd been there, but like so many things in Oxford, virtually nothing had changed. The boathouse was shuttered and dark. The water was dappled silver in the moonlight, fringed with tiny eddies where black willow trees dipped their branches into the water. Dozens of shallow wooden punts were moored side by side against the duckboard jetty. A few were half drawn up a stone slipway next to a wall.

Stepping into one, Matt rearranged the seat cushions into a makeshift bed.

'Oh my word. Now I see what you have in mind,' said Natasha.

Matt took off his jacket and laid it on the cushions.

'I'm afraid it's a bit damp in here, but there's not a lot I can do about that.'

'I think I can cope,' said Natasha. She was purring again, which he took to be a promising sign.

The punt wobbled a little as he helped her climb inside, barefoot. Natasha let out a giggle.

'What's up?'

'Have you seen the number of this punt?'

'What?' Matt glanced at the figures painted on the back of the seat. 'Sixty-nine. How appropriate. I hope we can live up to it.'

He kissed her, softly and deeply, and started to unbutton the front of her dress, knowing she had no bra on underneath and that her golden breasts would spill out. But Natasha clamped her fingers firmly over his hand. 'Now, Minty, slow down. I want to make the most of this.'

He propped himself up on one elbow, watching her open her tiny evening bag. He guessed what was coming next, and sure enough, she drew out a wrap of white powder and held it out to him, licking her lips seductively. Matt had been offered almost everything in his time, including some substances he didn't think Natasha could possibly imagine existed, but he managed to look surprised nonetheless.

'Tasha. You disappoint me. There's no need for that,' he said sternly.

'Now don't be a bore, Minty. I didn't have you down as one of the thought police. You know how amazing this could be.'

He kissed her lips softly. 'It will be amazing. But there's no need for you to waste that when I've got a much more exciting alternative.'

Her green eyes shone like a cat's in the moonlight as he slid his fingers into the inside pocket of his jacket. He could hear her breathing quicken as he pulled out a twist of brown paper. Inside were two pieces of twig.

She seemed confused.

'I promised you amazing. You're going to get amazing,' said Matt.

'Is this from . . . from the jungle?'

He winked. 'Well, it's not from Boots, I can tell you that.'

'What's in it? Nothing made from the blood of cockroaches or anything like that, I hope!'

Matt smiled and ran his finger along her leg, and she shivered. He slid his hand under the hem of her dress until he reached the top of her thigh, which confirmed his diagnosis that she wasn't wearing any knickers.

'Tasha, if you want an extraordinary experience, you have to be prepared to go to extraordinary lengths. Now, just close your eyes and open your mouth.'

As he broke off a tiny piece of bark and placed it on her tongue, the warmth of her mouth around his finger made him realise he had no need of stimulants. He couldn't wait much longer.

'Do I shwallow or sthuck?' mumbled Natasha.

'Chew. I'll take some too. Now lie back and try and relax.'

'What will it do?'

He smiled. 'Wait and see.'

Some time later, Matt lay gazing up at the stars as Natasha regained her breath. He knew they'd have to leave soon; it was a miracle no one had heard them before, the noise she'd made as he'd made love to her the second time. The first time she'd expressed her pleasure by digging her nails into his backside until he'd almost squealed himself.

'What the fack was that stuff?' she demanded as they got dressed. 'And please, please can I have some more? That was the most amazing shag I've ever had, and you, Minty, were enormous, if you don't mind me saying. I want every time to be like that.'

Matt patted her bottom. 'I can't tell you. In fact, no one really knows. I was given them by some tribal elder and he said he'd have to shoot me with a poisoned arrow if I found out the ingredients.'

'Facking hell!'

'Quite. I didn't dare bring any more through customs. Now, you're getting cold. Shall we go and have a coffee?'

'Just a coffee?' said Natasha, her face crestfallen.

He kissed her as he ushered her into the car, trying not to laugh. He'd known the so-called herbal aphrodisiac he'd given her couldn't possibly work, but Natasha had believed it would give her the shag of a lifetime and that was all that mattered. 'You've had more than the recommended dose already, I'm afraid. If we do it again, I'll have to give it to you straight. You'll have to make do with the ordinary variety.'

# Chapter Fifteen

'*La isla bonita . . .*' Carrie sang her heart out above the noise of the juicer in the cottage kitchen. Today was the day and she felt like a new woman. A woman who was off on her holidays. A woman who'd packed four bikinis and three times as many shoes as she actually needed. A woman who had taken control of her life and was moving on.

The encounter with Matt and his friends in the Trout had been consigned to history. The shock of hearing Fenella was pregnant had been filed away under Lucky Escape. After all, she could never have cut loose and gone off on a road trip if she'd been married to Huw, especially if she'd had children. She knew she was rationalising, making the best of the situation, but that was the only way to survive.

She was crunching on her third slice of toast when she heard Dolly trundling up the village street. She felt a weird feeling of excitement that wasn't far off the way she felt when she was about to go on stage sometimes. She almost ran outside before slowing down to a pace more suited to someone about to turn thirty. Nelson slid open Dolly's side door, his expression more lugubrious than ever.

'Where's Rowena?' he asked gloomily.

'On the phone to someone, I think. Can I start loading our bags?'

'Yeah, but I hope you haven't brought too much crap. These vans don't hold a lot and it puts too much strain on the engine if they're overloaded. Doesn't do the road-holding any good either.'

'We've tried to keep it to the essentials,' said Carrie, determined to stay cheerful whatever. The last thing she wanted was for Nelson to have second thoughts and cancel the trip. She was now so desperate to get away, she thought she might explode if they couldn't set off.

Nelson gave a sigh but reached for her rucksack. Carrie wondered what he'd say when he saw their other luggage and the crate of beer, and decided to let Rowena break that one to him.

'Before you set off, I think I should give you a few tips for driving Dolly, show you around the engine, run through a few do's and don'ts,' he said.

'Well, I'm sure Rowena's fully up to speed with all the techie stuff,' Carrie replied firmly.

He grunted. 'What if Rowena's incapacitated or unable to perform her duties? You'll have to take over. No, I definitely think you should have a lesson. It's the least Dolly deserves before I let you take charge of her.'

Not being able to deny that Rowena might conceivably be unable to perform her duties at some point, Carrie had to give in. Twenty minutes later she was trying desperately hard to pay attention as Nelson rattled on about Dolly's big end and warned her about the van's asthmatic intake (not that it was Dolly's fault at her age, of course). He was particularly obsessed with the spongy brakes and mercurial gear-changing. Carrie wished he'd give her some credit. She'd been driving for more than twelve years. How hard could it be? All you had to do was point the thing in the right direction. She sighed in relief as Rowena emerged from the house. Then frowned at her friend's pale face.

'Are you all right, Rowena?'

'Fine. Totally fine.'

The *totally* said everything. 'Who was the phone call from?' Carrie asked.

'Mum. She worries about me, you know. Warning me about muggers and pickpockets. As if I needed warning. I see you've already started loading up,' said Rowena.

'Yeah. Seems like you girls took my advice for a change and didn't bring too much,' said Nelson sarcastically.

'I thought we'd better wait for you, Row. I didn't want to forget anything,' said Carrie, sensing trouble brewing over the luggage.

'Forget anything my arse. You'll never have room to sleep if you take all that stuff. There's the awning to go in yet,' grumbled Nelson.

'Oh stop rattling on, Nelson. You sound like an old woman!' snapped Rowena. Nelson's face dropped like a stone, and she threw him an apologetic smile. 'Sorry. I'm a bit tetchy this morning.' She lowered her voice. 'Time of the month, you know.'

Carrie knew the effect that any hint of female problems would have on Nelson, and sure enough he muttered something about carburettors and scuttled off to the rear of the van. She felt terribly sorry for him, and worse, she was now certain that there really was something wrong with Rowena, who was pacing about, chain-smoking.

Carrie almost dragged her into the kitchen. 'Tell me what's going on. You look like you're going for colonic irrigation rather than on holiday, and you almost took Nelson's head off.'

'And this from Miss Sweetness and Light,' snapped Rowena.

Carrie felt as though she'd been slapped. Rowena shook her head and said, 'Carrie, it's no good. I have to tell you, I can't come on the trip.'

Carrie couldn't speak. She couldn't believe what she was hearing. 'Can't come? Why? Is it your mum? Is she ill?'

'No, Mum's fine.'

'Then tell me why we can't go. If something has happened, I'll try to understand,' said Carrie, attempting not to burst into tears for Rowena's sake.

'You remember when we were doing *Grease*? On the last night? When that man with the bad wig got talking to me and you thought he wanted to get inside my knickers?' said Rowena.

'Yes,' said Carrie, puzzled.

'Well, Wiggy – the man – works for an independent production company. He was staying with a friend and got dragged along to *Grease*. He suggested I go for an audition in London for a new medical soap called *HeartAche*.'

'*HeartAche*? You are joking!'

'It's not that crap a title,' said Rowena defensively.

'It's not the title . . . I'm just amazed that you actually went to an audition for a soap.' That she'd managed to keep it a secret was what Carrie really meant.

'It was months ago. I'd convinced myself they weren't interested,' said Rowena airily.

'And you couldn't tell me?' said Carrie, realising just what she'd missed over the past few months. She really had been on another planet.

'Oh, you had enough to worry about without me going on about it.'

Carrie felt a lump form in her throat. Rowena hadn't wanted to lord it over her when she'd been so down.

'Well, yesterday morning the casting woman phoned to say that they wanted to offer me the part but I'd have to be in London later today. I tried to stall her for a few days but she wanted an answer first thing this morning.'

Horrified that she might have ruined Rowena's big chance, Carrie went into overdrive. 'I can't believe you'd turn down a part in a soap for me! Now I know why you were so upset when you came off the phone. You raving nutter, Rowena. You can't pass up a chance like this.'

'But I'd promised you we'd have this holiday. I know how much it means to you and I couldn't let you down.' Rowena chewed her lip nervously. 'I was stressing about it all day yesterday, wondering whether to accept or not. You know I'd sell my granny for the part but I also know how much you need this break. Either way I was letting someone down.'

Carrie felt physically sick at the thought of Rowena giving up her dream because she felt sorry for her. 'No. No way, Jose. You can't turn this down, not for me, not for anyone. You have to get back on that phone and tell them you've changed your mind. Grovel, lick their boots, do anything, but don't throw this away.'

Rowena's face lit up, her eyes suspiciously bright.

Rowena never cried, not for real. 'Do you really mean it, hon?' she said.

'Of course I mean it, you daft devil.'

'I'm so relieved you feel like that. You see, I haven't thrown my chance away. I thought you wouldn't want me to, so I phoned back first thing and said yes. It means I'd have to miss out on the first term at drama school and if they kept me in the show, I probably wouldn't be able to go at all, but this is my big chance.'

Carrie's heart skipped a beat. She was so proud on Rowena's behalf, so buoyed up by her delight and enthusiasm, that it almost felt like she'd got the part herself. 'I'm so glad you decided to go for it. I couldn't have lived with myself otherwise. What part is it?'

'Shameless Hospital Hussy,' said Rowena proudly. 'With an addiction to internet gambling and a secret conviction for stealing men's underwear from washing lines. She has a chequered past, you see.'

'How could they ever have given the role to anyone else?'

'Thanks for being so great about this. I should have had more faith. I should have known you wouldn't mind, but I didn't want to let you down. You know we've always stuck together,' said Rowena.

'Now don't go all sentimental. No hysterical blubbing and overacting. Save that for the show.'

'Okay. But that leaves you alone with Dolly, and I can't have that.'

'Why not? Dolly and me get along just fine,' said Carrie, hoping she was making a convincing job of the 'heroine puts on brave face for friend's sake' act.

Rowena was all smiles now. 'Ah. Now that's the tricky

part. I didn't want you to miss out on your holiday because of me. I didn't want you to go off on your own and I couldn't think of anyone else who was free at short notice or had sod-all to do for a month.'

'No,' said Carrie, as she realised what Rowena was about to say. 'No. You haven't. You'd better not have.'

'Honey, it was the only thing I could come up with at short notice.'

Just then, the stable door of the kitchen crashed open and Matt stood in the doorway, a rucksack on his back and a broad grin on his face.

# Chapter Sixteen

'Absolutely, definitely not.'

'Carrie. Be reasonable,' pleaded Rowena as they stood at the front of the van. Matt was by the gate, talking on his phone.

'No. *Non. Nein.* There, you have it in three languages. How's that?' said Carrie, still reeling with shock at Rowena's bombshell.

'Shhh. Matt will hear you,' hissed Rowena, desperation creeping into her voice.

'I don't give a toss. I am not going on holiday with Matt Landor.'

'Come and sit in the van and listen to me. This is the best solution.'

Inside the van, Rowena shut the door. Nelson and Matt were leaning over a map on the bonnet of Matt's Mini, Nelson's plump backside nestling next to Matt's firm one. Matt's jeans tautened over his backside as he picked something up off the ground.

'The answer's still no,' Carrie said. 'I don't need a babysitter. I'll be fine on my own.'

'But it's not that simple, hon.'

'What d'you mean, not that simple?'

Rowena glanced out of the window and lowered her voice. 'Nelson isn't too keen on letting you loose with Dolly.'

'But he was going to let us go off together.'

'Yes. *Us.* But you, on your own, that's a different matter. Please don't blame him, Carrie. You know he's a worrier. Dolly means everything to him. You do as well, of course,' she added hastily.

'I think what you're really trying to say is that Nelson thinks I'm unstable and can't be trusted to handle Dolly on my own without driving her over a cliff.'

'Well, I wouldn't say that exactly, but he was at the church that day. He saw what happened. He doesn't know you as well as I do.'

'I wish people would forget about that. I wasn't myself, and why would he trust Matt to come along anyway? What does he know about vintage camper vans?'

'Quite a bit actually.' Matt popped his face inside the van, grinning. 'One of my mates at school had one in the sixth form. We spent months bumming about round Wales in it before I went to uni. Best time I've ever had in my life. I've just been admiring the Love Machine.'

'It's Dolly, actually,' said Carrie sarcastically.

Matt let out a low whistle. 'Great name. Come to think of it, great singer. I've always rated her version of "I Will Always Love You". Much better than that OTT Whitney Houston crap.'

To her horror, Carrie saw Nelson's jaw drop in astonishment and admiration.

'Would I be right in thinking that Dolly had the original Canterbury Pitt conversion?' added Matt with a disarming grin.

'One of the finest examples in the country,' said Nelson, almost smiling. Carrie watched him turn to putty in Matt's skilful hands. Within minutes, they were both poking around in Dolly's engine, touching up her paintwork and drooling over her big end.

'That is a truly disgusting sight,' murmured Carrie.

'I knew I should have turned down the part,' said Rowena, seeing her face.

'No you shouldn't. You absolutely shouldn't. But I don't need Matt to hold my hand on this trip.'

'I know that, but I can think of worse blokes to share a confined space with. He knows about camper vans, and if you chop your finger off or catch a life-threatening disease, who better to have around?' Rowena gave a sly smile. 'You have to admit that he's pretty easy on the eye, and he was so nice the morning after Huw's wedding, phoning to see how you were.'

Carrie folded her arms but said nothing. She wanted Rowena to suffer.

'And I had his number in my mobile and I just thought . . .'

'Just thought what?'

'Well, it might be totally bizarre and I might be horribly wrong, but I thought there might be some sort of, um . . . chemistry between you.'

'Spark? Chemistry? Oh yeah, put us together in a confined space and we'll both explode, you mean!'

'Carrie, be reasonable. After all, they say hate is only the flip side of love. Look at Rhett and Scarlett. Beatrice and Benedick . . .'

'They're fictional, Rowena. Made up. Not real.'

She held up her palms. 'Okay. Okay. Maybe you're not

destined for each other, but you definitely need a ... distraction, and even if you really don't fancy him, can't you at least agree to get along and hide the daggers for a few weeks?'

Rowena was almost pleading now, and Carrie forced herself to imagine whether she could bear the prospect of sharing a tin box with Matt for a month. No. It was unthinkable. No matter how good looking, he was just too patronising and arrogant.

Seeing Carrie hesitate, a hopeful smile stole over Rowena's face. 'Matt seemed very enthusiastic when I asked him. He's going back to Tuman in October and he was looking for something to do. He's had a bad time out there. I'm not sure exactly what happened, but ...'

'Really?' murmured Carrie, her attention focused on the way Matt was caressing Dolly's dipstick with an oily rag as Nelson drooled.

'Look, if you're scared of being with him or something ...' said Rowena.

Carrie's head snapped back to Rowena. 'Scared? Why should I be scared?'

Nelson appeared in the doorway. 'Right. We've checked Dolly's oil levels again and I'd rather you went easy on the gas pedal, but she's ready to go. If you have any problems, Matt'll sort them out. Why don't you finish loading your stuff?'

'Do you want a few minutes to yourself?' said Rowena gently.

Carrie climbed out and stood by the gate to the cottage. She knew she was standing on the brink. Stay here in Packley, static, waiting to start the rest of her life, or set off in the van with a bloke she hardly knew. If she'd

112

been looking for an adventure, a metaphorical journey as well as a literal one, this was her chance. She should be mature about the situation and seize the opportunity. They might even get along.

'If you're scared I might jump you the moment we get out of the village, you'll be quite safe. I'll even wear shorts in bed just for you,' said Matt from behind her.

Any hope of getting along evaporated as he grinned down at her, but she turned round and squared up to him. 'I'm not scared of a man called Minty.'

He smiled softly. 'Look, Caroline, I think we should try and make the best of this for everyone's sake. I've got to go back to work in Tuman in a few months. Until then, I've got time I don't want on my hands. I can't see myself hanging around Oxford until the autumn with a load of tourists. I was thinking of getting away for a while, and when Rowena phoned me about coming along with you, I decided it was fate.' He grinned and she knew he was bullshitting her.

'Look, Matt, I don't believe in fate any more. Life is just a random series of events over which we have no control.'

'I prefer to see it as actions with consequences, and if you won't go on this trip for yourself, then do it for Rowena. She cares about you. She wouldn't have taken the job if I hadn't agreed to come along.'

'That's blatant emotional blackmail.'

'And I have no qualms about using it,' he threw back, looking down at her with that strange mix of irritation and concern she'd seen before.

'You're going to miss the boat if you don't go soon,' called Rowena anxiously.

Matt's eyes challenged her to back down. 'Carrie's still making up her mind about whether she dares to come along.'

*Dares!* The cheeky, arrogant sod. 'I'm coming,' declared Carrie.

'Thank God for that,' cried Rowena.

A few minutes later, as Matt strode off to the van and climbed behind the wheel, Carrie and Rowena exchanged a last hug.

'Why do I feel like Bruce Willis setting off to destroy the asteroid in *Armageddon*?' Carrie whispered.

'Bruce never made it home, but you will. Now go on. You might even enjoy yourself.'

Then she was inside the van, next to Matt, wrestling with the old-fashioned seatbelt. The engine revved suddenly and Dolly let out a tortured groan before kangarooing forward.

'I thought you said you could handle these things,' she shouted above the clattering engine.

Matt grinned at her and winked. 'I said my mate had one once. I never said I'd driven one.'

# Chapter Seventeen

The thunderclouds gathering above the motorway seemed like towering castles of doom to Carrie. She and Matt hadn't gone very far when they'd hit a jam. They'd just managed to get going again but Dolly's wipers were struggling to cope with the torrents of water sluicing down her twin screens. A blinding flash rent the sky, followed by a huge clap of thunder that almost shook the van off its chassis.

But that was nothing to the storm Carrie was about to unleash on Matt after what he'd just confessed. Instead of turning off towards the ferry port, he'd headed in the opposite direction, towards the motorway that led west.

'You're going the wrong way,' she'd protested. 'This doesn't lead to the ferry terminal.'

'We're not going to the terminal. I don't have my passport.'

She was so stunned she hadn't spoken for a few seconds. Then she'd realised he was winding her up. She gave a little tinkling laugh.

'Matt. You should be a comedian. Come on, you've had your joke. We can take the next exit and double back for the ferry.'

'I'm not joking, Carrie. I wish I was.'

She gripped the edges of her seat in shock. He meant it. He actually meant it. She'd agreed to go away with him to help Rowena, clinging on to the consolation of a month in hot and glamorous places. But now? They were going to miss their ferry. They were going to miss Paris and Rome and Provence. The Eiffel Tower, the Alps, St Tropez . . . Her dreams were flowing away down the gutter. And it was all Matt's fault.

'Noo-oooo!'

Matt swerved and the van lurched sickeningly. 'Jesus Christ. I nearly ran into that truck. What the hell's the matter?'

'What's the matter? You are. You just destroyed my holiday!'

'Now just calm down. This isn't the end of the world.'

'Calm? Stay *calm*? After what you've just told me?'

'I can't help it if my passport's expired. It's a good job it happened now, rather than when I was queuing at the check-in to go back to Tuman. I did the responsible thing and sent it off as soon as I got back. How was I to know I'd be invited on a road trip round Europe?'

'But you knew you'd need it when you agreed to come,' said Carrie, knowing she was wailing but not caring. 'You knew where we were planning on going. How could you have done this? You've ruined the whole bloody trip!'

'With respect, I haven't ruined the whole bloody trip. It's just going to be different, that's all.'

'With respect,' snarled Carrie. 'You're just a fucking idiot!'

The wipers swished. The rain hammered down. The engine of the giant truck next to them rumbled like an impending earthquake.

When Matt spoke, his voice was icily calm. 'Caroline. In my professional opinion, getting all worked up like this is bad for you. You should watch your blood pressure.'

'Stuff your professional opinion. I'm not even thirty yet. I don't have anything wrong with my sodding blood pressure!'

'I could check for you. I brought some kit with me,' he said, raising his eyebrows. 'Shall I?'

'You . . .'

'Yes?' He stared at her, challenging her.

'Oh just turn off for the bloody services!'

'Well, it seems a shame when we've finally got going, but if that's what you *really* want.'

The only thing that had stopped her from saying something very rude again was the futility of it. Nothing she could say would change the situation, and ranting and raving would only play into his smug, arrogant hands. If only he'd told her before they'd set off. She'd never have agreed to go. Never! Now, all she could do was steam in the passenger seat as the traffic jam began to ease and Dolly started to move again.

At the services, Matt seemed to spend a ridiculously long time finding a space big enough for Dolly. In the end, they were miles from the entrance and Carrie knew she'd be drenched when she went to the loo, but she couldn't care less. As he shunted the van back and forth to get it straight, she saw people scuttling through puddles into the service station. The pools of water shimmered with dirty diesel rainbows that seemed to sum up her life over the past few months. The hope of a brighter future, but tainted. 'It's only a holiday,' her rational side whispered. 'But it meant so much to you and he's destroyed it,' said her bruised and battered heart.

'I think we should discuss this like adults,' said Matt, killing the engine.

Carrie focused on a family picnicking in the car in front. A little boy stared at them from the back seat.

'If it's any consolation, I am genuinely sorry about the passport,' he added, not sounding the slightest bit apologetic. 'But I will not be called a fucking idiot, Carrie. Not by you or by anyone.'

Carrie bit her lip. Winding down the window a few inches, she let the raindrops spray her hot cheeks. The little boy in the car put his tongue out at her. She stared him out, then did the same back. Terrified, he hid behind the seat.

She decided to hold out an olive branch, convincing herself that she was being gracious rather than, actually, just a teeny bit in awe of Matt. 'Okay. I'm prepared to admit that, in hindsight, fucking idiot was a bit strong. You're only a stupid prat.'

'Still inaccurate but slightly more acceptable.'

'But why didn't you tell Rowena about your passport before we set off? Why wait until we were on our way?'

'Would you have come with me if you'd known?'

Carrie rolled her eyes. 'Don't be ridiculous.'

'There you are then. What was the point in telling you? We'd never even have got out of Packley.'

More silence. Raindrops ran in snail trails down the

screen and the motorway was a dull roar through the glazing. The thought of turning the van round and crawling all the way back home was a deeply depressing one. She didn't need to go backwards, that was for sure, but then again, riding round the West Country in a camper van was hardly going to solve her problems. Matt's phone beeped. He glanced down and the corners of his mouth tilted.

'Natasha?' said Carrie.

'No. My boss in Tuman.'

'How nice. I need the loo,' said Carrie, feeling very insignificant.

Matt dropped the phone in the door pocket. 'Wait a minute. It's pissing down out there. There's an umbrella in the back.'

'Don't bother. I'll run.'

The rain had slowed to a drizzle but she was still wet by the time she ran through the doors and into the service station. Locking herself in a cubicle, she sat down, her mind racing. This was the second time recently she'd hidden in a toilet. What a mess her life seemed to be. She ripped a handful of loo paper off the roll to wipe her wet face. She needed what this trip represented. A chance to break away, to put distance between the old Carrie and the new one she was desperate to find. The trouble was, she wasn't really sure who the new Carrie was, and finding out under Matt's watchful eye wasn't going to be easy.

After blasting herself under the hand dryer, she held her head high and strode out into the service area.

Matt was waiting at the entrance, two takeaway coffees in his hands. 'Latte or mocha? I wasn't sure which.'

Carrie grunted.

'That sounded like latte, but it's a dialect I'm not familiar with.'

'Mocha,' she mumbled.

'Ah. It is English. Of sorts. Mocha it is.'

'Thanks.'

'Would you feel safer having this discussion in public or in Dolly?' he asked.

'It had better be Dolly. I don't want to be arrested for GBH.'

He raised his eyebrows. 'Is that a threat?'

'No, a promise.'

Inside the van, the steam from the drinks misted up the windows.

'I'll pay for the ferry tickets,' said Matt as she sipped the mocha. It was far too hot and burnt her tongue, but she needed something to focus on. 'It's my fault you've lost out on the trip abroad. It's the least I can do.'

She hesitated before replying. He'd held out a great big olive branch and it was going to be difficult to refuse it. She didn't feel like being ten any more, but she didn't feel like growing up either. She certainly didn't feel she should turn into Miss Sweetness and Light just for Matt. Since Huw had left her, she didn't feel she owed anyone anything, except her parents and a few close friends.

'Look. It's not the money. Not just that, though I'm not in a position to say no. It's the fact that I was look-ing forward to going somewhere new . . . somewhere different. We didn't have much time, Huw and me, when we ran the farm . . .' She stopped, already conscious of having said too much. Of letting her guard down.

'I can understand that. I can see why you're disappointed and I will get you some new tickets for another time, but that doesn't mean we should abandon the trip. We can still carry on. We can still have a good time.'

She buried her nose in the chocolatey steam from her drink. 'Are you saying I get to choose where we go and you have to agree?'

He hesitated that bit too long. Hmm. For all that laid-back calm, she suspected Matt Landor was a bit of a control freak.

'If you want.'

She hid her smile with a sip. 'That's just my first condition. My second condition is that I drive whenever I want, starting now.'

'Be my guest,' he said, popping the lid back on his empty cup. 'And is there a third?'

'I'm saving that for when we get where we're going. Hand over the keys.'

Taking her place behind the wheel, Carrie adjusted the seat position and mirror. She could only just reach the pedals. She turned the key and pushed Dolly into reverse. The van gave a rattle, then a rumble. Carrie pushed down on the gas and lifted her foot off the clutch. The van shot backwards like a cork from a bottle and there was a scraping noise.

'Shit!'

The rear mirror was a mass of green bush and tree. She'd backed into some kind of hedge. 'Oh, bugger.'

'I should have warned you. Her clutch is a bit temperamental, but I'm sure you'll get used to her whims and foibles,' said Matt, leaning back in his seat. He closed his eyes and let out a long sigh. 'Now, I got up at the crack of dawn this morning, and if you don't mind, I'm going to get a bit of sleep and leave everything in your capable hands.'

# Chapter Eighteen

Until his accident, Matt had always had the gift of being able to drop off anywhere, a useful side effect of the sleep deprivation he'd endured while training as a junior doctor. But since he'd got back from Tuman, his sleep patterns had been erratic, to say the least. Some nights he'd lain awake for hours before falling into a fitful doze. Other times, he'd sat down to watch some late-night crap on the TV and the next thing he'd known it was three a.m. and he was waking up dry mouthed on the sofa. For the first twenty miles after the services, he'd only been pretending to sleep, he'd been so on edge at handing over responsibility to Carrie, but soon, despite the noise, the fumes and the rattling, Dolly had somehow managed to lull him into oblivion.

When he woke up, he watched her through half-shut eyes. Her knuckles were white with tension as she gripped the big steering wheel. Her eyes were wide as they concentrated on the road. She'd be stiff as a board, he guessed, by the end of the day, but he wasn't going to interfere. He felt guilty about the passport fiasco and even guiltier about lying to her, but he'd known she'd never have agreed to the trip if she'd known. He was still wondering about his exact motivation for going along. He was certainly going mad in the flat with nothing to do.

'I hope you're not working,' Shelly had said in her text. 'Or I'll find out and fire you. ☺'

He smiled to himself. Dr Whiplash they called her at the base, but he had to admit she was a great boss, apart from her error of judgement in sending him home. Still, now he was here he might as well get into the best shape he could. Get some fresh air and exercise. He had a few diving buddies at a hospital in the South West; he decided he could look them up and give Carrie some space to herself. He opened his eyes and squeezed them shut again. The sun was blinding. All the clouds had miraculously disappeared and it was verging on warm, even by his standards. They weren't on the motorway any more. The roads were scarily narrow and a glance in the wing mirror showed an alarming queue of traffic behind the van.

'Where are we?' he asked drowsily.

'Somewhere in north Devon.'

'Bloody hell. How long have I been asleep?'

'Nearly three hours.'

'Shouldn't you take a break or something?'

'I did. I stopped and went to the loo at Taunton and bought some lunch from a shop. When I tried to wake you up, you muttered something about leaving you alone because you deserved to suffer. So I did.'

'Thanks.'

'I got you a bottle of water and a pasty. They didn't have much left.'

The pasty and water were rolling around the footwell. 'Looks delicious. Do you want me to take over the driving?'

'Not much point. We're nearly there.'

Rescuing his lunch from the floor, he took a long swig of the water. He was incredibly thirsty and also very hungry. He must have stepped on the pasty while he'd been asleep because it was squashed flat at one end. But then he'd eaten plenty of things almost as bad, if not in Tuman, then at school.

Outside, the countryside had changed from fields to rolling hills and, in the distance, dark moorland. Dolly let out a groan of protest as they started to climb a steep hairpin bend. Carrie changed down the gears and the van slowed from gentle amble to snail's pace as she laboured up the hill. From behind there was the sound of tooting horns. Matt turned round to see an irate BMW driver shaking his fist. He waved back and blew him a kiss. The driver gave him the finger.

'Don't do that! Haven't you heard of road rage?' said Carrie.

'I was only trying to defuse the situation with humour.'

'Then don't.'

Dolly made it to the top of the hairpin, and at the top, a glorious vista opened up. Sea and sky merged in a sparkling palette of blue.

'Can you tell me where we're going? Bloody hell!'

There was an ear-splitting squeal of brakes. Matt was catapulted towards the windscreen. His seatbelt snapped tight round his chest. The smell of burning rubber rose from the road as a horn blared from behind.

'What the hell do you think you're doing?' he said, his heart thumping in his chest.

Her mouth was set in a grim line. 'Turning left. We're here.'

The BMW driver was screaming abuse through his window as he roared past, and Carrie didn't blame him. But it was too late to worry. Dolly was bumping her way down a lane that was barely more than a farm track. It wound its way down the side of a deep valley to the sea. It was a boneshaker of a ride and Carrie knew it was fortunate that they hadn't met anyone driving up it, as she was none too sure there would have been passing room.

She didn't dare look at Matt but she was sure he was holding on to the grab handle. Eventually the valley widened out and she spotted the patch of sand and gravel that served as a makeshift car park. There were no houses, just a few cars, a couple of motorbikes and another camper van.

'This is it,' she said, jumping down on to the gravel. She had pins and needles in her legs and her back was stiff from the long drive. She pushed her hair back out of her eyes so she could get a proper look at the view. The sand and shingle beach shelved steeply into a dark blue sea.

Matt joined her, shading his eyes. 'We're not staying the night here, are we?'

'No.'

'But you chose this place for a reason?'

'Yes.'

Oh yes, she thought as the waves thundered up the beach. A few people were surfing and a couple had let their dog off the lead. It was barking as it chased the waves.

'This is where Huw proposed.'

'And you think it was a good idea to come here?' said Matt.

'I don't know if it was a good idea, but I do know there's something I have to do.'

'Do you want me to come with you or wait here?'

'I don't mind,' she said, but she had already started walking on to the sand. The truth was, she really didn't mind whether Matt was there or not. He'd already melted away, and all she could see now was Huw.

Huw racing her along the beach, slowing down until she'd nearly caught him then setting off again. Teasing her. They'd come to Devon on a rare weekend away from the farm. She'd booked them into a gorgeous country manor hotel and they'd walked to the beach before they'd even unpacked.

She smelled the air again, sharp with the tang of seaweed. She tasted the salt on her tongue. She saw Huw lose his footing as he glanced back at her. He'd tripped on a piece of rock and hit the sand like a falling tree. When he hadn't moved, she'd rushed to his side, gasping for breath. He'd lain so still, she'd thought he'd really hurt himself but as she'd leaned over him, he'd opened his eyes, grinned and pulled her down on top of him.

'I thought you'd knocked yourself out!' she'd told him.

'After tripping over on a beach? What d'you take me for. A bloody wuss? Carrie, I've played front-row forward for Packley.'

'Then I should be angry with you for making me think you really were hurt.'

'But you aren't angry with me. You love me.'

She'd thrown back her head and laughed. 'You hope I do.'

She could feel his arms around her now, pulling her face to his, kissing her deeply, with little finesse but loads of enthusiasm. When he'd finally stopped starving her of oxygen, he'd kept his arms round her and said: 'You'd better love me, because I want us to get married.'

And she'd said yes.

She'd hesitated over bringing Matt here because she'd thought she might make a fool of herself. Yet strangely enough, now that she was here, she felt calm. Slipping her hand inside the pocket of her jeans, her fingers found the smooth circle of her engagement ring and drew it out. She'd collected it from the farm along with all her other worldly goods and kept it ever since, not knowing what to do with it. She'd taken it on the trip hoping to find some place to get rid of it. She'd thought of chucking it off the Eiffel Tower or into some Italian lake. Anywhere that took her fancy at the time. Yet now she was here, back in this place, there was only one option.

She heard footsteps on the shingle and felt Matt beside her.

Twisting round, she stared at him. He held her gaze steadily but she tore her eyes away. She walked towards the waves, lifted her arm and threw the ring high into the air. The instant it left her hand, it disappeared against the sea and sky and didn't even make a splash.

'Was that supposed to be symbolic?' he asked as she picked her way over the shingle towards him.

'I've no idea,' she said, watching the surfers laughing as they came out of the water, dragging their boards behind them. 'I know you think I'm certifiable, but I had to do that. I can't expect you to understand.'

'Then I won't try to, but I do know this. I'm bloody starving, and if I spend much more time in that van, I'm the one who's going to need certifying.'

She scanned his face. Even though he'd been asleep, he looked tired. There was stubble on his chin, and though it was no business of hers, she hoped he wasn't thinking of regrowing the beard. Without it he was ... she could admit it to herself because she had no connection to him ... he was actually very handsome. Like a dirty Mr Darcy, she thought.

'What's so funny?' he said as she caught her lip in her teeth, trying not to laugh.

'You are. Where's your stamina? We've only been together half a day and you can't cope,' she teased.

'What I need is some food, and a place to stretch out. I'm six foot four, if you hadn't noticed.'

'Then we'd better find a campsite and you'd better hope you can get the cooker working,' she said, laughing inwardly at the expression on his face.

After rejecting one or two places, they finally pulled into a small site next to a hideaway beach.

'It seems a bit basic. What do you think?' Carrie asked at Matt surveyed the field.

'Have you ever lived in the jungle?' he said.

'Right. I see what you mean. It'll do fine then.'

They managed to fix the awning to Dolly and Matt started getting out the camping gear. Carrie was struggling to light the gas on the stove when she heard his mobile go off. She tried not to listen to the conversation, realising there were going to be a lot of moments like this over the next few weeks. Moments of intimacy.

After a few minutes he popped his head inside the van. 'You managed to get it going?' he asked, seeing the old-fashioned kettle hissing merrily.

'Easy peasy,' she said, covering the pile of spent matches by the stove. She wondered if it was Natasha he'd been speaking to on the phone.

'Matt? What does Natasha think about you coming away with another woman?'

When he answered, he sounded faintly annoyed, and she almost wished she hadn't asked.

'Natasha doesn't think anything. In fact, she doesn't know yet. I didn't know myself until this morning, remember.'

'And will you tell her?' she said carefully, pouring water into two mugs. She turned to find him standing in the entrance to the van, hands resting on either side of the frame.

'Next time I speak to her. But she's far too busy with her job to worry about stuff like that.'

He took the mug with a gruff thanks and they stood drinking their coffee, talking about the site. After a while, Matt drained his mug and said, 'I'd better fetch some food. We passed a shop up the road on the way here. I'll only be ten minutes. What kind of beer do you drink?'

'Anything will do,' she said, surprised and amused at his domesticity.

An hour later, when he still hadn't returned, she was just pissed off. Slamming the door of the van, she headed off towards the sea.

# Chapter Nineteen

The RNLI lifeguards were just packing up their pick-up ready to leave when Carrie walked down the sand. It was a glorious evening, with a scarlet sun slipping into the sea. The surf was pounding the beach and a few hardy types were still making the most of the waves. She rolled up her jeans, kicked off her flip-flops and walked into the sea, flinching at the water temperature. Then, enjoying the sensation, she dared herself to go in a bit further. An unexpected wave caught her and her jeans were soaked.

'Why don't you just strip off and go for it?'

One of the surfers was watching her, an amused smile on his face. He was standing in waist-high water, holding on to a surfboard as if he'd been born with it, while she was paddling around like a little kid.

'God, no. It's freezing,' she said, embarrassed.

He laughed out loud. 'In the buff, yeah, but if you've got a wetsuit on, it's fine. You and your bloke should try it.'

'What bloke?'

'The tall dude you were with at Combe Strand. Unless you just picked him up off the beach. Your splitty's pretty hot, by the way.'

If it was a chat-up line, she thought it rated high on the scale of originality. His interest is Dolly made her wonder if he might be something to do with the green VW that had been parked by the sea earlier that day.

'She's called Dolly and she's not mine, only borrowed,' she said, as he tugged his board into shallower water.

'And what about your boyfriend?' he asked.

Carrie pulled a face. Still, she supposed it was a reasonable thing to assume; she and Matt had been together in the van. She shook her head firmly. 'My boyfriend? Oh, you mean Matt. He's just a . . . total prat. Some bloke put on this earth to torment me.' She smiled. 'He's just a mate.'

'Okay. I'm Spike, by the way.'

'Carrie.'

'Hi, Carrie,' he said, wading out of the sea like some kind of hippy Neptune. Carrie pushed her feet into her flip-flops and grimaced as her wet jeans hugged her thighs.

'You two must get on pretty well to share a van together,' said Spike as they crunched up the shingle beyond the tide line.

She smiled and shook her head. 'To be honest, we hardly know each other.'

'Am I missing something here?'

'No. I was supposed to be coming on this trip with my friend – a girl.' Spike raised his eyebrows – which was interesting, as he had a couple of piercings through one of them. 'A girl *friend*,' she added.

'It's no business of mine what you do. Girlfriend, boyfriend, bit of both. Each to their own, I say.'

'Matt's just someone I went to uni with. He had some time on his hands and Rowena – my friend – thought I'd like to have some company.'

'And do you? Want some company, I mean?'

Did she? She didn't know what to say that wouldn't sound desperate or smart. She wasn't sure what she wanted from this stranger on the beach, so she just shrugged.

'I'll take that as a "don't-know-and-wondering-if-this-weirdo-in-a-wetsuit-might-be-an-axe-murderer".'

'Maybe, but I just don't know about anything right now, full stop.'

'Going with the flow, eh? I can buy that.' He flipped a thumb in the direction of the camping field. 'That's cool. How d'you feel about meeting another guy? He's a lot better looking than me.'

She saw the green VW at the other side of the field. 'That your splitty?'

'Sure is. He's called Ron. After Ronald Reagan.'

'I've never been introduced to a president.' She laughed.

He winked. 'Then maybe there should be a first time. If you plan on sticking around for a few days, maybe you and Ron can get better acquainted.'

'Hey, Spike!'

At the shout he twisted and waved at a group of surfers dragging their boards along the edge of the waves.

'See ya then,' he said, picking up his board.

'Yes. See you again soon,' replied Carrie.

Spike loped away down the beach. For a while Carrie watched him surfing, thinking of his lazy smile and casual confidence. She wondered if he and his mates lived down here on the beaches or whether they were only here on holiday. They seemed to be catching waves effortlessly, and she found herself envying them. They were drifting further and further down the strand and she watched until her eyes ached, before turning for the site.

When she got back, Matt was leaning against the van, chatting to two girls, both with beers in their hands. A carrier bag of groceries lay at his feet.

'Hi there,' he said, raising a bottle of beer to her. 'Cara, Siobhan, meet Carrie, my travelling companion.'

The girls shot brief smiles at her then turned back to Matt. Gazing adoringly up at him, the taller of them said, 'Bye then, Matt. See you around?'

He nodded. 'Sure.'

'You got the groceries then?' Carrie said lightly.

'What I could find. Which wasn't much. Baked beans. Tinned mince. Pasta.'

'And the beer?'

He glanced down. There were three bottles left in the eight-pack. 'I met the girls in the shop and we got talking. Then we realised we were at the same site and . . .' He paused, levelling his eyes at her. 'You were nowhere to be seen, so we had a drink together.'

'I guess I'll have to use up whatever's left in the crate then. I went for a walk to the beach. I got talking too,' she said meaningfully.

Matt picked up the groceries. 'Really?'

'Yes. To some of the surfers.'

'Good. Glad to hear you're settling in. Now, shall I cook dinner or are you going to do the honours?'

\*

That night, Matt slept out in the awning while Carrie took the roof bed. Despite being six feet off the ground under a roof that flapped like a demented crow in the wind, she slept better than she had done for weeks. She put it down to fresh air and finishing the beer with Matt. When she woke, he was already up, showered and lying outside the awning in his shorts writing a letter.

'Do you mind if I go for a walk?' she said.

He hardly even glanced up from the page. 'Fine by me. I might go and find an internet café later. I need to send some emails to the base in Tuman, so don't rush back.'

That was plain enough, she thought. She'd stay out as long as she wanted, not that she needed Matt's permission. It was a fine if breezy day; if she found a sheltered spot on the beach she could do a spot of sunbathing and get her head together. She might even see Spike. He'd certainly intrigued her and she wanted to speak to him again. She knew nothing about him, and in a way she didn't want to. *You're free now*, she reminded herself. *You can talk to sexy strangers on the beach and no one will care.*

She'd been lying on the sand for an hour, trying to get into a bonkbuster novel, when Spike arrived with his friends. He waved immediately, then trotted down to the water almost directly in front of her. The tide was coming in so she didn't have to move to find herself closer to them. The wind was strong now and the roar of the surf was louder. She sat up and hugged her knees, catching snatches of their shouts and banter on the breeze. Spike caught a wave almost immediately and stood up.

'Respect, mate,' called one of the guys paddling out to him. Even to Carrie's untrained eye, Spike was by far the best surfer, catching the waves cleanly and riding them for longer than anyone else.

After another hour, she'd pulled on her T-shirt as the wind gusted more strongly. The waves seemed massive to her now and there were fewer people out in the surf. Spike's gang was standing at the edge of the water; all of a sudden he peeled off and strode towards her. Pulling off his wetsuit hood, he ruffled his hair and said, 'Awesome.'

It was not a word Huw had used very often and Carrie felt like laughing but managed to nod nonchalantly. 'Looks great.'

'Do you surf?' asked Spike, shaking water from his face and hair.

'Not as such. I've done a bit of body-boarding once or twice.'

Once actually, she thought. When she was about thirteen.

Spike winked. 'Then you should have no trouble progressing. Maybe I can persuade you to try something a little more adventurous?'

The surf thundered on to the shore. The waves looked as big as trucks.

'Hey. I don't know. Those waves look very big to me.'

'Big? Man, those waves are tiny. You should see some of the surf at Thurso or off the Atlantic in France. This is baby stuff, Carrie.'

One hell of a baby, she thought, eyeing the waves. No way was he getting her out there, no matter how cute he was.

'No need to look so petrified. I know what I'm doing but I won't force you if you don't think you can do it,' he said with a look that left her in no doubt that he thought she was a prize wuss if she didn't at least try. 'So. If you won't come surfing, are you ready to meet Ron yet?'

'Oh yes,' she said, a bit too quickly.

'Then come on.'

Back on the campsite, Carrie stole a glance across the field towards Dolly but there was no sign of Matt. Spike propped his board up against the camper van and unzipped his wetsuit. He wasn't very tall but he was sturdy and fit looking. He also had a silver ring through his left nipple. Carrie found her eyes drawn to the ring, then realised he was checking her out too, but far more unselfconsciously. She felt the warmth rising from her neck to her roots. With her chestnut hair and fair skin, there was no hiding a blush. She wasn't used to flirting, and the cast of Packley Drama Society, gloriously camp to a man, didn't count. She was used to being Huw's partner. Used to Huw's hand on her bum, telling the world she was his.

Spike didn't look as if he was bothered about owning anything except his surfboard. He ran his hands through tangled, sun-streaked hair, mussing it up even further as if to say, 'You see, I don't care about convention.' She laughed at herself. For all she knew, he could be a chartered surveyor from Surrey who ironed his underpants.

'After you,' he said, showing her into the awning.

If he did iron his pants, she'd be very surprised. Even she could see that Ron hadn't been as lovingly cared for as Dolly. The awning was ripped in a couple of places and must have let the rain in at the slightest shower. There were cans and fast-food cartons littering the ground among a couple of crumpled sleeping bags. Ron's bodywork was rusting, and inside the cabin he smelled of neoprene, stale beer and something sweet and sickly.

'Sorry about the whiff. It's Sex Wax,' Spike said.

'Sex Wax?'

'You put it on your board to help your feet grip.'

'Oh. I see.' My God, now she was blushing again. 'Um . . . do you come here often? I mean, do you surf here – in Devon – a lot? If you see what I mean.' No, she was crap at flirting. She was ten years out of practice. Spike let her keep digging the hole, his blue eyes appraising her as she sat on the bench seat. 'I think I should be getting back. Matt has no idea where I am,' she said at last, feeling embarrassed.

'Whatever,' he said. 'And the answer to your question is yes. We do come here often.'

'We?'

'Me and the guys.'

'Where are they?'

'Still riding the waves, I guess. They'll be back later.'

'Oh,' said Carrie, realising that Spike must have spotted her and homed in specially.

'Why don't you and Matt come over here tomorrow night? We'll probably go down the beach, light a fire, hang out with a few beers.'

'What time?'

He laughed at her. 'We don't do time, Carrie. Time? Hey, just watch for the smoke.'

She'd started to leave when he called after her. 'You should try surfing. I think we've got a spare suit. I'll get you on a board before you can think about it. What have you got to lose?'

'I'm not sure,' she muttered, without turning round.

She suddenly realised her heart was thudding. She fancied Spike. Who wouldn't – faced with that ripped body and bad-boy smile? He also had the enormous advantage of being completely the opposite of bloody Huw, and there was something else attracting her to him too. It was the idea of hooking up with someone she'd only just met – of picking a guy up just because she *could* – that appealed to her. Huw would have been shocked, angry and amazed. Carrie smiled. Surely this was what freedom meant, and it felt heady; exciting and scary all at the same time. Rowena had been right: this road trip was exactly what she needed.

# Chapter Twenty

Later that evening, she was lying outside Dolly with a beer. Spike and his mates must have gone out, because Ron the van was nowhere to be seen. As Matt listened to his iPod and read some weird medical journal, Carrie flicked through a copy of *Cosmo*, hoping he wouldn't see her unhealthy interest in an article entitled 'Avoiding the Walk of Shame: Top Ten Tips for Your Best Ever One-Night Stand'.

She hadn't had a one-night stand since the sixth form, and she wasn't even sure that shagging Kieran after her sixth-form prom counted. They'd done it in his parents' bed, while they were away in Lanzarote, then he'd taken her home on the back of his scooter. No walk of shame there, although it had been embarrassing enough. After that, she'd gone out with a lad from work, but they'd always known they'd split up when she went to uni. The next man she'd had sex with had been Huw – the only man she'd had sex with since, in fact. She closed the magazine with a sigh and lay back, gazing up at the stars. On *Cosmo*'s 'one-night-stand-o-meter' she rated a 0.5: 'Have you ever considered becoming a nun?'

Matt appeared overhead, blocking out the stars. The

angle accentuated his height. He looked like Nelson's Column with stubble. 'Tea or bed?'

'Oh, let me see now. Why don't we be devils and have a nice mug of hot chocolate?'

'I'm afraid we don't have any hot chocolate, so it looks like our only option is bed.'

She sat up quickly because she'd felt a kick low in the pit of her stomach. The feeling wasn't unpleasant but it wasn't comfortable either. It felt like a tightening, a tension. She wasn't sure whether it was hearing Matt talking about bed or because she was thinking about sex at the time.

'Do you want to sleep in the roof again or take the awning tonight?' he asked.

'I don't mind.

'I think you'll be more comfortable in the roof,' he said.

'Okay, but you don't have to make any sacrifices for me.'

He grinned wickedly. 'I'm not. There's more room in the awning. My feet will stick out of the roof bed.'

'You take the roof then,' she said as the light from the lamp flickered between them. This wasn't going to be as easy as she had imagined. Then she thought of Spike, and how she'd felt drawn to him so quickly. She also thought of the years she'd spent being faithful to Huw and how meaningless that now seemed. Nothing was going to stop her doing what she wanted.

'Matt, this is a bit awkward, but I think it's probably a good time for us to agree some ground rules. Earlier, when you asked if there was a third condition to me carrying on with the trip . . .'

'Hmm.'

'Well, we need to discuss another possibility that may arise.'

He folded his arms. 'Go on. It can't be worse than you wanting to drive.'

His eyes gleamed but she didn't rise to the bait. 'Okay. There's no easy way of saying this, but Rowena and I had an agreement, a pact, and I think we should have the same deal.'

'A pact? That sounds serious.'

She knew he was laughing at her but she carried on. 'Yes, a pact. Sexual ground rules for us both to stick to.'

He blew out a little breath. 'Sexual rules? Gosh, you girls do know how to have a good time. Bring them on. I hope they're very strict.'

Carrie wanted to throw something at him but she refused to be put off. 'I think it will be easier if we get some aspects of this trip straight from the start. I'm sure you'll be relieved to hear what I'm going to say, so I won't mess about, I'll just come out and say it . . . You see, Rowena and me, we arranged this trip for a break, for fun. After what happened with Huw, I decided that if I . . . we, that is, met anyone, we'd . . . well, we'd just go for it.'

Matt was listening intently, as if she was one of his patients. She almost expected him to sit back, steeple his fingers and peer at her over the top of a pair of horn-rimmed spectacles.

'And if you don't mind, I've met someone I'd like to get to know better and I was hoping we could stay here for a few days, maybe longer. I expect you have people you want to get to know better too. You do understand what I'm saying, Matt?'

He looked at her gravely, as if he was going to tell her

she'd caught something nasty, then his face broke into a smile.

'Well, thank God for that!' he said, blowing out a breath. 'I was wondering how I was going to tell you this. You see, I've got the chance to go diving with some nurse mates from Exeter tomorrow. There are some fantastic dive sites on this coast and there's a wreck not too far off Hartland Point.'

'Oh. That's great then. If you're going to be busy too . . .'

'It's perfect. In fact, the weather forecast is pretty good all week, so I may not be around much. I emailed my mates this morning and a couple of them are on leave. Haven't seen them for two years, so it worked out well in the end.'

'Oh. Well. If you're happy for us both to do our own thing . . .'

Matt laughed out loud. 'I thought that was the idea. My God, we don't want to be joined at the bloody hip, do we? No disrespect, Carrie, but I can't think of anything worse, and I know you can't either.'

'Absolutely. Nothing could be more horrible than having to spend all day with you.'

'In that case, shall we get an early night, as we're both going to be so active tomorrow?' he said.

'Good idea.'

Matt picked up a towel from the table. 'Right. I'm going for a quick shower before I go to bed. I expect you'll be asleep when I get back, unless you're staying up.'

'Not if I'm going to be *active*, no. I'll need my strength,' she said. 'I'll see you in the morning, then.'

143

'Not unless you're an early riser. I've got to be out of here by seven.'

'Seven a.m.?'

'Yeah. My mates are picking me up first thing. I don't expect you'll see me until it's dark.'

'So you won't be back for dinner?' she said casually.

Matt winked at her. 'No, I won't be back for dinner, and if your day goes as you're obviously hoping, I'm sure you'll have better things to do by tomorrow night.'

# *Chapter Twenty-one*

When Carrie woke up, all she could hear was the cry of seagulls and the distant roar of the sea. It was a much hotter, calmer day than the one before, so she spent the day sunbathing, swimming and listening to her iPod. The first few hours were bliss, lying in the shelter of the rocks on the beach with her bonkbuster and her music for company. It was just a shame that Rowena was not there. She pictured her friend hanging out with the cast of *HeartAche*, maybe trying out the costumes. Rowena in scrubs ... She suddenly wondered if Matt wore them at work and what he looked like.

She was sitting outside Dolly, painting her toenails a gorgeous shade of shell pink, when she finally saw Spike's van bumping across the field. It stopped outside the awning, a gaggle of shirtless people laughing inside as Spike poked his head out of the driver's window.

'See you tonight?' he called.

She tried to sound cool, which was difficult when you were wearing toe separators. 'Yeah, sure.'

'Bring Matt if you like. Lola here wants to meet you both.'

A hand shot out of the window and waved. It belonged

to an elfin-faced girl with wonderfully wild hair. 'Hello, Carrie!' she called.

'Hi, Lola,' said Carrie, waving back.

'See ya later then!' shouted Spike.

Carrie felt a little knot of excitement in her stomach. Tonight looked like it was going to be a lot of fun.

As the sun sank slowly over the sea, she saw Spike and his friends heading for the beach, armed with crates of beer and driftwood. Matt still wasn't back and Carrie wasn't sure whether she wanted him to come to the beach party or not. Spike had specifically asked him and Carrie felt uncomfortable about not including him. But she felt awkward about him being there, as if he might be watching her; judging her.

'Well, tough,' she said out loud as she wriggled into her best pair of shorts and the lace-up cami top she'd worn at the wedding. It was slightly too tight and made her look what her mum would have called buxom. Tonight, buxom was exactly what she wanted.

She was surprised how nervous she was as she headed down to the beach, where smoke was already spiralling into the sky from the fire. Spike and his mates were standing and sitting around it drinking beer and smoking joints. They were all barefoot, so Carrie slipped off her flip-flops as soon as her feet hit the sand. Spike had his back to her as she drew near. He was wearing an over-sized T-shirt and shorts. His calves were sturdy and strong and sprinkled with strawberry-blond hair. Her stomach was fluttering with nerves. She was so crap at this. So out of the loop. 'Hello.'

He turned and grinned. 'Hi there. This is Carrie,

guys,' he said as the others waved hi with their bottles. He went on to introduce them all: Baz, Jim, Stig and Lola, who close up looked so sporty, she'd probably been conceived on a surfboard. She reminded Carrie of a mermaid from a book she'd read when she was little.

'Beer?' offered Spike, leading Carrie closer to the fire. 'Thanks.'

Her arms were covered in goose bumps and she was grateful for the warmth. As he passed her a bottle, he ran his eyes over her body. She hoped he liked what he saw. After a day in the sun, she thought she looked good, glowing, and she realised why she fancied Spike so much. He made her feel sexy. Desired just for her body and absolutely nothing else, such as her brain or her book-keeping skills. She hardly knew him and yet she felt a connection with him. Lust, largely.

'Your mate not with you?' he asked.

'He's gone diving with some friends. I have *no* idea when he'll be back.' Carrie didn't want to talk about Matt and she didn't want to think about him. This was her chance to start again. Free, casual, not expecting anything other than fun.

'Maybe he's decided to stay the night,' said Spike.

'He might have. Probably has. Where've you been today?' she asked, desperate to change the subject.

Spike gave something approaching a sigh of ecstasy. 'Croyde. We caught some awesome waves. D'you want to come out with us tomorrow, or are you still making your mind up?'

'Why not?' she said, determined not to chicken out but knowing she was going to lose any ounce of mystique once she got on a surfboard. Not that she thought she had any mystique in the first place, but she was still going to take to a board like a stone. Spike held out his joint to her but she shook her head. Her one and only experience of weed at uni had ended up with her dancing round the student union in her knickers.

Spike shrugged. 'No need to look so terrified. There's always a first time for everything.'

'It's not the first time,' she said.

'I meant the surfing.'

'Oh. Yeah. *Sure*.'

He gestured to the sand beside him. 'Come and chill out. Tell us what a nice girl like you and a nice boy like Matt are doing down here. Together. But not.'

She told them as much as she wanted to about the road trip and her job on the farm, leaving out the details about her break-up with Huw. She also told them about Rowena and the acting, but mostly she listened to them talk about surfing, like it was the answer to life and the universe. The flames from the fire had died down by the time she saw Matt walking down the beach towards them. The sand was littered with empty bottles and roaches. She was feeling relaxed and mellow after finally succumbing to a few drags on a joint. Huw would have gone mad. He hated anything that smacked of hippydom.

'How was the diving, dude?' she asked, stifling a giggle.

'It was good,' said Matt. 'Sister.'

Spike laughed. 'You should try staying on the water rather than under it. Carrie here was worried you'd been eaten by a shark.'

'There aren't any sharks round here,' said Lola, running her hands through her hair.

'You look like a mermaid,' said Carrie suddenly, not knowing why but feeling it was exactly the right thing to say at that moment. 'A beautiful mermaid with a silvery tail.'

Lola seemed surprised but then she smiled in pleasure. 'Do you really think so?'

'Definitely. You could sit on a rock, waiting to lure sailors to the bottom of the sea.'

Spike let out a snort. Even Matt smiled. Carrie was delighted she'd amused everyone so much, especially Lola, who crawled over and handed her a joint.

'Please try this. It's really good stuff,' she said.

Carrie felt it was only polite to accept as Lola seemed so sweet and nice.

She saw someone hand Matt a beer and hold out a joint to him. He took the beer but refused the smoke, saying, 'No thanks, I'm diving again tomorrow.'

Carrie had an insane urge to titter. She took a drag on the joint and sat back, feeling as if life couldn't get any better. Really, things were looking up for her. Even Matt, sitting opposite on a driftwood log, looked very attractive tonight. Lola was curled up at his feet, her long mermaid fingers caressing the tribal tattoos on his forearms.

'Where'd you get this work done? Down here or in London?' she asked.

'In Tuman,' said Matt.

'Where the fuck's that?' drawled Baz.

Lola held out her own joint to Matt and this time he decided to take a drag on it.

'It's an island in the Pacific Ocean, north of Australia. I was out there for a while earlier this year,' he said.

'What the fuck were you doing in a place like that, man?'

Here we go again, thought Matt, really not wanting to talk about his bloody job. He'd had a good day and he wouldn't have come down here at all if he hadn't wanted the keys to Dolly from Carrie. Frankly, he hadn't expected her to be on the beach; he'd been sure she'd be shagging the surfer guy by now. Then he'd seen the smoke and decided, sod it, he wanted his mobile, which was inside the van.

'Come on, tell us. Don't be shy,' said Lola.

'I work for a medical charity and we help to run a small hospital in one of the villages. We also go into the jungle and hold clinics for people from outlying tribes.'

'So you're a doctor? Cool,' said Lola.

He laughed. 'Far less cool than it sounds.'

'So you actually do operations on people out there?' she asked.

'We do some basic surgery, yes, and we've got a labour ward and a small theatre, but we can only operate when the generator's working, otherwise we have no electricity. Sometimes we go out to outlying communities by canoe or light aeroplane. We run health clinics in the main village, which is about fifty miles from the nearest big town.'

'What kind of stuff do you do?'

Matt turned down Lola's offer of the joint this time. He really did want a clear head in the morning and he didn't give a toss if they – or Carrie – thought he was uptight. 'Nothing spectacular. Minor ops, preventative healthcare and education. We see a lot of malaria and TB too. You probably know the sort of thing.'

Their blank faces showed they probably didn't. Their

eyes were glazing over and he couldn't tell whether it was his fault or the hash. He felt Lola's fingers on his arm again. 'And you got the tattoos done at some place in the city or in the actual jungle?'

He smiled. Her expression was almost childlike. 'In the actual jungle.'

Baz was lying on the sand, staring at the sky, a blissful smile on his face. With a bit of luck they'd all be so spaced out, they wouldn't care what he told them.

'Just these?' said Lola, kneeling next to him. 'Or are there more?' She pushed her hands inside his T-shirt and lifted up the fabric. She blew out a breath. 'Oh my God. You have to see this.'

Matt pretended to laugh as she tried to pull his T-shirt off. He hated this kind of exhibitionism, hated being the centre of attention. It only led to awkward questions.

'Hey, man, let's see it!'

'Yeah. Get the shirt off!'

They started banging bottles on rocks and driftwood and chanting, 'Off, off, off!' Matt caught Carrie's eyes. She was watching him from her spot next to Spike. She was quiet but she didn't look too stoned. Yet.

'Show us,' said Lola huskily.

He gave in. Stood up, pulled his T-shirt over his head and stretched his arms out wide. Then he turned round slowly, letting the cool night air lick his skin. He could feel the prickle of salt on his flesh, still clinging to him from the sea despite his shower. The banging and laughing stopped. Then someone let out a low whistle.

'Jesus . . .'

Slowly he turned full circle until he was facing Spike and Carrie again.

'That is truly awesome,' said Spike, raising his bottle in salute.

Matt felt Lola's fingertip tracing the patterns that flowed across his skin in whorls and loops. They covered his back, across his shoulder blades and down his spine, disappearing into the waistband of his low-rise jeans. They were tribal patterns, some kind of rite of passage for warriors, but he wasn't going to tell Spike and his mates that.

'Where do they end?' Lola asked, awestruck.

Matt was embarrassed. 'Where do you think?' he joked.

Lola said nothing. She'd switched her attention to Carrie, who was staring at Matt, her face a strange mixture of emotions. He couldn't fathom her. She seemed as fascinated as the rest of them.

'Did they hurt?' The voice was small and quiet. He hadn't expected Carrie to ask that.

'If I said no I'd be lying, but tattooing is part of life for some of the people out there. The village elders – the local leaders – asked me if I wanted these after I'd been running a clinic for them. It was a great honour. I couldn't say no.'

'How long did it take, man?'

'How do they do it?'

'Did they – like – give you anything while they stuck you?'

The questions came from everywhere except Spike, who was silent and, Matt thought, trying to look bored.

'My back took all day. They use a sharp thorn and a small mallet to hammer the design into the skin, then they press bits of burnt tree trunk in it,' he said.

'A thorn?' said Lola throatily.

'Fuck me,' said Baz.

Right, thought Matt, he'd provided enough entertainment for one night. He shrugged his T-shirt back on, refusing to titillate Lola with any more gory details.

'Any chance of more beer?' he said, even though he didn't want one.

Spike indicated a pile of bottles sitting in a bucket of water. 'Help yourself, mate,' he said from his place next to Carrie.

Matt watched her hugging her legs. She was definitely cold and probably nervous, he guessed. She was also a big girl and could make her own decisions. Downing his beer quickly, he made his excuses, and as he'd expected, Lola came with him.

# Chapter Twenty-two

The first time is always the worst, Carrie told herself as she lay next to Spike in the van in the early hours. He was propped up one elbow, lighting a joint. She took a drag herself and hoped she wouldn't throw up or pass out. The sex had been furtive and graphic but that was okay. She hadn't expected fireworks – hadn't wanted them. She'd wanted sex that was dirty and real. But maybe not so short.

'Where are the others?' she asked Spike.

'Probably stoned. They'll sleep on the beach. Apart from Lola, that is.'

She pressed her cheek against Spike's chest, trying to block out an image of Lola astride Matt in Dolly. Nelson would go nuts if they were smoking stuff in there.

'Told you there was a first time for everything,' he said.

She lifted her chin to look at him. 'It wasn't my first time.'

'Your first time playing away, I meant.'

'I'm not playing away. There's no one else.'

'No one else *now*. Bastard, was he?'

She realised she didn't like Spike calling Huw a

bastard, even though he was. She'd said it herself, and much worse, many times.

'Let's forget him. Sorry if I was nervous.'

'You were great, but you folded up your top when you got undressed. Force of habit?'

She closed her eyes. 'Oh shit, did I? I don't remember.'

'That's what happens when you stay in the same place with the same guy too long.'

'And you never do?'

He took a long, lingering puff of his joint and stared up at the ceiling of the van. She wasn't quite sure if he was going to speak again or just pass out. 'I never say never. Too final. I just see where life takes me. Making plans scares me,' he said eventually.

'What about money. How do you live?'

'I did have a job until last year, but one day I was on the beach at Croyde with a load of other dudes. They were all living in vans by the sea and I realised: life's too short for work. This is where I want to be. So I sold my car and the flat, and cashed in the pension plan.'

'You had a *pension*?'

He turned to her languidly, running a finger over her stomach. 'I *did*.'

She shivered as his finger stopped at her navel. 'What did you do for a living?'

'Some boring-as-shit office work. I can barely remember. What about you?'

She laughed softly. 'You know what I did. I worked for my boyfriend running his farm.'

'Oh yeah. Sorry. I forgot. But who cares about all that stuff? I only care about now.'

His hand crept to her breast. He took her nipple in his thumb and forefinger. Her stomach swirled again as he said, 'I think I short-changed you last time. In fact, I think it would be a good idea if I put that right now.'

Shifting his weight, he rolled on top of her and kissed her. His mouth was wet, his tongue slippery. She wrapped her legs around his back and arched her pelvis. She wanted to screw Spike on the beach, in a cave, up against a wall, *everywhere*. She was smoking weed and having sex – not making love – with him in a sleazy camper van. She really hoped he hadn't been an accountant. She hoped he was on the dole, never paid his council tax and sold the *Socialist Worker* on street corners. He was everything Huw hated, and she couldn't believe how good that felt.

Sunbathing, sex and surfing. What more could a girl want? Less of the last one, actually. A huge wave spun Carrie round like a stray sock in a spin dryer. She wasn't going to come up this time. This time she was going to drown. Her battered body would probably be hauled out of the sea a few weeks from now, minus a few bits the fish had taken a fancy to. She wondered if Huw would come to the funeral . . .

A hand reached down, grabbed her wrist and hauled her to the surface. She came up spluttering and coughing, gasping for air.

'You can put your feet down if you like. It's not that deep,' shouted Spike.

'I th-think I might take a b-break.'

He laughed as he paddled off. 'It's awesome out here today. I'm staying. Catch you later.'

Dragging the board behind her, she waded out of the sea, spitting out water. Her eyes were raw, she was aching all over and there was water in orifices she didn't know she had. *A week*. She'd spent a whole week of her life surfing and managed the amazing feat of standing on the board for about five seconds. Spike said she was doing great, but as far as Carrie was concerned, surfing was definitely not the orgasmic experience the others made it out to be.

Sex with Spike hadn't been quite as orgasmic as she'd hoped either, but that hadn't seemed to matter. They'd done it in the van, on the beach, in a cave – the last two not as much fun as you would have thought, with seaweed stuck to your bum and sand everywhere. It had been rough and ready and so unlike making love with Huw that she'd felt, at times, as though her whole world had been tumbled around and washed away. Maybe this was the only life she'd ever known. This life of shagging and lying on the sand. With Huw, she'd worried about mortgages and rents, milk yields and subsidies. With Spike she worried about drowning and whether they'd got enough condoms.

Shading her eyes with her hand, she watched Lola catch a wave, surfing it as if she was part of the foam. She hadn't seen Matt with Lola again and she had no idea if they'd slept together that first night. It was none of her business. Tugging down the zip, she wriggled out of her wetsuit. She was freezing; she needed a hot shower. Spike was wading out of the waves, dragging his board, as she gathered up her stuff ready to go.

He grinned. 'Had enough already?'

'I thought of swallowing a bit more of the Atlantic but

decided, hey, why not leave all that to you guys.'

He laughed. 'A few more months and you'd crack it.'

Months? She searched his face. He was thinking months?

'See you later on the beach? We're having a special party. It's Lola's birthday today.'

'Is it? I must get her something.'

He winked. 'No need. I've got her a present already. From all of us.'

# Chapter Twenty-three

Later turned out to be *much* later. The sparks from the fire were white and orange and scarlet against the darkening sky as Carrie sat on the beach that evening. She had Spike's arm around her back and they were sharing a joint. Well, it was a birthday party – even if Lola hadn't actually turned up.

Baz was playing the guitar and Carrie felt mellow. Mellow yellow. Baz was really, really brilliant. He was fantastic. He should go on *The X Factor*, she thought. Maybe she should phone up Simon Cowell and tell him about Baz.

'You should be on the telly,' she said to Baz when he'd finished his song, but no one seemed to hear her. Oh well, she thought, maybe she was invisible. Now that would be fun. She could sneak into the men's locker room at the health club . . . She laughed, laughed until her sides hurt and she was rolling about in the sand.

'How are you, Caroline?' said a voice.

She turned her head, which took ages. Spike was next to her, grinning, and his mouth was huge, like a big open cave. 'Can you get up, sweetheart?'

'I'm amazing, and . . .' She lowered her voice to a whisper. 'Did you know I'm invisible?'

'I think not,' said Spike.

'Oh, I am. You know. I think we've all become invisible,' she said. 'Which is tricky, because if we can't see each other, we're going to be bumping into one another and—'

'Carrie, you're talking out of your arse.'

His voice sounded harsh but she didn't care. 'You know, I might be. Or you might be because I can't see you but I can hear you, so maybe you're *really* talking out of your arse.'

'Come on. Get up. It's five o clock in the morning.'

He pulled her up off the sand like a puppet on a string. She was bouncing slowly up and down and it felt so mellow. She blinked. Her eyes weren't working very well so she tried to hold them open really wide. She needed matchsticks to prop them open like Tom and Jerry did in cartoons. But hey. This was totally *weird*. 'You smell nice,' she said. 'You're not Spike. You're Matt.'

'Have a gold star. Now come home.'

'Nah. Don't be silly.'

'You're stoned.'

'No. I'm just enjoying myself. You're a boring old fart.'

'You know, Carrie, I'm trying very hard to be patient here. But if you carry on like this, I'm going to get—'

'*Very* cross. Very very cross. I know. You'll report me to the head and I'll be expelled.'

'For God's sake, woman, stand up.'

It was funny, being on her feet. It was so funny, she was laughing. Laughing like a drain, whatever a drain laughed like.

'Ow! You're hurting me, you spoilsport prefect,' she protested.

'Whatever you say. We need to take you home.'

'I don't wanna go home. I want to stay here with my friends. Whoa . . .'

'Your friends aren't here, Carrie . . . Be careful, Lola. She's heavier than she looks.'

'I am *not* fat.'

'It's fine. I can manage her,' the other prefect said as she took flight again. That was it. That was *it*! She was a kite caught by the wind, and Matt and his friend were flying her. *Wheeeee!*

'For fuck's sake,' said Matt, as Carrie collapsed on top of him and he struggled to wriggle free. 'She weighs a bloody ton.'

'Do you think she'll be all right?' asked Lola.

Carrie lay in the sand, waving her arms and legs. 'Lola? Is that you? Look, I'm an angel.'

Lola knelt beside her. 'Yes. It's me. Are you all right?'

'Please don't let that nasty man take me home. I want to stay with you and my friends. I'm having such a great time. I can fly, you know.'

'You *are* home,' said Lola.

'Oh, lovely,' said Carrie, snuggling up under her warm Take That duvet, fresh from the airing cupboard. 'You are so lovely, Lola. Like a beautiful mermaid. Will you wake me up when Terry Wogan comes on?'

The next morning, Carrie had a stomach like the contents of a hoover bag. She wasn't in a fit state to have a conversation, but she knew that she'd been brought back to the van in the early hours by Matt and Lola. She remembered having a beer, and then oblivion. It was like the whole night had been erased. She might have ended up in the sea, or Tuman, and she'd have been none the wiser. She thought that Lola or Matt – or both – had been stroking her hair as she knelt beside the loo, then held her up as she nearly passed out.

'Ganja shouldn't make you sick. Unless you had some other stuff with it,' said Matt.

'Is she okay?'

As Lola spoke, Carrie tried to turn her head. Big mistake.

*Bleurghhh* . . .

'I don't deserve this,' she muttered.

'Me neither,' said Matt grimly.

When she'd stopped being sick, when she'd sat there on the floor of the cubicle for half an hour without throwing up again, he left, leaving her a pile of clothes and a toothbrush. She staggered back to the van, where Lola was sitting on the steps, her chin on her hand, like a Gothic pixie.

'Are you feeling better now?' asked Lola, looking very worried.

'Yes thank you,' said Carrie in a teeny, tiny voice.

'Can I get you a cup of ginger and chamomile tea?'

Carrie smiled weakly. She was grateful for Lola's help, but the thought of chamomile tea made her want to barf again. 'A glass of water would be nice. Matt said I was on my own. What happened to Spike and Baz and the others?'

Lola seemed embarrassed. 'They were stoned in their van. I don't expect they meant to leave you. They might not have known you were there.'

Carrie was confused. Surely they hadn't just left her. 'But how did you find me?'

'I went out with Matt. We went clubbing in town, and when we came back we went for a walk on the beach.' Lola faltered as Matt appeared. 'Then we found you.'

'Oh God. Was I that bad?'

Lola nodded. 'You were stoned. I think you had my birthday present.'

'Thanks for bringing me back here. I don't know where I'd have ended up without you. Probably washed ashore on a desert island.'

'Oh there was no need to worry about that. The tide was going out, but Matt said you might have choked on your own vomit if we'd left you.'

'Nice,' said Carrie, feeling nauseous again.

'Not really. I've seen it happen a few times,' said Matt, grinning.

Lola glanced up at Matt with an expression close to hero worship. 'Do you think she's going to be okay on her own? Do you think one of us should be here to watch her? I don't mind staying with her but you're the professional.'

'Oh, I think she can be safely left, if she behaves herself for the rest of the day,' he said.

Carrie bit back a very rude word.

'The guys will be along to pick us up in about twenty minutes,' said Matt. 'Why don't you go and get your stuff, Lola?'

Lola seemed reluctant but Matt spoke firmly. 'Carrie will probably be better left on her own, and anyway, I promised to teach you to dive.'

'Okay. I'll get my things. Back soon.'

When Lola was out of earshot, Carrie said to Matt, 'You think I'm an idiot, don't you?'

'No. I don't think you're an idiot. We've all been there. Don't you remember what I got up to at uni?'

Carrie watched him pack his diving kit into a bag, thinking that she hadn't really known him that well at uni at all. He'd been Huw's friend but they hadn't hung out together that much. He'd just been one of the rugby crowd and a drinking buddy. Matt had existed on the outer edge of her universe, while Huw had been at the centre.

Today Matt was wearing board shorts and a grey T-shirt that was a little too tight to cope with his broad shoulders. His thick, coal-black hair was wet from the shower and glistening in the morning sunlight. She could see why so many other woman *had* noticed him at uni, and how easily he might have occupied the centre of their universes. Lola certainly seemed to have an enormous crush on him.

Hoisting the bag on his shoulder, he said, 'You seem fine now, so I'm taking Lola diving. Despite what I said about leaving you alone, you can come if you want to,' he added gruffly.

'I think I'll pass if you don't mind, but thanks for asking,' said Carrie, knowing they both wanted her to come diving about as much as they wanted a hole in the head. But at least he'd asked ... Suddenly she felt horribly emotional. It must be the drugs, she told herself, rather than how touched she was that Matt and Lola had cared when Spike hadn't given a toss.

# Chapter Twenty-four

Carrie was getting some fresh air on the beach that afternoon when she saw Spike. He was surfing and seemed as fresh as a daisy. Lucky bloody Spike. She watched him for a while and thought he hadn't noticed her. Then he walked out of the waves.

'Hi there. How you doing?' he said, as if the previous night hadn't happened.

'I've felt better.'

Carrie waited for him to elaborate or apologise. He ran his hand through his hair. 'Yeah. Sorry about losing touch last night. I was so out of it, I can't remember what happened, but I knew someone would look out for you.'

He'd left her there. He knew he had and he didn't care.

'I went home with Lola and Matt,' she said, leaving out the part about being carried home. The odd snatch was returning to her. She remembered something about flying a kite . . .

'Are you coming in the water today?' Spike asked.

The sea was seething and boiling, the waves shifting and rolling, rather like her stomach had been. 'Maybe not today, thanks.'

'Like I've said already, in a few months you'll start to get the hang of it. You might even get to stand up for more than a few seconds,' said Spike with a grin she guessed was meant to be cheeky but just seemed guilty.

'I'll take your word for it.'

He seemed twitchy and picked up his board. 'I'm going to catch some waves. Not every day you get surf like this; it's too good to waste. I'll see you tonight then?'

'Maybe. Maybe tomorrow,' she said.

'I think you should know, I was planning on tonight being my last one here,' he said casually.

So he was moving on already. She waited for the pang of regret, the twist in her stomach, but only felt a kind of freedom. Like she'd been scoured out and cleansed, though that could have been her hangover. He carried on. 'I've been off work long enough so I can't hang around here any longer. You should, though. You might even get Matt on a board.'

'I don't think so. I thought you said you were going to spend the whole summer surfing. I thought that was why you quit your job in the first place.'

He toed the sand, and Carrie realised this was the first time she'd ever seen him look anything other than totally sure of himself. 'Yeah. I know it's crap, but I'm twenty-eight. I can't spend my life surfing. I need a job. A place to live.'

'You said you used to work in an office and you hated it. What are you going to do back home?'

If it hadn't been so tanned, his face might have turned red as he looked away at the sea and then, almost, back at her. 'I was a tax inspector.'

Carrie burst out laughing but Spike didn't. He looked

like a schoolboy who'd been caught cheating. 'Somebody has to do it,' he said.

'But a tax inspector? I just didn't think you . . . You mean you worked for the Inland Revenue?'

'So what? We all get shafted by society in the end. We all get in our family saloons and trundle off to the rat race. I can still surf at the weekends and holidays. So I'll see you tonight on the beach? We can have a farewell party,' he said, a wheedling note creeping into his voice.

Carrie knew he was hoping she'd sleep with him again. After what he'd done, he expected just to pick up where they'd left off. The scales had fallen from her eyes with a resounding clatter. Spike wasn't a free spirit. He was selfish and shallow, and his world revolved around him alone. She didn't want that; she deserved better.

'Why not?' she said, but she knew she wouldn't be at the party. He leaned forward and gave her a salty kiss before jogging back to the sea, his board under his arm.

When she got back to the van, Matt was lying outside the awning, flicking through some medical journal. He was lying on his stomach, in shorts. His bronzed back was bare and his tattoos were startlingly obvious. They really were something, and she had a strange urge to reach out and touch them.

'Had enough of the ocean?' he said without turning round.

She dumped her stuff on the grass. 'For today. You had enough of hunting mermaids?'

Flipping over, he propped himself up on one elbow. He had dark hair around his nipples, a trail arrowing down his stomach.

'My friends are on the night shift at the hospital. They had to get back and get some rest.'

She sat down next to him and hugged her knees. 'Matt?'

'Yes, Caroline?'

'Do you mind if we move on from here?'

'What? Now?'

'Yes. I'd like to see somewhere different. We've spent long enough here.' She hesitated. 'If that's okay with you. I don't want to ruin any plans you might have.' She was thinking of Lola.

'What about your plans for tonight?' he said carefully.

'I don't have any plans for tonight. I've never had any plans other than to enjoy myself.'

Matt still didn't know, of course, that Spike had asked her to stay one last night and that she had decided to pass on the invitation. She wasn't sure why she'd decided to walk away, but it definitely wasn't the fact that he'd turned out to be a tax inspector and more to do with his obsession with himself.

'If we are going, I need to say goodbye to Lola first,' Matt said.

'Oh. Yes. Of course. I don't want to ruin anything . . .'

'She won't mind,' he said, pushing himself to his feet.

Carrie thought he was wrong and that Lola would mind very much, but it was too late now to withdraw the request. Maybe Matt needed to walk away too. But poor Lola . . . Could any relationship be simple? Couldn't you just shag someone and forget about it? And if not, why not?

# Chapter Twenty-five

Peace had broken out as they headed south through Devon and down into Cornwall. Slowly they'd wound their way round the creeks and inlets, beaches and fishing villages of the South West, ending up almost at Land's End. They'd taken it in turns to drive and to choose the next day's destination. Now they were lying on the beach in the late afternoon sun, drinking beer, when Matt's phone went off. Carrie was pretending to be interested in one of Matt's journals, but out of the corner of her eye she caught his mouth twitch into a smile.

'Your nurse friends?' she said casually as he texted back a message.

He laughed softly.

'Brushing off their sexy outfits, are they?' she said.

'Unfortunately no. We all wear scrubs now. The short skirts and black stockings went out with Carry On, most unfortunately in my opinion.'

'You're just a pervert,' teased Carrie.

'Believe me, Stewart and Bryan would look crap in skirts.'

She sat up. 'You didn't say they were guys.'

'You didn't ask. You just assumed they were girls.'

Carrie couldn't resist it. 'Your eyes are twinkling . . .'

'Twinkling?'

'They do when you're pleased about something.'

'Carrie, I do not twinkle. Nobody twinkles.'

'No. You definitely go all twinkly eyed when you're pleased. Now you're blushing too.'

'And you're bullshitting me,' he said, annoyed at last.

'Are you pissed off with me?'

'I'm not pissed off, no. That's not the word I'd use at all.'

'Then what word would you use? Are you cross with me? Am I in trouble again?' she teased.

He raised his eyebrows. 'Are you saying you want to be in trouble with me? If so, I can arrange it quite easily.'

Carrie swallowed. Just in time she realised they were almost flirting. Just in time she caught herself imagining Matt in scrubs and nothing underneath. She bit her lip. Having a doctor fantasy was understandable if you were thinking about Luka from *ER*, but Matt? Yet she was prepared to admit that to some women, like Natasha for instance, he probably came across as broodingly sexy. Or maybe just moody. Turning on to her stomach, she idly flicked the pages of his journal, wrinkling her nose at some of the graphic photos of some bloke's bunion surgery. Yuck.

'This is truly disgusting. Do you really find all this crap useful?'

'Some of it,' he said slowly. 'Do you find all *this* crap useful?'

'Hey . . .'

He'd got her copy of *Cosmo* in his hand and was reading from it.

'*How to give any guy mind-blowing oral. If you want to know how to drive your man wild, we'll tell you how.*

*The tips, the techniques, the sure-fire ways of making him your slave for ever. In your hands, he won't be putty, he'll be rock hard . . .'*

'Matt. Pack it in. Someone will hear.'

'Let them. This is vital sexual health information. Everyone should hear it. Bloody hell, I didn't know *that* actually worked.'

She snatched at the magazine but he'd whipped it away. 'Give it back, please!' she pleaded, as a middle-aged couple a few yards away stopped arguing and stared at them. On his feet now, Matt held the page aloft. 'She did *what* to him? My God, I've been deprived all my life.'

Carrie leapt to reach it but he was too fast, and she started to giggle.

'Oh . . . but no way. How disappointing. That one's medically impossible. The anatomy's all wrong.'

Carrie was laughing and squirming at the same time. 'You're making fun of me.'

'And now you're blushing.'

'I am not!'

Finally he held out the magazine. 'Really, I'm shocked at you, Caroline. This is truly obscene. Do you fancy going out tonight?' he added suddenly.

Carrie was totally taken aback. 'Where? To the pub? Clubbing?'

'Not quite.'

'Where then?'

'Wait and see.'

'Well, aren't you going to say something?'

The truth was, she couldn't take in the scene in front of her. It was beautiful, weird, surreal . . .

'It's a theatre,' he offered helpfully.

'Yes. I can see that.'

They were standing on a small stone platform at the top of a cliff above the sea, looking down on a theatre that had been literally carved out of the granite rock face. Steep staircases plunged down between the aisles and benches, where grass served for cushions. The seating, the stage, even a little Juliet balcony, had all been hewn from the solid rock. The backdrop was the Atlantic Ocean, wild breakers crashing on the rocks below the stage as gulls screamed overhead.

'It's incredible,' she said at last.

'Incredible good or incredible weird?'

'Hard to believe that there's a theatre at all. This place is just so wild.'

Matt was amused. 'I can't believe you're an actress and you've never been here before.'

'I had enough trouble persuading Huw to come to my performances, let alone go to a theatre for pleasure.'

'Yes. I can imagine that. I can't see my old mate here either, but it's a shame you've never been. On a fine night, when the sun's going down, it's a pretty good place to be.'

'I wouldn't have thought it was your kind of thing either. I thought the only entertainment you were interested in was who could pee furthest up the rugby club wall.'

'That's where you're wrong. Mum used to bring us here when we were on holiday in Cornwall. We pretended we hated it – which we did, of course – but when I got older, I came back a couple of times without having my arm twisted.'

Carrie had to admit that the round stage, bare and

inviting, was almost making her drool. 'Do you think we can take a look?' she asked.

He glanced at his watch. 'I think they're closed to visitors. There's a show tonight, but maybe we can sneak in. Come on.'

They'd managed to duck under a rope barrier and get halfway down the steps when a loud voice behind them boomed, 'Excuse me, can I help you?' A woman in a voluminous velvet kaftan cast a stern eye over them. 'You can't go down there. The theatre is closed.'

'We only wanted a quick look. We've come all this way, you see, and we're going home tomorrow,' pleaded Carrie.

The woman's face was as stony as the cliff face. 'It's out of the question. Sorry.'

Carrie didn't think the woman looked at all sorry, but Matt climbed back up the steps and started talking to her in a low voice. After a few nods, the woman pursed her lips and said grudgingly, 'You have five minutes, and believe me, I shall be counting every second.'

Matt grabbed Carrie's arm. 'Quick. Come on.'

'What did you tell her?' she asked as they trotted down the steps to the stage.

'That I was going abroad on a dangerous mercy mission but first I needed to propose to you on the stage of the Minack Theatre.'

'You said what!'

He shrugged. 'It was the only thing I could think of on the spur of the moment. Just make sure you look happy on the way back up.'

She forgave him when she stood on the stage. The atmosphere was sending actual shivers up her spine. She imagined the stone seats packed with people, felt the heat of the lights on her skin, heard the gasps and laughter and applause, the stamping and shouting of the audience. Matt was standing behind her, his breath warm against her neck.

'Carrie, I need to tell you something,' he murmured behind her.

She tensed instinctively as his arms encircled her body, then forced herself to relax. Watching them intently from her perch, the kaftan woman would be expecting a performance. She and Matt had better make this convincing. 'I've been trying to find a way to tell you this for ages,' he whispered in her ear.

'Is it something I'll like?' she breathed, getting into character and enjoying herself more than she wanted to admit.

'It's something important . . . but it's awkward.'

'What do you mean, awkward?'

'Well, it's not an easy thing for a man to have to say to a woman.'

He was overdoing it now and she hoped he wasn't going to take too long. His arms were helpfully warm against her bare skin, but the hairs were tickling her.

'Matt, can you get on with it, please?' she said briskly.

'But darling, I'd hate to hurry this special moment.'

She tried not to laugh. 'I think you're just hamming it up now.'

He spun her round to face him, his face stricken with anguish. 'Hamming it up? Caroline, this is serious. Don't you know how I feel about you? How I've longed for this day?' He pulled her against his chest, banging her nose against his breast bone.

'Ow!'

174

He thrust her backwards, gripping her arms. 'Oh Caroline, sweetest, don't tell me I've hurt you.'

'You bashed my nose, you twerp,' she said, rubbing the tip.

'I got carried away. It's just that . . . I haven't told you what I need to say yet.'

Reaching up, she broke his grip. 'I think I can guess.'

He winked theatrically. 'Perhaps not, Caroline.'

She grinned cheerfully. 'Goodbye, Matt. I hate to hurt you, but I've decided to leave you. And by the way, don't give up the day job.'

'Okay. But I only wanted to tell you that you snore.'

'I do not snore!' she said indignantly.

'I'm afraid you do. Just a tiny bit. Nothing that can't be solved by a spot of ENT surgery. It's not my forte but I can have a go with the vegetable knife if you want.'

She threw up her hands in disgust. 'Matt, thanks for showing me the theatre. It was a nice thing to do but you are still a git.'

As she stomped up the steps, the woman was looming, her kaftan billowing in the breeze.

'So that's a no, then?' called Matt.

'Sod off!' shouted Carrie.

'Don't leave me, Caroline, I can't live without you!'

Kaftan woman gave an outraged gasp as Carrie passed. 'Are you completely off your head, young lady? You don't deserve a good man like that. He's as fit as a butcher's dog, and if I were you, I'd have him up the aisle and into bed before you could say Jack Robinson.'

# Chapter Twenty-six

It was after midnight as they sat drinking shots at the table inside the van. Carrie was still buzzing from the show. They'd managed to get two returns for *A Midsummer Night's Dream*. The performance had been breathtaking, played out against the setting sun and the stars. As the final scene had come to an end it had begun to rain, so they'd dashed back to Dolly and fallen inside, laughing and damp. Now they sat wrapped in towels round the little dining table. Matt lifted the vodka bottle and pushed a bumper bag of crisps towards her.

'Not for me, thanks.'

'What, no vodka?'

'No more crisps. I'll have another shot, though,' she said, holding out her glass.

'So you enjoyed the play?' he asked as he filled it.

'It was amazing. That setting was just made for *A Midsummer Night's Dream*. Mind you, I didn't think much of Bottom, and Titania was a bit over the top.'

He shook his head. 'And you'd have done a much better job?'

'Abso-bloody-lutely. I'd have been fabulous, darling.'

His eyebrows shot up. 'Really? I thought Titania was fit.'

'You would. She's just your type.'

'And what type would that be?'

Carrie stifled a tiny burp. She knew she was slightly pissed but she didn't care. That was what being slightly pissed was all about.

'Well, let me see. I'd say that your type could be summed up as Top Totty. Long legs, long hair, voice like Radio Four crossed with the Pony Club.'

He rested his chin on his hand.

'I'm right, aren't I? I can see I'm right because you're trying to look enigmatic. You do that when I'm right. And this time I can tell. I'm absolutely spot on, Minty darling.'

'I think you need another drink.'

She pointed a finger at him. 'So I *am* right. You just don't want to admit it.'

'Why don't you tell me about your dream role? The part you'd really like to play.'

'Oh, that's a hard one. Oops!' She giggled. 'Hadn't meant that to sound like a line from a Carry On film.'

'Nothing wrong with the Carry On films, as I've said before,' said Matt, pouring himself another shot. 'Now, what part would you like?'

'A very big one.'

He laughed out loud and it suited him, but she wasn't so squiffy that she couldn't see what he was trying to do: draw her out, steer the conversation on to her. Cunning, but not quite cunning enough. He really wasn't that bad when he'd had a drink and pulled the poker out of his arse. And the kaftan woman might have got one thing right: he was quite fit. His face came into focus. She liked the way his dark silky hair curled against his neck, and he did have lovely eyes; they were smoky blue-black fringed with dark eyelashes. She wondered, suspiciously, if he used mascara, and when she giggled, her bare knees bumped against his under the table.

'I want to be Lady Macbeth,' she declared, much too loudly. 'Well, don't look so surprised. Don't you think I can play a cold-hearted murdering bitch?'

'On the contrary, I think you're perfectly capable of it. I'm just getting rather worried about sharing the same space as you.'

He drained his glass but made no attempt to pour any more, which was a good thing. A very good thing actually, because she had her beer goggles clamped to her eyes and she needed to see Matt for what he really was. Ugly, withered and troll-like.

'Matt . . .' she began.

He rested his chin on hand again, listening intently. 'Yes, Caroline.'

He didn't look like a troll; she'd be lying if she didn't admit that he was, in fact, horrendously sexy. Maybe some black coffee might render him less attractive.

'Can I ask you something personal?'

'Mmm. That depends how personal.'

She wished he wouldn't do that. Lean even closer and *murmur*.

'I want to know,' she said, leaning dangerously close herself, 'just exactly what you did in Tuman that got you into trouble?'

'So this is Truth or Dare, is it?' he said.

'If you like.'

'In that case, you have to offer me something too.'

'Okay. Name it,' said Carrie, more boldly than she felt. 'Anything goes?'

She knew she was a bit tipsy but she didn't care. Matt was so close now that she could feel his breath on her neck. 'Absolutely anything.'

'Okay. Here's my question. Do you still love Huw?'

Now that, she thought as her heart sank, really was a hard one. He backed off slightly but he must have seen her swallow as she tried to keep her composure.

'Crafty,' she said, waving her glass at him with a wink, 'and below the belt, even from someone whose job is asking uncomfortable questions.'

'Yes, but I thought we were playing hardball. That anything goes.'

She blew out a breath. 'Do I still love Huw? What does that mean? I suppose I still think about him. I still feel . . . cut up when I think of what he did to me, and I definitely still hate him sometimes. The trouble is, I still think about the bastard far too much.'

Matt shook his head gravely. 'Sorry. You'll have to be more specific than that. What do you mean by too much? For instance, have you thought about him today?'

'This morning on the beach, I thought about him and what he might be doing right now. Him and her.'

'You mean Fenella.'

'Yes. Fenella.' There, she'd managed to get her tongue round the name without gagging. That must be progress. 'And I thought about him – and Fenella – on the journey here a few times.'

'This doesn't sound very promising, I have to say.'

'Yes, but. You haven't heard the full story yet. It might not be quite as bad as you think.'

'And why's that?' said Matt.

'Because I didn't think about him tonight while we were at the play. Not for a single moment. In fact, he might not have entered my head unless you'd just asked your question.'

'Which you still haven't answered.'

'Because I know this is Truth or Dare and I want to be honest, and being honest, I don't know.'

There. She'd been as open as she could, but Matt wasn't going to let her off the hook that easily.

'Would you take him back if he walked in here now?' he asked.

'No way.'

He raised his eyebrows.

'Okay. If we're being strictly accurate, I don't *think* I'd take him back. Will that do? That's the best I can do right now. Now, I've kept my side of the bargain and it's your turn.'

'I'm quaking,' he said, but his hands were rock steady.

'It's the same thing I asked before. What happened to make you rush home from Tuman? Because if you're planning on going back there, why are you back here now?'

'I didn't want to come home. I was sent back. For four months.'

'Really? Robert said you'd done something heroic. Why would they send you back for that?'

'My brother is a total wanker.'

'I'm sure he loves you too. Now come on. I gave you an honest answer. You have to give me one.'

Matt raised his eyebrows again. 'Well, if you insist . . .'

She kicked him under the table.

'Ow!'

'Don't try and wriggle out of it, Matt.'

He watched her while he rubbed his knee. She could see in his eyes that he was desperate to escape. For a moment she thought he might try to leave, but then he sat up and raked his hands through his hair.

'Okay. The reason I was sent back was because of an accident. Well, they called it an accident; I prefer to call it a bloody stupid mistake. But that's why I'm here now.'

'When did this happen?' asked Carrie.

'About a month before Huw's wedding. I'd already declined the invitation. I wasn't even supposed to be there. You were unlucky, you see.'

He looked to her to laugh but she folded her arms and said, 'Don't stop now.'

# Chapter Twenty-seven

He was aware he was playing with the shot glass and desperately wanting another drink. Also wishing he had a cigarette and wishing he didn't want one so much.

'I was on my way back from one of the villages in a Jeep and we hit some debris. A stump or a log, I don't know what happened exactly,' he told her. 'The next thing I knew we were off the track, not that there was much of one. There was an almighty crash . . .'

Then shrieking or screaming. Of birds or people he was no longer certain. When his colleagues had arrived from the medical centre, they said he'd been knocked out. He wasn't sure, though as soon as the Jeep had hit the tree, he knew he'd broken his nose. He must have smashed it against the windshield, because there had been blood on the glass.

The one thing he'd never forget was the smell of petrol. It had made him retch. Then he'd known he'd got to get out. The instinct to run had been more powerful than he could ever have imagined. His heart had literally been trying to punch its way out of his chest as he'd forced open the door of the Jeep, the stench of fuel in his nose, knowing that it could go up at any moment. He'd fallen on to the ground, dazed but aware enough to know he had to get away from the vehicle.

He would have run, he was sure of it, but then he'd heard a groan next to him and realised that he couldn't get away because Aidan, his colleague, was still trapped in the Jeep.

'I didn't know what to do,' he said. 'You see, I was fucked either way, or rather Aidan was fucked. My God . . .'

He thrust both hands through his hair, feeling the sweat on his palms, his heart pounding, and the agony of the decision he'd had to make in a few seconds.

'Matt?'

At Carrie's prompt, he forced himself to carry on speaking. 'I knew that he probably had some kind of spinal injury and if I moved him I could be making it worse. I knew that if I pulled him out like that with my bare hands he could end up paraplegic, but I had no choice. It was that or let him burn.'

He stopped, seeing the scene again, hearing the sounds, smelling the fuel and remembering his own terror and confusion as he'd weighed up the options. No one was coming to rescue them, not for hours maybe. It was his call. His decision. His error of judgement, and Aidan had to live with the consequences.

'I had no choice,' he repeated as Carrie listened, hugging her knees to her chest. The first person he'd ever told. Ever really talked to about how he felt.

'So you pulled him out.'

He couldn't look at her; he looked out of the window and against the night saw only his own reflection – and hers, white faced, opposite.

'I managed to crawl to the other door. It was already open but I still had to drag him out. Do you know the only way I could do it? I told myself that he was just a great big bastard; a wing forward I had to tackle to win a rugby match. If I got him out, I'd have helped England beat Australia in the World Cup final. All I had to do was stop him from reaching the line and scoring a try. How bizarre is that?' he said, shaking his head at himself.

'Not bizarre at all. Who knows the way our minds work when . . . when we're pushed to the limit,' she said.

*You mean when you flipped at the church,* he was thinking. *Carrie, it's not the same thing* . . . but he said nothing. Didn't want to hurt her.

'Then what happened?' she said softly.

'I dragged him out of the Jeep and away from the wreckage until I blacked out. Totally fucking stupid thing to do, of course, but I was out of my head,' he said. 'Adey could have had all kinds of internal injuries but I didn't have time to think. I wasn't thinking at all. I don't think I was even on the planet.'

'But you got him out,' she said.

'What?' he said, hardly hearing her now as the guilt overwhelmed him. She was going to want to know what happened next.

'You pulled this Aidan – your mate – out. You saved him . . .'

It was then he knew he'd said far too much. *Way* too much. It was the first time he'd spoken about it properly since he'd got back. It had been more unpleasant than he'd thought. All that bollocks they told you about baring your soul being therapeutic. He must remember never to tell a patient that talking helped – or to become a better liar.

'The Jeep went up like a rocket; not, I have to admit, seconds after I'd got Aidan out, though that would make a better story. It must have been a good few minutes later, because the noise woke me up. I'm not sure what happened, to be honest, but I managed to find the radio in a bush and eventually the cavalry arrived from the base. It was them who saved Aidan, not me.'

'And is he okay?'

'He's in a wheelchair. Unlike me, he won't be going back to Tuman or playing rugby again, and that's my fault. I probably caused the paralysis getting him out.'

'Surely you can't know that for certain. I'm not a doctor, but you—'

'Had no choice? Carrie, I've heard all that from my colleagues. Maybe I didn't have a choice, but it will never stop me blaming myself.'

She said nothing, just hugged herself tighter, and his heart went out to her. She was like a little girl, over-whelmed by what she'd just heard and, like most people, at a loss about how to respond. But then she surprised him.

'What about you?' she asked.

'Me? Oh, just this,' he said, touching his nose. 'Plus a couple of cracked ribs. Serves me right for trashing a Jeep and Aidan in one go. Two for the price of one, eh?' He laughed at himself to avoid telling her about his other – ha! – injuries. That he was not quite himself afterwards and had to be persuaded to come home after he'd lost it during one of the clinics they were running. He'd been about to stitch someone up after a minor op when suddenly he'd smelled burning. That smell, sickly, acrid, of burning metal and rubber had made him gag. He could no longer see his patient, let alone focus on what he'd been doing. All he could see was Aidan lying in the Jeep, the flames as the whole thing exploded. His hands had started shaking so much he'd had to hand over to his colleague. Then Shelly had turned up to find him sitting in the office with his head in his hands. It turned out that some of the kids had lit a fire in the clearing and thrown an old tyre on it, but it had been enough to earn him a ticket home to England.

Matt knew that even a moderate head injury could make you act out of character; could affect your emotions and perceptions for weeks and months afterwards. But the scans had shown nothing sinister and he was self-aware enough to know that blaming a bump on the head was easier than admitting he'd been shaken up and that he'd felt guilty.

'I was driving too fast, I wasn't paying attention. No wonder we went off the road,' he said out loud.

He and Aidan had been up all night attending a difficult birth in the outlying village, but being tired wasn't an excuse. His colleagues had told him he'd been tired; he wasn't to blame. But they weren't the ones who'd crashed the Jeep.

'You're very hard on yourself, Matt. I'm sure it wasn't your fault. It could have happened to anyone,' Carrie was saying.

Okay, thought Matt, she was trying very hard to be kind now. She was speaking in a soft voice, because she felt sorry for him and wasn't quite sure what to say. Inside he felt angry, embarrassed and very much like lashing out at someone. He felt like saying: 'Stick to the acting. Leave the sympathy and understanding to me. I'm a professional at it, remember, and so much better than you.'

But he couldn't bear the thought of seeing her face crumpling like a little girl's, so he leaned forward and kissed her very gently on the forehead. Then he got up and headed outside before he said something he'd really regret.

# Chapter Twenty-eight

'Would you like to drive?' said Matt as they packed up the next morning. 'You might feel safer, considering.'

She tried not to rise to the bait. Neither of them had mentioned the night before; neither the vodka-fuelled confessional nor the kiss. She'd felt the kiss was the equivalent of a pat on the head: a signal to back off from his personal life. She'd felt dismissed, gently but firmly.

'Actually, I've got a bit of a headache. Maybe you should drive. You haven't got any paracetamol, by the way?'

'Sorry. No. Try a cup of coffee. If it gets really bad, I'll stop at a chemist's.'

'You are such a caring person, Dr Landor.'

Ignoring her, he pulled the map from the dashboard and opened it, frowning.

'Where are we going?'

'I thought St Ives?'

She shrugged. 'Sounds as good a place as any.'

They ended up at a site just outside the town. Matt claimed he'd stayed there when he was in the sixth form at school. They headed down the steep streets into the town centre, splitting up so that Matt could visit the Tate Gallery. Carrie was longing to go there too, but she was longing for some time on her own even more. Making an excuse, she wandered round the surf boutiques, window-shopping. She wouldn't have admitted it to Matt, but money was becoming an issue. She'd be starting her teaching course soon and she needed to talk to Huw and sort out their finances, but the thought of seeing Fenella, her bump maybe showing by now, didn't appeal.

When she reached the Tate again, Matt was outside, chatting to a tall, dark-haired girl in jeans and a T-shirt so ostentatiously free of patterns and logos, Carrie knew they'd cost a fortune. He was whispering something to her and she turned round sharply.

'Hello, Natasha,' said Carrie. 'This is a surprise.' She could have kicked herself. She hadn't meant the words to sound sarcastic.

'Isn't it?' trilled Natasha.

'Not really,' said Robert Landor, emerging from a nearby newsagent with a packet of cigarettes. 'Seeing as Matt knew we were here.'

'I didn't know until yesterday,' said Matt evenly.

So the text Matt had received on the beach the day before wasn't from Nurse Bryan or Stewart; it was from Natasha or Rob.

'Does it really matter? I'm sure he meant to tell you,' said Natasha.

Carrie squashed down the unlikely but horrible thought that Natasha and Rob might want to share Dolly with her and Matt. 'Where are you staying?' she said, mentally crossing her fingers.

'Not in a bloody camper van, that's for sure. Bryony's

godmother has a gin palace down at the marina. We're staying on that,' said Rob.

'That sounds very luxurious. Cosy too. Is Bryony here too?' said Carrie, generous now she knew there was no chance of them sharing the van.

'Fenella wouldn't let her have time off, the evil witch.' Natasha's hand flew to her mouth, then she lowered her voice. 'I am so sorry. I'm sure you never want to hear her name again.'

'It's fine,' said Carrie, gritting her teeth. Matt's face was impassive.

'Of course. Anyway, you asked me about the yacht. Frankly, it's dreadful. Really vulgar, all white leather and gold taps. You must come and see it,' she said, stroking Matt's arm as if he were a small furry animal.

Rob gave a sigh. 'Yes, you simply must, but for God's sake let's get something to eat first. I'm starving. Is there anywhere in this place that doesn't serve bloody pasties?'

Surprisingly there was, and the four of them were soon sitting in a restaurant overlooking the harbour.

'That was rather good, considering,' said Natasha with a sigh, wiping a tiny trace of raspberry coulis from her mouth with a table napkin. 'You know, I think I saw this place mentioned in *The Sunday Times Style*. A.A. Gill gave it four stars so I thought it would be heaving with men in patterned sweaters, all outraged by the size of the portions.'

'The portions *were* outrageous. I might have to suggest we stop for fish and chips on the way home,' said Matt.

Natasha laughed. 'Is that what you've been living on for the past month?'

'Only as a treat,' said Carrie. 'Mostly we've existed on beans on toast.'

'Not much fun in a confined space, but we do know each other a hell of a lot better, don't we?' said Matt, winking at Carrie.

Taken aback at this unexpected display of comradeship, she was slow to react.

'Well . . .'

'Matt used to set light to his own farts at school,' declared Natasha, hastily marking her territory.

'Do you mind? This is a classy establishment,' said Rob, topping up Carrie's glass from a bottle of wine.

'So, Matt's filthy habits apart, you're having a wonderful time together. As you mentioned, sharing a confined space like that must be hell.'

'Dolly's been lovingly restored,' said Carrie loyally.

'I'm sure she has, but come on, it's just a tin can on wheels.'

'It's a lot better than boarding school, as you'd have to admit, Tasha,' said Matt unexpectedly. 'I'll go and get the bill.'

'Excellent,' said Rob.

'I ought to pay my share,' offered Carrie, dreading how much they'd spent.

Natasha patted her hand. 'Let the guys pay. It makes them feel useful.'

While Matt was at the bar, Tasha slid into his seat next to Carrie. She smelled spicy and expensive, probably courtesy of Jo Malone. Huw had brought Carrie some JM cologne once and she'd kept the bottle long after the last drop had evaporated. Natasha was chattering about the boat and where they were planning to go on it. Carrie thought it sounded really awful, all that white leather upholstery, the comfy beds, the proper toilet . . .

When Matt came back, Natasha was back on their boarding school days. 'Do you remember what a dump it was? Never any hot water, gross food. Matt rebelled against it all, of course.'

'*Quel surprise*,' said Rob.

Natasha ignored him. 'Carrie, you might find this hard to believe, but he actually kidnapped the bursar and held him for ransom in the lower sixth common room. He got into the most terrible trouble. The head sent him on a ten-mile cross-country run.'

Carrie couldn't resist. 'It all sounds like a spiffing prank. Did you have midnight feasts too, like Malory Towers?'

She smiled broadly to show she was joking but Natasha called her bluff. 'Well, not quite, darling. We weren't really there to enjoy lemonade and buns. There were cakes involved but not of the chocolate variety. I seem to recall they were Matt's contribution – though my memory is naturally a bit foggy now.'

'Ah, but Matt's a reformed character these days. He doesn't do naughty things any more. Do you, Matt?'

Natasha's eyes glinted. 'Really? That's not what I heard. Is it, Matt?'

Carrie cringed. They were behaving like a couple of rival sisters, and Matt did what any indulgent parent would when asked to choose. He linked both their arms in his and said: 'You know what I think, girls. I think we should all go down to the harbour and look at the pretty boats.'

\*

Later, back at the campsite, Carrie returned from the shop with an out-of-date copy of *Heat* and a Twix to find Matt shirtless. He was shaving, using her make-up mirror wedged in the frame of the awning. She'd grown used to the back view of him by now; the tattoos, so weird at first, were now just part of him. She didn't think he'd noticed her watching him. He was scraping the blade over his neck, skimming his throat. Every so often he'd dip the razor in a bowl of water, leaving shaving foam and stubble behind. His hair was still damp at the ends, curling into his neck.

'Hot date?' she said, dropping her shopping on the table.

'I'm having dinner with Natasha.'

Right. Of course. Why shouldn't he? 'Isn't it the same thing?' she said.

He gave the razor a final rinse and laid it by the bowl. 'If you say so.'

She opened her magazine and sat down as he took a white shirt from the back of a deckchair. After he'd buttoned it up, he squinted in the mirror and ran his hand over his chin.

'What's so funny? Do I have spinach on my teeth or something?' he asked when he caught her smiling at him.

'No spinach, though if there was I probably wouldn't have told you.' She flicked the pages and stared hard at a photo. Now that was interesting . . . Paris Hilton had had a cat specially bred to match her favourite pair of stilettos. 'I don't suppose I should wait up for you?' she said casually.

'Probably not.'

Matt pulled on his socks and stuffed his feet into a pair of chunky black boots.

'You look ravishing, darling. Divine socks.'

His smile when he turned was wry and knowing. 'Thanks. I do like to make an effort. Clean underpants and all that.'

'That's more than I need to know,' she said, trying to take an interest in J-Lo's new yoga regime instead of Matt's mating ritual, but it was almost impossible. As he rolled up his cuffs midway to the elbow, she was heartily wishing that he would just bugger off. She didn't want him to linger any longer, preparing himself to have sex with another woman. It was just too intimate.

Relief came at last. Picking up his wallet, he shoved it into the back pocket of his jeans. She tried not to look for the telltale circle of a condom in his back jean pocket, but of course Natasha would have that covered. When he was ready, he said, 'Carrie, if you're not comfortable being here alone tonight, I can stay. This may be old fashioned, and I expect you'll be sarcastic, but I don't really like leaving you on your own like this.'

She laughed. 'Matt, you sound like my mum. Go and have a good time. To be honest, I'm looking forward to having a night on my own. I think it will do us both good to have a bit of space. I can do without your smelly feet for one night.'

'In that case, I'll see you tomorrow. My taxi will be here in a minute. Goodbye.'

'Don't fall off the boat,' she said after he'd gone.

# Chapter Twenty-nine

'So how are you getting on?' asked Rowena the next day.

Carrie clamped the phone firmly to her ear. She'd been determined not to be in when Matt got back from his night of passion with Natasha, so she'd walked down to the town. She'd finally succumbed to the Tate and spent several hours wandering round it, sitting in front of the artwork and installations. Huw would have had to be bound and gagged to enter a gallery.

'Sorry, Rowena. I can't hear you. There's a demonic seagull trying to attack me.'

She flapped her arm and the gull flew off, but not before it had swiped her ice cream. 'Get off, you horrible bird!'

'Where are you?'

'On the roof of the Tate in St Ives. You have got to see their new Damien Hirst installation. And the naïve fishermen's paintings are incredible . . . Oh, and did you know that the Barbara Hepworth sculpture garden is here—'

'Yeah, yeah, but how *are* you getting on?' cut in Rowena.

'Fine.'

'Only fine? I thought you might have had more to report by now.'

'Okay. I get it. If you expected us to fall into each other's arms, it hasn't worked. Matt's just spent the night with Natasha on some skanky old luxury yacht.'

'Sounds totally crap. I can see why you'd rather stay in a rusty old camper van.'

'Wash your mouth out, Rowena. Nelson would faint if he heard that. Look, I'm sorry to disappoint you, but I'm not the slightest bit bothered about Matt. He isn't my type.'

'What about Spike?'

'I passed on Spike. I'm a free agent these days.'

The seagull was back, eyeing her paper carrier bag of groceries. She gave it her best death look.

'That's a shame. He sounded cute,' Rowena went on as the gull stared at Carrie like the creepy little boy in *The Sixth Sense*.

'He turned out to be a tax inspector,' muttered Carrie, deciding to leave out the fact that he'd also left her on the beach stoned out of her skull.

'Well, it's not exactly grounds for dumping the guy, but I suppose it's your life.'

'How are *you* getting on, Rowena?'

'The truth? It is bloody manic. Mayhem. I don't want to go on about me, but you won't believe who was on the set this morning . . .'

Half an hour later, Carrie's mobile was beeping to show the battery was running low and the seagull had dive-bombed a family into handing over their chips. It was late afternoon. She figured Matt would be back by now, unless he'd decided to stay on the yacht for another night. She wanted to get back to Dolly, have a shower and wander into town for the evening. She'd seen flyers saying there was a band playing at one of the waterfront pubs. One of those Ye Olde Something or Other places by the harbour. Gripping her bag of supplies tighter, she peered at the leaflet in the pub window. It was a Nirvana tribute band.

'It is you, isn't it?'

She turned to see Lola smiling at her.

'What are you doing here?' They both said it at the same time.

'You first,' said Lola, flicking back her long hair. She seemed nervous, shy even.

'Matt wanted to revisit old haunts,' said Carrie. Trying to avoid the seagull muck, she deposited the groceries on the pub table.

Lola hopped about nervously, then said, 'We missed you and Matt.'

Carrie was glad Matt wasn't here now with Natasha. She had a feeling Lola still had a major crush on him.

'Have Spike and the others gone home?' she asked, but the question was answered by the man himself strolling out of the pub.

# Chapter Thirty

He was shoving his change and a box of matches into the pocket of his board shorts.

'Sorry,' mouthed Lola.

'It's fine,' said Carrie, gritting her teeth. Behind him were Baz and Stig, both grunting hello before scarpering faster than hares out of a trap. So, they all knew he'd dumped her, thought Carrie; though that wasn't strictly true, because she'd walked away from him. Her face heating up didn't help.

'What a surprise to see you here. Down for the weekend?' she said, hardly bothering to keep the edge out of her voice.

He gave her his best lazy smile but she could see he was beyond his comfort zone. 'No. We decided to stay on a couple more weeks, catch some more waves while we could. How're you doing?'

He'd obviously been planning to stay on surfing and was too cowardly to tell her the truth. Yet she could hardly complain: she'd buggered off too. He owed her nothing, but she didn't like being lied to.

'You know. We get about. We've been round the south coast to Land's End. Matt took me to the Minack Theatre to see *A Midsummer Night's Dream.*'

Spike's eyes flickered momentarily to two girls in bikinis laughing by the harbour. 'Where is Matt?' he asked, refocusing on her.

'Out with his friends. We're not joined at the hip.' She bit her lip as he raised his eyebrows. 'I have to go. My fish fingers are melting.'

He laughed. 'Well, we can't have your dinner defrosting. Maybe I'll see you around.'

She wanted to sink into a hole. 'Maybe.'

Hoisting her bag, she scuttled off along the harbour. It was the opposite direction to the site but she didn't care if she ended up in Glasgow as long as she got out of Spike's sight. However, the pub table must have been damp, and the bottom of her bag disintegrated, sending cans and packets rolling out over the cobbles. Everyone turned, of course. She was now more entertaining than the seagulls dive-bombing a traffic warden as he tried to ticket a motorbike.

'Hey. Let me help.'

Lola was behind her, picking up beans and rice as deftly as a Wimbledon ball girl.

'Thanks. What a plonker I am.'

'Nah. You just need a stronger bag. Hang on.' She pulled a jute carrier out of her backpack and handed it over.

'Thanks,' said Carrie, shoving the shopping inside. 'Love the logo. *Say no to plastic.*'

'I printed it myself,' Lola said, her cheeks turning pale pink, her eyes shining.

'It's great, Lola. You're really clever.'

The girl smiled modestly, and Carrie could see why

Matt liked her. Her heart went out to Lola. It was all very well shagging people you picked up on the beach, but it also meant casting them aside like driftwood. If you weren't careful, if you got into any kind of relationship that went beyond mutual-bonk level, someone ended up feeling discarded.

'Do you want to go for a smoothie or a herbal tea? There's a great Fairtrade café up the hill,' said Lola.

Carrie smiled. Herbal tea. Daring. 'What about Spike? Won't your friends miss you?'

'They said they're going off to Perranporth for the day.'

'And you don't want to go surfing with them?'

'I'd rather talk to you.'

Carrie smiled, but inwardly she knew that talking about Matt might mean she was going to have to tell Lola about Natasha.

'I've been wondering how you were,' said Lola as they walked up the cobbled street, drinks in hand.

'I'm fine, why would you worry about me? If you think I'm upset about Spike, then don't. We both knew it was just a bit of a fling.'

'Oh no. I know you don't care about Spike. It's Matt I was thinking of.'

'Matt? Why would you be worrying about me and him?'

Lola looked puzzled. 'You like him, don't you?'

'Like him? I suppose that's one word for it. He's okay in his way. As a friend.' She felt his lips on her forehead, putting her in her place in the gentlest yet hardest of ways.

'I think he's amazing,' Lola said dreamily.

There was no hope now. Should she tell her? *Matt's got a girlfriend. She's called Natasha and last night they went out together, had wild sex and he hasn't come back yet.*

'He's incredible. Working out in Tuman as a doctor, helping all those people, and I like his tattoos.'

Carrie wasn't sure the message would get through, but she didn't know how far to push things. 'Lola, I think you should know that Matt's not the type to settle down. He never has been and I've known him a few years now.'

'Yes, I know all about that. He told me about when you were at university together. And all about your fiancé and what you did at the church. I thought it was funny, actually. I mean, I was upset for you but I'm sure I'd have reacted the same way if the person I loved did that to me.'

Carrie stopped and rested the bag on a wall. She'd been puffing all the way up the hill but Lola's remark had taken away what was left of her breath. 'I really wish Matt hadn't told you about the wedding.'

'Why not? He was only being nice.'

Nice? Well, hey, why not put an ad in the *Cornish Times* and the *Devonshire Bugle*; maybe even the *John O'Groats Gazette*, she thought. No. Why not tell Sky News and broadcast it to the whole world?

'He really cares about you,' said Lola hastily.

'I'm sure he does care, but he needn't worry about me. What happened is all in the past now. It's light years away. I'm a completely different person.'

Lola picked up Carrie's bag from the wall and her face brightened. 'Are you? Are you really different?'

There was no point taking things out on Lola, who was really very sweet if slightly not of this earth. 'Yes,

I am. The woman Matt told you about – the mad, stupid one—'

'I'm sure you could never be stupid!'

'Oh, I could. Anyway, she's history. This is me now.'

They'd reached the gates of the campsite and Carrie was hoping Lola wouldn't want to come in with her. Bloody, bloody Matt. He'd allowed a nice girl like that to get a crush on him, discussed all Carrie's embarrassing secrets with her and then gone off and shagged Natasha. Lola's eyes were fixed on the orange beacon that was Dolly.

'Isn't that your camper van? And look, there's Matt! Do you mind if I say hello?'

'Of course not, but I need some stuff from the shop first,' said Carrie, hoping Lola wouldn't ask what stuff because she had no idea. She just didn't want to be a witness to their reunion. In fact she was a big coward and desperately hoped Matt would tell Lola about Natasha himself.

'Shall I take your groceries back to Dolly?' offered Lola.

'Oh, would you mind?' said Carrie, before realising she sounded exactly like Natasha.

She'd queued for ages in the shop behind a group of teenagers trying to scam bottles of cider out of the assistant. Which turned out to be lucky, because by the time she got back to the van, Matt had evidently done the deed. He was standing in the awning with his arms round Lola, giving her a distinctly fraternal hug. Carrie slowed her step. Matt was kissing the top of Lola's head, rather like he'd kissed her after the play at the Minack. A gentle but firm dismissal.

She just was wondering whether to creep away when Matt saw her and mouthed, 'Wait.' She froze as he gave Lola a large white handkerchief and she blew her nose noisily. It could only be moments before Lola realised she was here, so she strolled towards the van making as much noise as possible without coughing or humming too obviously. Matt whispered in Lola's ear and she wiped her face hastily. When she turned, her eyes were bright and her cheeks pink but she was smiling.

'Did you get your stuff?' she asked, so courageously that Carrie's heart went out to her.

'Yes thanks.' She rattled her paper bag loudly.

'I'd better be getting back,' said Lola.

'Do you want me to walk you home?' said Matt.

Lola shook her head and threw them both a brave smile. 'No thanks. I'll be fine.'

'She's not fine, is she?' said Carrie after Lola had gone.

'She will be,' said Matt.

'No thanks to you.'

His face darkened. 'What did you say?'

'Forget it.'

'No, Carrie. I won't forget it. Are you blaming me for Lola being upset?'

Furious at his self-righteousness, she exploded. 'Yes, I am. Can't you see that you've hurt her? She worships the ground you walk on and you've just used her for sex and chucked her away like a . . . like an old chip wrapper! The minute Natasha came sniffing round, Lola may as well have not existed.' She was trembling but she didn't care.

'Have you finished?' he snapped.

'No. As a matter of fact, I haven't. I'm pretty pissed off actually, Matt.'

'Again?'

Her heart was thumping. 'Yes. Again.'

'And what is it this time?'

'You told Lola all about the wedding. About me trashing the flowers. Why did you do that?'

'I wasn't aware your horticultural vandalism was classified material and I'm sorry if I embarrassed you, but Lola wanted to know about you so I told her. Yes, I mentioned Huw and I said you were here to try and get away from what had happened. To try and change your life.'

'I never said I was here to change my life. I've never discussed how I feel about Huw, so how can you presume to know me?'

'I've shared Dolly with you for nearly a month. I think I've gained some insight into your moods by now.'

'Really? So you know me, do you? You like discussing me like I'm some . . . some kind of *specimen*?'

He laughed out loud but she was like a rocket now, a rocket with the blue touch paper ablaze. 'I expect you talk to Natasha about me too, don't you? I expect you laugh your bloody heads off at me while you're shagging each other.'

For a moment, as she stood there simmering with indignation, she thought Matt was going to shout at her. God, she wanted him to shout at her. It wasn't fair, arguing with someone who stayed so horribly calm. But he didn't shout; instead he picked his wallet up carefully from the table, turned to face her and said softly, 'Firstly, Carrie, I would never discuss you with Natasha.

Secondly, when I'm making love to Natasha, the only person I'd ever discuss or think about is Natasha.' He reached out and touched her cheek. 'And thirdly, if you're jealous about me having a relationship with Natasha or Lola, and the reason you're so angry with me is that you want to have sex with me yourself, you only have to ask.'

# Chapter Thirty-one

When Matt had left, she couldn't cry, she was too shocked and angry. She was right. Matt was wrong. His words rang in her ears, stung and tormented her more than anything he'd ever said. Jealous? About Matt?

Eventually she fell asleep. She was woken the next morning by Matt shaking her gently by the shoulder.

'I know you're not asleep.'

'I am. Go away.'

'Then wake up, because I want to talk to you.'

She squinted. 'Are you going to apologise?'

His face was puzzled. 'What for?'

'For being a git.'

He didn't apologise, just said, 'I want to talk to you about something else and I think it would be best if we got out of here. Why don't we walk down by the beach and get some brunch there?'

They wandered down the path towards the great sweep of sand, where the surfers were already out catching the morning waves. A few brave families were sitting inside tents or huddling in the dunes. The breeze blew hard, whipping Matt's hair across his face.

'You need to understand something about Lola.'

'Like she's crazy on you and you've broken her heart?' asked Carrie.

'She's not crazy on me. Not in the way you think.'

'Yesterday, when we walked back to the site, she couldn't shut up about you. How wonderful you are. She's mad on you, Matt, can't you see that?'

'She likes me as a friend, that's all. Did she tell you what happened to her a few years back? Did you know she got a place at medical school? She was just about to start uni when her brother was killed in a motorbike accident.'

Carrie swallowed hard. That only made it worse that Lola was hurt now, but she contented herself with, 'That's terrible. I'm really sorry.'

'She didn't feel she could leave her mum, so she decided not to take up her place. Then she had some kind of breakdown and university went out of the window. But she's much better now and she wants to try again. I've promised to help her reapply for medical school.'

'Are you sure that helping her is a good idea? Wouldn't it be better to make a clean break and get someone else to support her? I saw you yesterday. You were holding her and she was upset.'

'Yes. Unrequited love hurts,' he said.

Carrie gave a little snort. 'It hurts more when you've loved and lost.'

'Maybe.' He paused. 'But Lola isn't suffering from an unrequited crush on me. We spent a lot of time talking while you were with Spike.'

Ah. Now she saw. 'Oh bugger.'

'Yes.'

'It must be awful for her,' she admitted. 'It must have been terrible seeing Spike and me together all the time.' Though 'together' was an understatement, she thought. They'd been practically hoovering each other up every night. No wonder Lola had spent so much time with Matt. 'I wouldn't wish being in love with Spike on any woman,' she said. 'Oof!'

A football had bounced into the middle of them and the two young lads skittering to a halt after it had almost knocked Carrie off her feet. Matt steadied her with one arm as the boys grunted an apology and collected the ball.

'Carrie, sometimes you can be so naïve,' he said as she straightened up.

'What's that supposed to mean?'

'It isn't Spike she has a crush on. It's you.'

# *Chapter Thirty-two*

Matt had to buy her a hot rum chocolate and a plate of pastries to help her recover from the shock. Of course she was used to having gay friends of both sexes, but she had never had a girl with a crush on her before. It was her first time for that one and the last thing she expected from Lola, whom she had been convinced had something going on with Matt.

'She was rather hoping you might feel the same way,' said Matt, stirring sugar into his coffee. 'She thought you might be over Huw, she knew you weren't interested in Spike, and I'm completely out of the frame, of course.'

Carrie picked up a croissant. 'Of course.'

'I hope I did the right thing. Lola asked me what I thought; if you would ever be interested in a relationship. I suppose I could have lied, I could have carried on fuelling her false hopes, but I decided to be honest.'

She dropped the croissant back on the plate, replaying her conversations with Lola to see if she'd said anything that might have given the wrong impression. 'But I'm sure I never gave her any encouragement. I hope not. I wouldn't want to hurt her.'

'I know that. But apparently you said something about being a different person now.'

'Not that different!'

He smiled. '*I* know that, but when someone's looking for a glimmer of hope, it doesn't take much.'

'Maybe.'

Unrequited love was fairly horrible from both sides, Carrie decided. It didn't really matter who was in love with you – man or woman – if you didn't feel the same way and if you actually *liked* the person, as she did Lola, it was not a nice feeling. Their happiness depending on you? Or yours on them? It seemed like way too much responsibility. She wondered if Huw had felt like that about their relationship. Was that what he'd meant when he'd talked of being suffocated? The two of them still hadn't discussed what had happened. With Fenella on the scene now, she didn't think they ever would.

'You might have told me all this last night,' she said.

'A, I promised Lola I wouldn't, and B, I was bloody pissed off with you.'

Mentally Carrie counted to ten. Matt could be so infuriating; so sure he was right. 'Look, I'm sorry I spoke to you like I did, but I didn't know what was going on.' And, she might have added, what he'd said to her was off the scale.

He shrugged. 'Just promise me you won't tell Lola that you know how she feels. If she talks to you about it, that's different.'

As they walked back home along the sand, Matt said, 'By the way, I suppose I should also apologise for what I said to you last night.'

'Well, don't trouble yourself too much.'

'No. I have to be fair. I should have explained about Lola straight away but I was too bloody minded.'

Carrie held her breath, waiting for him to mention what he'd said about her wanting to have sex with him. But he didn't. Instead, he just quickened his stride as if he couldn't wait to get out of her company.

With such an atmosphere hanging between them, it was a huge relief when Rowena phoned to say she was coming down for a few days. She wasn't needed on set for a while because her character had been kidnapped by a deranged patient who was holding her hostage in the old hospital boiler room.

'I've done all the scenes where he tries to give me a lethal overdose and I get rescued just in time by the Hunky Paediatrician, so I can come down and see you,' she'd said.

Carrie was over the moon that Rowena had been kidnapped. She hadn't realised how much she'd missed her friend until now and was dying to share all of Rowena's news and parts of her own. When she told Matt, he immediately offered to move out.

'I might be a new man but I don't think I can cope with lying awake listening to you two gossiping all night.'

She ignored his teasing. 'You don't have to move, but I can see your point.'

'And of course there's a spare berth for me on *Prospero*,' he said.

Of course. There was nowhere else he was going to stay unless he booked into a hotel, and she'd have felt too guilty to let him do that. Even though she didn't believe for a moment that Matt would use the spare berth, she said, 'Have a good time.'

'Don't do anything I wouldn't do,' he said, hoisting his rucksack on to his shoulder.

'And don't you get seasick.'

'There's no danger of that. We won't be going anywhere for a few days. In fact, I've been asked to pass on a message by Natasha. She wants us to take the *Prospero* out for a day trip next week and I wondered if you'd like to come with us.'

Carrie was so surprised she didn't know what to say. Natasha had asked? That didn't seem very likely. It was Matt that wanted her to go. Then it hit her, almost sucking the air from her lungs and the moisture from her throat. How could she ever have thought him unattractive or just not noticed him before? Even with his tangled hair and unshaven face – no, especially with both of those things – he was incredibly sexy. He had the kind of dark sensuality that crept up on you, slowly easing its way into your consciousness until it had gripped you and there was no wriggling out of it.

'I'll think about it,' she said, wishing him gone instantly.

When he'd left, Dolly seemed suddenly much larger and emptier. Carrie couldn't brood for long, though. She had to meet Rowena at the station and they were going to spend the weekend making up for lost time. The clubs and bars of St Ives wouldn't know what had hit them.

# Chapter Thirty-three

Rowena arrived at the station wearing huge shades and an even more enormous grin. Carrie hugged her enthusiastically and they headed straight for the beach, parking Dolly by the esplanade and wasting no time wriggling into their bikinis. They were planning on relaxing in the sun before going on to one of the seafront clubs, where Rowena had blagged VIP tickets on account of being about-to-be-on-the-telly-in-a-soap. As they spread their towels on the sand, Carrie told her about the yacht invitation.

'Okay. Let me get this *straight*. You've been invited to spend the day on a luxury yacht with free drinks, free food and two gorgeous doctors, and you don't want to *go*?' said Rowena.

'It's not that I don't want to go on the yacht. It's just complicated,' said Carrie, rubbing sun cream on her stomach.

'Complicated in what way?' said Rowena sarcastically.

'Well. Natasha's going to be there too.'

Even though Carrie couldn't see Rowena's eyes because of the floppy hat and Jackie O shades, she knew her friend wasn't impressed. 'So?'

'I don't want to be a spare part.'

'Spare part! I'm not buying that. Why should you be? The luscious Robert will be there so you won't be stuck on your own.'

'Maybe . . .'

She *really* didn't want to go into all that had happened between her, Matt and Lola right now or Rowena would never let her hear the last of it. So she decided to change to a subject that Rowena couldn't possibly resist.

'How are you managing getting from Packley to the studio every day?' she asked casually.

Rowena took the bait immediately. 'Well, actually, I'm not. The guy playing the Cocky But Gorgeous Hospital Porter has offered me a room.'

'Sounds perfect. You being the Nympho Nurse With a Heart of Gold. Have you snogged him yet?'

'Well, we do share a brief on-screen fumble in the sluice room, but there's nothing going on in real life. The woman playing the Bitchy Hospital Administrator is going to be sharing with us too, and she watches us like a hawk. She used to be a prison warder on *Bad Girls*.'

'Not the one who murdered the governess with a frozen chicken then ate the evidence?' gasped Carrie.

'The very one,' said Rowena. 'And she's even scarier in the flesh, but we can't afford the rent between the two of us so we had no choice but to say yes.' Rowena took off her hat and shades, lay back on her towel and carefully arranged a copy of *Inside Soap* over her face.

'Is that in case you're recognised?' teased Carrie.

'No. I daren't let my face get tanned. I'm supposed to have been in a boiler room for two weeks. Continuity will kill me if I go home looking like Dale Winton.'

Carrie turned on to her stomach, loosening her bikini strap. She planned on wearing a backless top tonight and didn't want any white lines. She didn't want anything, no matter how trivial, to spoil her night out with Rowena. It would be just like old times, though as she rested her cheek on her hands, she knew the old times were gone for ever. Rowena might never come home to the cottage in Packley. Why should she want to with an exciting new job, London on her doorstep and the CBGHP to share with? Carrie felt very sorry for Nelson, who had definitely lost Rowena now.

When she got back home, she decided, she must start looking for a place of her own, or at least pay Rowena a proper rent on the cottage, though that wouldn't be easy on a student teacher's grant. Maybe she could get a part-time job in a theatre bar or a box office to earn some extra cash. She also needed to sort out her share in the farm business with Huw. For now, though, with the sun on her back and the sound of the surf in her ears, she definitely wasn't ready for anything other than a good time.

Later, when they'd taken Dolly back to the campsite, Matt surprised her by turning up.

'I left some stuff in the van,' he said, pulling out a small black overnight bag. 'I'll be gone in a minute.'

'Don't rush for us,' said Rowena flirtatiously.

'It's okay. I'm done now. Are you having a good time down here?' he asked.

'Fabulous. We're off to a club later. I've got VIP tickets,' she said, then added casually, 'is your brother down here?'

Rowena's next move was as obvious to Carrie as an express train hurtling down the tracks.

'I've got a few spare tickets I could let you have. I'm sure they won't mind me asking guests,' she said, her voice becoming husky, as if she was about to seduce a co-star.

Matt gave her his best smoky-eyed smoulder. 'Rob said he'd back later, but I'm not sure he's going to make it because he's been in London at a conference and I expect he'll stop off for a drink after. But thanks for the offer. Natasha loves clubbing,' he said.

'It's only one of the town clubs. Nothing sophisticated. Probably a bit of a dump really,' Carrie cut in hastily.

'It is not a dump! I don't get VIP passes for dumps,' said Rowena.

Matt gave Carrie a knowing look. 'I'm sure it's a great club. Thanks, Rowena. That's really kind of you.'

Rowena shot a triumphant glance at Carrie. 'Here you are,' she said, scooping a handful of VIP passes from her beach bag. 'And if Rob does decide to come back early, make sure you give him one for me. If you know what I mean, that is.'

'I know exactly what you mean. I'm sure he'd be happy to return the favour,' said Matt, ignoring Carrie's open mouth. 'I'll see you later then.'

# Chapter Thirty-four

The frosty atmosphere between Rowena and Carrie didn't last long, and soon they were spilling out of a taxi in front of the Cabana, a garish club situated in a side street just off the seafront. There was no sign of Matt or Natasha, much to Carrie's relief. After bopping away until their throats were raw, Carrie went to the bar. She felt like the invisible woman, trying to catch the barman's attention among a load of blokes built like brick outhouses. Then she noticed the guy next to her was grinning.

Carrie didn't think he looked like an axe murderer so she smiled back. He was quite nice, in fact, with smiley eyes and spiky gelled hair like David Tennant. David Tennant on steroids, she thought; judging by his bulging biceps, he obviously worked out a lot.

'I was just getting my friend a drink,' she said, seeing Rowena's blond head bobbing away on the dance floor.

'Is that her? The tall, thin one in the yellow dress?'

'Yes. How do you know?'

'My mate Jake just bought her a drink.'

So, Rowena had worked fast. She smiled at the guy.

'I'm Gav,' he said.

'Carrie.'

The barman was asking her what she wanted. 'What are you having?' she asked Gav, intending to buy the round.

Reaching in front of her, he slapped some notes on the bar. His arm was well muscled and very tanned.

'A Corona, and sorry, but I'm old fashioned. I believe a bloke should pay for a woman. Shall we go somewhere a bit quieter?' he said, flipping a thumb in the direction of some booths at the far side of the dance floor. 'Ladies first,' he added, his hand on her back. It was slightly sweaty, but it was a warm night so she overlooked it.

As they sat in the booth, Gav's teeth and T-shirt glowed a curious blue-white in the strobe lights. Carrie slurped her drink nervously, trying not to be judgemental. He had very interesting hair, she told herself, and very firm biceps. As he picked up his beer bottle, she saw the thick gold ring on his little finger.

'You're a fantastic dancer, and that top really suits you,' he said, his eyes travelling over her body appreciatively.

Hmm. Verging on the cheesy, but he seemed to be sincere so she smiled back. 'Um. Thanks. Are you here on holiday?' He roared with laughter, as if she'd said the earth was flat. 'Bloody hell, no. I'm a local, but I can tell you don't come from round here. You on holiday with your blond mate? Two girls out for a good time?' he said.

Carrie realised that there was no way he would possibly understand the Matt thing, so she said, 'That's it.'

Gav shifted closer. 'Well, you've chosen exactly the right place to come if you're looking for a good time, and exactly the right bloke to have it with.'

'What do you do down here, Gav?' said Carrie, realising she'd shuffled a few inches away from him.

Gav put down his drink and leaned towards her, filling her nostrils with a powerful waft of aftershave. He lowered his voice and said huskily, 'Actually, Carrie, I'm a firefighter.'

He paused as if he expected her to gasp, so she blew out a little breath. 'That's very impressive,' she said.

'Most people seem to think so, but I don't tell many people, to be honest. You see, Carrie, the problem with my line of business is that some women get really horny when I tell them about it. The last girl I took home from a club turned up at the station crying while I was at work. She was begging me to take her to bed. Can you believe it?'

'Not really,' mumbled Carrie into her drink.

'The lads on my watch never let me hear the last of it.'

'I'm sure they didn't,' she replied, suddenly catching sight of Matt and Natasha on the dance floor.

Gav carried on. 'Do you know what they did? Stuck photos of me up all over the station, with "Stud Muffin" plastered across them. Mind you, it's an occupational hazard in my job, attention from women. One whiff of that uniform and they're like putty in your hands. You know, you probably won't believe this – and I don't really like talking about it – but my last girlfriend had counselling after she split up with me. "Keely," I said, "I know you're going to be devastated, but I need to be honest with you . . ."'

Carrie was nodding, hopefully in all the right places, not that her contribution to the conversation was required. Natasha and Matt were making their way towards the VIP booths, Matt with a beer in his hand and Natasha with a blue cocktail with an orange umbrella in it.

Gavin was still talking. 'Did you know, I can carry a fifteen-stone man for twenty metres?'

Natasha waved at Carrie and flashed a smile. Matt nodded but didn't smile. Gavin was still talking and had now virtually pinned her to the far end of the booth. Carrie was being gassed by Lynx fumes. 'So, Carrie, my secret's out, but I hope you won't hold it against me. You're a mature woman. You know the score. You seem like you're up for a good time and I can show you one.'

Natasha and Matt were in the next booth. Carrie heard Natasha complaining, 'My God, this place is totally unbelievable. The people are like something off a reality show. Urggh. What is that smell? Matt, darling, I'm going to have to perch on your knee. I can't sit on these seats.'

She couldn't hear Matt's reply, but it sounded like a growl so she guessed he was having as much fun as a day at the dentist. Carrie cringed as Gav continued to feed her more cheesy lines than a deli counter. She was going to drag him out for a dance when she suddenly found herself starved of oxygen as he dived on top of her. The combination of mouthwash and lager filled her senses.

'Are you okay, baby? Or are you lost for words?' he said when they finally surfaced.

'You could say that,' she mumbled, desperate to wipe her mouth. 'Can I have another drink?'

'What? Now?'

'Yes. Please. I'll have one of those big blue cocktails,' she said.

'Anything for you, babe.'

She heard Natasha snort.

'And make sure you get me a pink parasol,' she called after him.

'Matt, can you get me a tonic? God knows what's in this vile cocktail,' said Natasha.

As soon as he'd gone, Natasha leaned over the back of the booth. 'So nice to see you enjoying yourself. You deserve a bit of happiness after Huw,' she said.

'I'm only having a drink,' said Carrie.

'Well, I think you've pulled, darling. That guy was practically hoovering you up. What is he? A bricklayer?'

'A firefighter, actually,' said Carrie, thinking bad things about cocktail umbrellas and where she'd like to shove them. 'He can carry a fifteen-stone man twenty metres.'

'How thrilling, darling. I enjoy the odd bit of rough myself. Is that Rowena?'

Rowena was snogging the bloke from the ice-cream van on the beach.

'You girls do get about,' said Natasha.

'We know how to have a good time,' said Carrie.

Matt came back. 'Hello,' he said to her, with a face like thunder. Natasha immediately sidled on to his knee and wound her arms around his neck. His expression was impassive; his hands were on the seat. Carrie tried not to think of how much she wanted to sit on Matt's knee and snog him.

Gav arrived back and squashed Carrie against the end of the seat again. 'Thanks for the drink, Gav. Mmm. These Blue Heaven cocktails are so delicious. And the parasol is so-o pretty. Mmm,' she declared.

'The cocktails aren't the only thing that's delicious,

baby, and I'm going to send you to Blue Heaven.'

There was a squeal of laughter from Natasha, but Carrie couldn't see because Gav was thrusting his tongue into her ear and growling, 'You little wildcat.' Then he pounced on her again and clamped his mouth on hers. His hand was on her thigh, creeping up her skirt.

'Gav, sorry, but I can't do this.'

'Don't be silly, we've only just started getting to know each other.'

'I'm going now,' she said in her best assertive mode. His eyes were hard and cold as she pulled his fingers off her thigh.

'You're a bit of a prick tease, aren't you, Carrie?'

Her heart rate quickened. 'No, actually, I'm not teasing. Thanks for the drink but I can see my friend over there.'

'I told you, she's with my mate,' he said.

'No. I don't think so. Look, she's waving at me.'

'I don't think so, babe.' He crushed her against the seat, shoving his hand up her skirt again. She tried to push him off but he was strong. Her heart was pounding now and her mind whirling with a mix of fear and anger at her own stupidity. She relaxed, allowing Gav's fingers to slide up to the lace of her knickers.

'That's better, baby. Just go with the flow. Let Gav do the driving,' he grunted.

As his hand slipped under the elastic of her pants, Carrie raised her knee ready to hit him where it hurt. It was then that she heard Matt's voice. He was standing in front of her with his arms folded, like a Victorian father crossed with a pro footballer.

'Is this man bothering you?'

Carrie's heart sank. Bugger. Matt was going to play hero.

'Matt, I can take care of myself.'

'Really? Because it looked to me like he was bothering you.'

Gav sneered. 'The lady was just having fun. Now I'll overlook your interfering if you just piss off and mind your own business. Carrie here doesn't want you poking your nose in.'

Gav squeezed her thigh and Carrie let out a squeak. 'See? She likes a bit of rough stuff,' he said.

Matt's eyes narrowed dangerously. 'What did you say?'

'You heard. She's enjoying herself. Now piss off, you posh twat.'

Matt's fist flew out like lightning and Gav fell backwards on to the table with a grunt of pain. Bottles and glasses smashed on the floor, alcohol spattering everywhere.

'Facking hell! My new dress!' shrieked Natasha.

Someone shouted, 'Fight!'

Momentarily distracted, Matt doubled up in pain as Gav's fist thudded into his stomach. He managed to grab Gav's ankle and the two of them ended up on the floor, grunting.

'Stop it!' screamed Carrie, but people had already swarmed from the dance floor to shout and cheer them on. They grappled with each other but Matt managed to get on top of Gav. Carrie was on the verge of trying to separate them when three huge bouncers, two blokes and a woman started to muscle their way through the crowd. Natasha had disappeared.

'Leave him alone! We're all going to get thrown out, you stupid prat!' shouted Carrie, whacking at Matt with her bag.

'Ow!' Matt groaned as the metal frame crunched down on his skull. 'What the fuck was that?'

'A fake D&G clutch. Now come on, you idiot!'

Gav took his chance to get up and was dragged into the crowd by a group of his mates just as the bouncers pounced on Matt and Carrie.

'But I haven't done anything,' wailed Carrie as the woman bouncer twisted her arm behind her back. 'Ow! That hurts!'

'We don't like catfights. Out you go,' boomed the woman.

'But I wasn't fighting!' shouted Carrie, propelled through the cheering crowds by the woman. In a moment she was being thrust through a black hole, with no idea what had happened to Matt, Natasha or Rowena. 'Don't think of trying to get back in. You're lucky we haven't called the police,' said the woman, slamming the door behind her.

It took a few seconds for Carrie's eyes to adjust to the dimly lit alleyway behind the club. The wind was whistling in from the sea, blowing rubbish around her ankles. Her skirt was torn and her knees were grazed from where she'd stumbled as she'd been thrown out. It was damp in the sea air, and she could smell chips, cigarette smoke, maybe worse. Where was Matt? She was frantic. What if he'd been hurt by the bouncers? Then she heard him. He was doubled over a few metres away in the shadow of a skip, gulping in air. His shirt was ripped, his jeans were stained with beer and there was blood trickling down from his lip. As he straightened up, he spat, then wiped the back of his hand over his mouth. He looked very, very pissed off.

'I didn't plan for this to happen,' Carrie said.

He was glaring at her. 'Really? And I thought you might have wanted to get my attention. What the hell did you think you were doing with that prat?'

'I can take care of myself, and I was just having a good time,' she said defiantly. 'I made a bad choice, that's all.'

'Again?'

'How dare you judge me! Who I choose to talk to or sleep with is none of your business. There was nothing wrong with Spike.'

'I didn't mean Spike,' he said, advancing towards her. She backed away. The wall was behind her. Matt kept on coming and planted both hands on the wall either side of her head. She flattened her palms against the brickwork. It was cold and rough against her bare back. 'Ah, now I get it,' he said.

'What the hell do you mean by that?'

'I think you know exactly what I mean. Every time I find a woman attractive, shall we say, you get all arsey and start giving me a moral lecture. But it was okay when you wanted to have sex with Spike, or tonight with Mr Muscle.' His breath was warm against her face. 'I think what you really want is a night with me yourself. Am I right? Is that what you want?'

She couldn't answer him. His arrogance and presumption drove her mad but she just couldn't lie. Not when, roughed up, smelling of lager and with a swollen lip, he was as sexy as hell.

'I don't . . .' she whispered, turning her head to the side, unable to look him in the face.

'Sorry? Didn't quite get that.'

Her eyes met his. 'I don't know!'

Her words seemed to echo in the darkness. She felt her heart beating, thick and hard, as though it wanted to burst out of her chest. Matt took her chin in his fingers and gently turned her face to his. And then he lowered his lips to hers, so unexpectedly softly that it took her breath away. Her knees buckled as his tongue swept over the inside of her upper lip. His shirt was damp with sweat as she twisted it in her fingers. He stopped kissing her and moved his mouth to her bare shoulder, nipping her, gently but enough to make her cry out in surprise. Just as she thought she might melt, he pulled away.

'This is crazy,' he said, shaking his head. 'We both know that we shouldn't be doing this. I need to see if Natasha is okay,' he added, looking away from her as if he felt guilty.

Still stunned, Carrie nodded. 'I need to find Rowena.'

Stepping aside for her to go ahead, he followed her out of the alley to the front of the club. Rowena was hopping about outside, haranguing the door staff.

'Where are they? What have you done, you great big ape! Do you know who I am?'

'Rowena. It's okay. We're here,' called Carrie.

Rowena hugged her. 'Carrie! I was so worried about you! I saw the fight but those gorillas wouldn't let me get to you. What happened? You look awful, hon. And Matt, my God, look at your face. You look like you've gone ten rounds with Mike Tyson.'

'Worse. I got involved with Carrie,' growled Matt.

'Matt, darling, are you all right?' said Natasha, flinging her arms around him. 'Oh my God, is that blood on your face? You could have been seriously hurt, or even killed!'

'Stop fussing, Tasha. I'm fine,' said Matt.

Rowena punched numbers into her mobile and looked at Carrie. 'I'll call us a minicab – the door staff gave me the number. If I tell them who I am, they might come a bit quicker.'

Natasha stared at Carrie with contempt while Matt wiped his mouth with a tissue. 'You had a lucky escape there. It was a good job Matt and I were on hand,' she said.

'Yes. I'm, er . . . very sorry about your dress. I'll pay to get it cleaned,' said Carrie, goaded to the limit but desperate to avoid any more trouble.

'Don't bother. It's only fit for the bin now and I wouldn't put you to the expense of dry-cleaning. I'm sure you need to count the pennies now Huw's gone.'

'Carrie. Cab's here!' Rowena dragged her away before she said something she'd regret.

Natasha called sweetly after them as they got in the cab, 'Thank you for the tickets. It's been a very entertaining evening.'

# Chapter Thirty-five

'Well, he must fancy you rotten to start a fight over you,' said Rowena, as they huddled in a Häagen-Dazs bar the next day. Rain poured down the windows. Rowena was attacking a hot fudge sundae with a spoon while Carrie was toying with a banana split.

'He didn't exactly *start* a fight, and I expect it was just the testosterone talking. There was no need for Matt to jump in like that; I can take care of myself.'

'Yeah, yeah, but it's still so cool, having two blokes beating the crap out of each other for you. God, I wish it would happen to me.'

'You wouldn't really. In the flesh, it's scary. Somebody could get really hurt,' said Carrie, dipping a chunk of banana into chocolate sauce. Now that it was all over, she had to admit that Matt had been rather magnificent. In fact, she hadn't been able to stop thinking about him, bristling with fury, lunging in on her behalf. But what had happened afterwards, in the alley, had totally confused her.

'How's your banana split?' said Rowena, arching her eyebrows.

'Very nice,' said Carrie, realising she'd been staring

into space. As she dug into her ice cream, she could still feel Matt's mouth on hers. He was a wonderful kisser. Confident but tender. Even though he'd been furious with her and said some outrageous things, he'd been so gentle when he'd kissed her. And he'd been extremely turned on too. She'd felt him as he'd pressed against her.

'Fighting always gets a bloke's blood up. One of the medical consultants on the show told me. Makes them really horny,' said Rowena, scooping up a spoonful of squirty cream and eyeing Carrie over the top of her sundae. 'So will you be going on the yacht trip thing after what's happened?' she added, slightly too innocently.

Carrie remembered what had happened afterwards. Matt going all cold, and the humiliation of Natasha's contemptuous remarks.

'Of course I don't suppose you'd dare face Natasha after making her boyfriend defend your honour in a club,' Rowena said.

Carrie wiped her mouth with a serviette and smiled enigmatically. 'What time did you say your train was tomorrow, Rowena?'

Matt arrived back at the van the next day, rucksack over his shoulder. Carrie buried her head in her novel, pretending to be utterly absorbed.

'Hello,' he grunted.

'Mmm,' she grunted back.

'Your book.'

She glanced up. 'What?'

He grinned. 'Upside down.'

Gah! So this was going to be a battle to see who was first to mention the nightclub fight. She had no desire or motivation to back down. As a result, it was evening and her stomach was gurgling audibly before they progressed to monosyllables.

'Food?' said Matt.

'Yes.'

'Fridge?' he asked.

She shook her head and turned a page. 'Takeaway.'

'Oh. Chips then?'

The laughter was rising in her throat and her shoulders were shaking. 'Suppose so,' she managed sulkily.

'Shall I go? I need a bit of a walk and you'll forget the mushy peas and curry sauce. You can't get them in the jungle.'

When she looked up at him, his warm, sexy smile socked her as hard as any punch. She laid down her book and smiled back, wondering if he could see the way she'd lit up inside. 'Okay. See you later. I'll open some beers.'

Later, they sat on the grass, eating the chips with their fingers, steam curling in front of their faces. The damp paper crumbled under her hands; the smell of vinegar was sharp in her nostrils. Matt popped a chip in his mouth and Carrie squirmed inwardly. Even watching him eat chips was turning her on, which was really bizarre.

'Finished?' said Matt, seeing her lay down her paper.

He'd scrambled her brain now. 'Sorry? Oh, yes.'

He scrunched up the used paper, his eyes sparkling. 'Glad you enjoyed it.'

Carrie wished he wouldn't twinkle, or smoulder or brood or smile or be outrageous or gentle or tender with her, all of which seemed to drive her insane with lust. In fact, she wished he would just vanish away. But there again, that meant she'd never see him again. The awful truth was that she'd developed a monumental crush on Matt. Ever since she'd got back from the nightclub, she'd battled against how much she wanted sex with him; more, even, than she'd wanted Huw. Or maybe she'd forgotten what it was like to want someone so much; she must have wanted Huw this much, too, when they first met. Maybe Huw betraying her had tainted and twisted every memory until she couldn't trust her feelings. This trip was meant to change her life and it had, but not quite how she'd envisaged.

'Despite what you might think – how things might have seemed at the club – I really didn't mean to get you involved in a fight,' she said.

Matt shrugged. 'It's okay.'

'But Natasha's dress was ruined. She wouldn't let me pay for it.'

'She's forgotten about it now,' he said, gruff again.

'I didn't know what the guy was like,' said Carrie.

'Forget it.' His expression softened. 'To be honest, I haven't had a good scrap since some forward tried to elbow me in the face at uni. The linesmen had to drag us apart. I got a fractured cheekbone and was banned for three matches,' he said proudly.

'What happened to the other guy?' she said.

He gazed at her steadily. 'He's taken up ballet instead. I'm going for a run tomorrow morning, but I'll be back about ten. Be ready.'

'For what?'

'This bloody yacht trip.'

He held her gaze, daring her to answer him back. She

was so thrown, she didn't know what to say. It was almost as if he was challenging her to back down.

'Well?' he said, his brow creasing as she hesitated, lost for words.

'I suppose I'll have to if I've no choice.'

He jumped to his feet. 'Nope. No choice at all.'

# Chapter Thirty-six

'There it is. That's the *Prospero*.' Matt was pointing to the far end of the quayside. Even from here; the yacht was easy to spot. It was far bigger than Carrie had imagined, with a gleaming silver and white hull and scrubbed wooden decks, and it was attracting admiring glances from tourists and seen-it-all-before shrugs from the locals.

A familiar face was also waiting by the quay.

'You didn't mention Lola was coming too,' whispered Carrie as they exchanged waves.

'Yes. I thought you might be more comfortable if it was a group of us rather than couples.'

To Carrie, comfortable meant lying in bed eating a Flake while reading your latest great reviews in *The Stage*. Comfortable did not mean sharing a boat with a girl who had a crush on you and another who, possibly, would like to tip you overboard.

'And you're sure she'll want to see me?'

'I'm never sure about anything these days, but I thought it might be a good idea if you talked to her. This could be a good opportunity.'

'Has anyone ever told you that you interfere too much?'

'All the time. It's in my genes.'

In the distance, a minicab was pulling up. A man got out and wobbled his way along the quayside. 'Hold on. Isn't that Robert?'

Matt squinted into the sun. 'Do you mind going on ahead? I'll be with you in a minute.'

Lola caught sight of them. 'Hello again,' she said quietly.

'Hi,' said Carrie, smiling far too widely. 'Where are Spike and the others?'

'They said they might head off to Perranporth. You should come along with us again one day. You were doing really well.'

Natasha saved her from replying. 'Hello-ooo! Welcome to our humble abode,' she called from the deck. She was obviously cheery again, showing off the boat. Which, Carrie thought in total awe, really was magnificent. She and Lola walked up the gangplank to find Natasha every inch the yachtie, in white cropped jeans, a striped Bardot top and a Hermès scarf round her hair. Carrie had chosen a vest top from the extensive wardrobe in her backpack, teamed with a new skirt. It was a gloriously swishy affair she'd bought in a weak moment from a hippy shop in St Ives, and she'd hoped it gave her a touch of the gypsy maiden, but the way Natasha was looking down her nose, she felt more like a tavern tart.

'You look charmingly bohemian. Well done, it's a terribly difficult look to carry off,' said Natasha, air-kissing her before flitting off. 'And you must be Lola. Matt's told me all about you.'

Lola looked horrified. 'Has he?'

'Shall I show you round before we get under way? Do come into the saloon,' trilled Natasha.

*Saloon* conjured up images of a Wild West bar in Carrie's head, but this one couldn't have been further from the spit-and-sawdust of a whisky joint. In fact, there was no denying it, *Prospero* was the most luxurious place Carrie had ever been in her life. It was like a gentlemen's club crossed with one of Elton John's mansions. It oozed luxury, from the polished wood fittings to the leather upholstery.

Natasha beamed. 'Well?'

'Wow,' breathed Lola.

'Ditto,' murmured Carrie.

Lola raised her eyes in wonder to the leather ceiling. 'And this is your *auntie's*?'

'Godmother, darling.'

'She must be absolutely loaded.'

'She was a hedge fund manager, but she made so much dosh, she retired at thirty-five. She lives in Antigua now but she keeps the *Prospero* to stay on when she pops home for a visit.'

Natasha flung open a timber door. 'This is the master stateroom.'

Well, of course it was. It had a huge bed with a rounded end. Carrie tried not to think of the master and Natasha romping in it.

'There's an en suite of course, but if you want the loo, the main bathroom's next door,' Natasha said breezily. Carrie instantly wanted to have a pee, just to check it out, but Natasha swept them off. '*Voilà*. The galley. Bijou but adequate.'

Footsteps on deck led them all outside again. Matt was

standing by the wheel with a face like thunder. Robert was lolling across the seats, grinning. Carrie could smell the whisky fumes from several metres away.

'Hello, Rob,' said Natasha, kissing him briefly then stepping hastily back.

'Hello, ladies,' he said, attempting a wink but not quite managing it. 'Caroline, we meet again. Nice top you don't have on. And who is this?' he said, leering at Lola, who shrank visibly back against the bulkhead.

'This is Lola. Friend of Matt's,' said Natasha.

'Lola? *Lola lo-lo-lo-lo lola . . .*'

'Ignore him,' said Matt.

'Just having a bit of fun. *Lola lo-lo-lo-lo lola . . .*'

'Robert. Shut up,' snapped Matt.

'*You* shut the fuck up, Matt.'

'Shall we get something to drink?' said Natasha brightly.

Rob grabbed the wheel. 'And I'll drive.'

'You must be joking,' said Matt.

They glared at each other for a moment before Rob shrugged and said, 'Suit yourself. Make mine a double Scotch, Tasha.'

They followed their hostess down the stairs into the galley.

'Do you have any chamomile tea?' whispered Lola. 'And can I use the loo?'

While Lola was in the bathroom, Natasha extracted two bottles of champagne from the fridge. 'This was all I could get from the local supermarket but it will have to do. There are some nibbles in the cupboard up there.'

Carrie found a box of breadsticks and some very posh crisps made of parsnip and beetroot. 'Are these the ones?'

Natasha wrinkled her nose. 'Yes. Hardly a gourmet feast, but I managed to get some guacamole and olives from the deli by the harbour. I expect they're vile, but never mind. Let's open the bubbly, shall we? Glasses above the TV cabinet.'

Carrie took down the flutes from the cabinet while Natasha removed the wire from the first bottle and pushed her thumbs under the cork. It came out with a muted pop. 'Glass, please!' she cried as the foam bubbled out of the bottle. She wrinkled her nose before braving a sip. 'Go on,' she said, pouring a glass. 'Try it.'

Carrie doubted she could tell fine champagne from cheap plonk today, but she swished her glass theatrically, shoved her nose into it, downed a good swig and smacked her lips.

Natasha arched her eyebrows. 'Well?'

'Slightly corked, I'd say. And I'd guess it wasn't this grower's best vintage.' She held out the glass. 'I'd need a refill to tell properly.'

The engines started throbbing as Matt steered them out of the port.

'Seems like we're under way,' said Natasha as she refilled the glasses. 'So, have you slept with Matt yet?'

Carrie started coughing and spluttering, spraying bubbly all over the leather seats. Through streaming eyes she saw Natasha calmly holding out a serviette.

'Judging by that reaction, I'll take that as a yes.'

Carrie's evil twin took over, wanting to torment Natasha. 'We've shared the same tiny camper for weeks, of course . . .'

'I know that, darling, but have you *actually* screwed him?'

'Have you?' said Carrie.

'To ask that you're either being spectacularly naïve or deliberately obtuse,' said Natasha, sipping her drink and sighing appreciatively.

'Not that it's really any of your business, Natasha, but no, I haven't slept with Matt. Not in the sense you mean anyway.'

Natasha let out a little of sigh of satisfaction. 'I thought not. I know you think I'm being a bitch, but I'm not. Can you pass me those terracotta bowls, please? You see, I know your type, darling. A serial monogamist.'

Furious, Carrie clattered the bowls along the table. 'You don't know me at all, Natasha.'

'Ah, but I do. You tried to crash your ex's wedding, so don't try to tell me you're not a one-man girl.'

'Thanks for the advice, but you're wrong. We're just friends.'

Natasha gave a tinkling laugh. 'I'm sure you're the *best* of friends, darling. Maybe that is all you want, all he wants. Take my advice: Matt's not the kind of guy who will ever settle down. He needs to take risks, and frankly, he needs variety. He seems kind and caring, which he is of course, but there'll always be a part of him that he'll never show you.'

'And you'd know from experience, would you?' said Carrie, sloshing champagne viciously into the rest of the glasses.

Natasha gave a hurt pout. 'Darling, I'm only telling you this to save you from getting hurt. Matt's not the one to help you get over Huw. Screw him senseless if you like, but don't be stupid enough to fall in love with him.'

That was it. Carrie was definitely going to commit

murder on the high seas if she stayed a second longer. Wobbling horribly in every way, she set off with the tray of drinks and bloody nibbles. The boat was definitely bucking about more and she could see more white caps on the waves as she made it on to the deck.

'Let me give you a hand,' said Lola, taking two of the glasses from the tray. Behind her, Natasha emerged with bowls of guacamole and olives.

Robert swiped a glass. 'What, no whisky? I suppose this'll have to do, though I expect it tastes like lemonade.'

Sitting down next to Lola, Carrie tried to take some deep breaths and calm down. Natasha stood beside Matt like a loyal first mate beside her captain. But Carrie suspected that Matt was not so sure of his position. He didn't seem quite comfortable at the helm. Natasha constantly stroked his arm and even let her hand linger over his jeans pocket, patting his bottom as if to say: *Hands off, he's mine, darling.* Matt didn't reciprocate. He laughed at Natasha's jokes, was polite and friendly, but kept his hands firmly on the wheel.

At one point, Natasha went into the saloon to fetch a cardigan and Matt's eyes flickered in Carrie's direction. His lips parted as if he was about to say something, but Natasha came back before he could. She scanned their faces and frowned.

It was like some terrible period film where the wife realises that her husband has been shagging the parlourmaid. I feel like that parlourmaid, thought Carrie. I am a scarlet woman and yet I haven't *done* anything.

'Where's Rob been?' she said, desperate to change the focus to the figure that was stretched out across the seats, comatose.

'He stayed the night with some bloke he met at a medical conference, but I'm not sure he remembers that much about it,' said Matt quickly. Carrie was sure she heard relief in his voice.

'You can stop slagging me off. I *do* remember. Some of it. Did you know I can see an albatross?' said Rob unexpectedly.

'Is he all right?' asked Lola.

'With a bit of luck, he'll pass out properly in a minute,' said Matt, not bothering to keep his voice down. 'In fact, I think you'd better go down below where you'll be safer than rolling about half-cut up here in the cockpit.' Surprisingly Rob did as he was told with the minimum of fuss and was soon sound asleep in the palatial stateroom.

Natasha talked non-stop to Matt as they skimmed the edge of the coastline, past beaches and low rocky headlands.

Excluded from their conversation, Carrie started chatting to Lola about surfing. It was the only safe topic she could think of, but it led on to talk about travelling and what they both might like to do one day. As the wine took effect, she began to relax and really enjoy Lola's company again.

'I'll fetch us all a drink. Do you want bubbly or something else? I think they've got a full-blown cocktail bar down there. I could rustle up a margarita if you'd like one,' she said, seeing Lola's glass was empty.

'And an absolutely vile nibble?' whispered Lola, imitating Natasha's cut-glass accent.

Surprised at Lola being catty about anyone, Carrie laughed, then put her hand to her mouth, but they'd already attracted Natasha's scrutiny. She was craning her neck, a little like a giraffe, and that set them off some more. Natasha shot them a very disapproving look before turning her attention back to Matt. She was nodding her head enthusiastically at something he was saying as Carrie wiped her eyes.

As Carrie tried to stand up, Lola reached out and rested her fingers on her arm.

'Matt's told you, hasn't he?' she said quietly.

If you'd asked her first, Carrie would much rather have avoided this conversation, but she realised that it had been inevitable, so she managed to smile and say quietly, 'Yes, he has.'

'And you really like me as a friend?'

'Well, now you come to mention it. Yes, I do,' she said, and she meant it.

'And if you were gay, it would be me?' Lola was smiling ruefully.

'Well, of course. Absolutely,' stammered Carrie.

'There's no need to feel awkward. I knew you weren't interested in me in that way, even without Matt spelling it out. It was obvious, really, you and Spike being together, but I hoped for a moment.'

'And I thought you had a huge crush on Matt,' said Carrie.

'Oh I do, intellectually I suppose,' said Lola, giggling. 'He's an amazing doctor. Has he told you some of the things he's done in Tuman?'

'A few,' said Carrie, thinking of the night they'd seen the play at the Minack. 'He told me a bit about the accident but he hasn't gone into detail. I could see he hated talking about it. He doesn't like people making a fuss about him.'

Lola's face was puzzled. 'What accident?'

'He hasn't said anything to you about it?'

'No. You don't have to tell me if you'd rather not,' said Lola, smiling slyly. 'But I still think he's wonderful. If I was into guys, he'd be the one. He's rather beautiful, isn't he?'

For a horrible moment, Carrie thought Lola might do a Natasha and ask her if she'd shagged Matt, but realised she was far too polite for that. As for beautiful . . . She saw Matt standing at the wheel, one hand on it, one holding a beer. He was laughing at something Natasha had said, and yet Carrie knew he wasn't really happy or amused or entertained. Having shared so intimate a space with him for weeks, she could see he wasn't at ease from the way he pushed his hair from his eyes too often and the way he laughed that bit too loudly at Natasha's jokes.

There was something not quite right about the way he was standing, something brittle in the air that she couldn't put her finger on. The way Natasha was talking too quickly, supplying every silence with a joke, trying slightly too hard. She felt a lurch in her stomach, a pang not just of desire but of sympathy for Natasha. Empathy with her. *We ache for him*, a voice whispered to her. *We both want what we can't have*.

Lola shook her head. 'Don't try and deny you think he's gorgeous.'

Carrie laughed and whispered, Natasha style, 'There's nothing to deny, *darling*. Now I'm getting us all a drink. If you don't say what you want, I'll choose.'

After taking everyone's order, Carrie stood in the galley, sucking in deep breaths. From the stateroom she could hear Rob's snores; from above, Natasha's brittle laughter.

Matt *was* beautiful. He was all hard edges and uncompromising principles, yet she knew that if you could penetrate the surface, if he would let you in, he'd be so warm and tender, you'd never want to leave.

When she returned and handed over the drinks, Natasha was shrieking, 'No! I couldn't! I'm sure to have us on the rocks. Matt, no!'

'Don't be ridiculous,' Matt was saying. 'Of course you can do it. You should learn how to handle it.'

He was standing behind her as she held on to the wheel.

'Well, I'm willing to have a go, but you have to hold me, darling,' cried Natasha.

'Tasha. You will not crash this boat or have us on the rocks. Now I'm going to see if Rob's still alive. If you need a hand, just shout for me – or get Carrie and Lola to help you out,' he said.

'Oh, I think I've got the hang of it now,' said Natasha, casting a smile of triumph in Carrie's direction as Matt disappeared down towards the saloon. 'I'm learning fast.'

# Chapter Thirty-seven

Carrie and Matt walked back from the harbour in the early evening. Neither of them said much on the way home. Matt was silent to the point of sullenness, and it was obvious that something was troubling him. She had wondered if it was Natasha, but apart from the moment on the boat when she'd seen his expression as he stood behind her at the wheel, he'd acted very much as normal towards her. His biggest problem, she suspected, was his brother. Rob hadn't sobered up until they were turning round to head back to port.

At the top of the town he paused, taking her arm and steering her over to a wall. The touch of his fingers on her skin sent a thrill through her. They stood looking out over the town and harbour. Thick clouds had covered the sun and lights were flickering in one or two of the windows, even though it was only early evening.

'I know you spoke to Lola and I'm glad,' he said.

'Yes, I did. She's lovely. Someone I'd want to have as a friend; a good friend.'

He nodded but didn't say anything else. Carrie was disappointed. She hadn't been expecting praise but she'd been hoping he might open up a little more. She tried again.

'I decided it was better to get everything out in the open, though I wouldn't say it was the easiest conversation.' He smiled and her stomach flipped. She decided to take a risk, her heart beating thick and strong. She knew something had happened on the boat; it had been a turning point for her and for Matt, for everyone. 'But it's best to talk about these things, don't you think? Not to keep them bottled up and creating an atmosphere?'

Matt gazed at her steadily, just long enough to make her want to glance away, then he said, almost regretfully, 'If you're expecting some kind of outpouring from me, don't hold your breath.'

He made *outpouring* sound like some kind of disease or weakness, and she had to smile. 'I don't expect anything from you, Matt, and definitely not an outpouring,' she said.

'I think . . .' he said softly, touching her cheek gently and making her tingle from head to toe. She held her breath, waiting for him to say how he felt. Then he plunged her into icy water. 'I think it's time we moved on. In fact, it's time we went home. I think we've both got what we wanted from this trip. Am I right?'

Home. The word cut through her like a knife. She wasn't ready to go back yet. She needed more time here.

'Carrie? Have you got over Huw?'

She already knew the answer, and had known for a week now, maybe a lot longer.

'I haven't forgotten him, and I'm still angry with him and Fenella for how much they hurt me, but I just don't feel it's worth wasting any more emotional energy on them. The thing is, I did want to hurt him, but now it's as if I just can't be bothered to do anything about it, like all the anger has evaporated.' She stopped and swallowed hard. 'I did love Huw. Part of me always will, I think.'

'Maybe it would be dangerous to say that you don't love him any more,' he replied gently.

'Yes. It's probably safer to think that I do still care about him, but I've begun to wonder whether the things we shared aren't what I thought they were. Maybe our relationship had turned into a business partnership; you know, the farm, the way we lived, all the financial stuff. I realised today that even if I could, I wouldn't turn back the clock. I wouldn't have him back, not even as he was before he had the affair with Fenella. I don't need him any more.'

'Then I suppose you're cured.'

Of Huw, maybe, she thought, but now she had a new problem standing tall and gorgeous right in front of her.

'And what about you?' she said, ignoring her churning stomach.

'Me?'

'Have you got what you wanted out of this trip?'

He hesitated, then said, 'When I was sent home from Tuman, I was ordered to spend four months being bored out of my mind. And before you ask, Carrie, I think you know very well that I've been doing exactly the opposite.'

He held out his arm, an obvious signal for them to move on, in every way. She knew she'd get nothing more out of him, so she didn't push. She wanted to tell him, but she never would, that just because she didn't need anyone, that didn't stop her *wanting* someone. And that someone was him.

# Chapter Thirty-eight

They packed up Dolly the next morning and started the long drive back from Cornwall to Oxfordshire. Progress was painfully slow. Dolly didn't do above fifty, and some of the roads were tortuous and winding. They got stuck behind a tractor for miles and it was impossible to overtake, Dolly just didn't have the acceleration. Matt spent much of the journey drumming his fingers on the wheel and muttering under his breath. He hates anything getting in his way, thought Carrie, whereas she didn't mind trundling along at a snail's pace. She wanted the journey to drag.

By late afternoon they were only in north Devon again. Gasping with thirst and starving, they finally stopped by the side of an estuary for a break. Matt paced about as Carrie sat on a wall, munching on a pasty. She checked her watch. If they didn't get going soon they'd be hitting the rush hour and Dolly would have a trail of angry commuters behind her, all tooting their horns and showing no respect for her age. She was wondering whether to suggest they camped somewhere for the night when Matt threw his can of Coke into the bin with a clatter and jumped into the passenger seat.

'Let's go,' he growled, buckling up again and staring silently out of the window. A van had parked right in front of Dolly's bumper, leaving very little room to pull out on to the road. Carrie knew she needed to back up to make room. Thrusting the huge rusty gear stick into reverse, she pushed her foot down on the accelerator.

'Fuck it! It's no good!'

Matt's shout was followed almost instantly by an enormous bang from behind them. Carrie closed her eyes, knowing exactly what had happened.

'I think I've hit the wall,' she said in a small voice.

Saying nothing, Matt unbuckled and jumped out of the van. Carrie gripped the wheel. The crash, the noise and the impact of what Matt had just said had left her momentarily stunned. Then she came to her senses, climbed out and went to inspect the damage, dreading what she'd find. Matt was crouching on the tarmac, examining Dolly's injuries. The chrome bumper had crumpled like a foil takeaway tray, and Dolly's once pristine orange paintwork was scored with ugly black scrapes.

'Oh my God. Nelson is going to kill me.'

'Kill *me*, you mean. I was supposed to keep you under control,' said Matt. 'You've wrecked the rear bumper and quarter.'

'Me? If you hadn't shouted out, it wouldn't have happened!'

'I wasn't shouting.' He stopped, looked up at her and raked his hands through his hair. 'Does it really matter whose fault it was? It's Dolly that's suffered.'

'We can't take her back like this. Nelson might have a heart attack,' she said.

Matt scratched his head thoughtfully, then smiled. 'The van's still roadworthy. Get back in and I'll drive.'

Half an hour later, he was Googling VW repair specialists on the internet in the nearest tourist information centre while Carrie hovered behind him. Closing down the browser, he grabbed her hand and almost dragged her out of the centre.

'There's a repair specialist up the coast about fifteen miles away. It's four o'clock now. If we get a move on, we might make it before it shuts.'

As Matt slammed his foot down and Dolly protested loudly, Carrie's heart was in her mouth, but not because of his wild driving. She wanted to know what he'd meant in the van.

'What's no good, Matt?' she asked.

'This. Going home, playing these silly games, when we both know we're desperate to go to bed together.' He took his eyes off the road long enough to give her a look of pure lust that had her pressing her legs together.

'Matt. Watch out!'

The van swerved round a tandem, leaving the chubby riders wobbling in its wake.

'Isn't that what you want too?' he asked, putting his foot down harder.

Carrie's heart soared, willing Dolly to grow wings. 'Of course it is. I have done since we set off. Now, can't you make this thing go any faster?'

Harvey, the mechanic from the VW centre in the nearby town, gave a sharp intake of breath as he examined Dolly's bumper.

'Oh dearie me, you have been having fun.'

'Can you repair it?' asked Carrie anxiously.

'Yes, but it'll take time. I can't even order the parts till first thing in the morning, and I can tell you now the supplier won't have a new bumper in stock. I can get the damage to the bodywork beaten out and repaired in the meantime, but you'll have to wait three days for the bumper.'

Matt, sitting in Dolly's open doorway, smiled happily.

'So we're going to be without Dolly for *three whole days*?' said Carrie, trying not to jump up and down with glee.

'I'm afraid so, love, unless you want to take the vehicle home and try to get it done there. If you do want to leave it and I push the suppliers, I might have it ready sooner.'

'Thanks, mate. I know you're trying to do your best. Three days will be fine,' cut in Matt, acting all blokeish because that was what you did with a mechanic.

'Right. I'll go and get the ledger from the office and book her in,' said Harvey, probably surprised to have such docile customers. They followed him into a dilapidated Portakabin, where he wrote down Dolly's registration number in an oil-stained ledger and said cheerfully, 'Right. She's on my list. Shouldn't cost you more than five hundred pounds, possibly a bit more depending.'

Five hundred, thought Carrie. That was her rent money for the next few weeks, but she didn't care. She was going to spend three whole days in bed with Matt.

Harvey grinned. 'You can leave her here now or bring her back tomorrow if you want. I start at seven.'

Matt didn't hesitate. 'We'll leave her. Can you

recommend any hotels to stay in for the next few days?'

'Well, there's a couple of B&Bs in town if you don't mind basic. Then there's the Manor on the edge of the cliff. Bit pricey,' he said, but it was obvious to Carrie that he didn't think they couldn't afford the place.

'It'll do,' said Matt in a no-nonsense tone that made Carrie go weak at the knees.

Harvey grinned. 'Right. I can give you a lift there myself if you like. I go up the moor road on my way home.'

Twenty minutes later they were jumping down from one of Harvey's own camper vans – a chocolate-brown model called Dennis – on the gravelled forecourt of Hartland Manor, an imposing granite building scattered with plaques declaring its star ratings and awards.

'You'd better take out a mortgage,' advised Harvey as he left them standing in front of the stone steps that led up to the entrance.

Carrie hugged herself. She was in shorts and a vest top and the evening sun had gone behind a cloud. Matt didn't hesitate. In moments his arms were around her and he was kissing her thoroughly. She laid her head on his chest, feeling the warm cotton of his T-shirt under her cheek and his heart beating strong and steady.

'I'm not seeing Natasha any more,' he said. She lifted her chin to look at his face. 'We both knew it wasn't serious and we've known each other a long time,' he added, gazing down at her.

'I'm glad you've told me,' said Carrie, not knowing what else to say, because to say she was sorry would have been an outright lie. Her instincts on the yacht had been right, but she still thought Natasha might have different ideas.

'She told me she's been seeing a guy from work, but I'd have ended it – whatever it is – anyway. I've been lying to myself and her,' said Matt, stroking her hair.

'Me too,' whispered Carrie, still unable to believe she was in Matt's arms and that he was going to make love to her. His face was darkly sensual, the pupils of his eyes glittering in the evening light.

'You go in first. I'll bring the bags.'

At reception, he dinged the bell impatiently. Carrie tried not to hop from one foot to the other while she waited. From the depths of a leather buttoned sofa, a woman in a smart dress peered disapprovingly over the rim of a G and T. An old guy in a blazer was leering at her round a newspaper.

'Twin or double?' asked the receptionist.

'Double,' said Matt without hesitation.

As the receptionist turned to find a key, Carrie felt Matt's hand on her bottom and heard him whisper: 'I'm glad you crashed Dolly. There was no way we were having our first shag in a camper van.'

'I didn't crash her. You made me do it,' teased Carrie, almost bursting with anticipation.

'Are you going to start an argument, Caroline?'

She giggled. 'If I do, what are you going to do about it?'

'You'll find out soon enough,' said Matt cheerfully, smacking her bottom.

'Oh!'

The old man buried himself in his newspaper and the woman tutted audibly. The receptionist turned round, the glint in his eye showing that he'd heard everything. 'Your keys, sir,' he said to Matt. 'I hope you have an enjoyable stay.' He then beckoned Matt to come closer and muttered something in his ear, while glancing meaningfully at Carrie.

'I feel like Julia Roberts in *Pretty Woman*,' whispered Carrie as Matt led the way up the oak staircase to the bedrooms.

'What do you mean?'

'I'm hardly dressed as lady of the manor.'

'You look sexy as hell to me.'

'I don't think Hartland Manor does sexy as hell. I feel like a tart.'

'God, I do hope so,' said Matt, quickening his step and tugging her along the corridor by the hand. They stopped in front of a door at the far end and Matt pushed the key into the lock. He must have heard her tiny gasp of surprise.

'Sorry, but needs must,' he said, jiggling the key. 'They were full. It was all they had left.'

'I suppose it's ironic,' she murmured, tearing her eyes from the brass plaque next to the door that declared 'Bridal Suite'.

Inside, the room more than lived up to expectations. It was a country-house fantasy complete with high-backed chesterfield sofa and totally clichéd (and totally wonderful) four-poster bed draped with chintzy fabric.

Matt was amused. 'Hmm. The Manor's clearly a hotel of the old school. Do you want me to carry you over the threshold?' he asked.

The way her legs were wobbling, Carrie reckoned it

wouldn't have been a bad idea, but she couldn't resist saying, 'I wouldn't want you to get a hernia.'

He gave a laugh. 'I suppose I deserved that. Now I don't know about you, but I can't wait much longer.'

She didn't know how she'd waited this long either; not just a few hours, but weeks. He was dark and sexy and arrogant and infuriating and she couldn't wait to get him into bed. Her hands were shaking as she started to undress him. She forbade him to help and he didn't object, holding up his arms as she pulled off his top, sucking in his stomach as she ran her tongue over his bare chest, teasing him, wanting to savour him yet painfully impatient. Wound up like a spring inside, yet feeling a delicious languor, a need to linger over every muscle, every inch of skin.

She sank to the floor, the carpet velvet soft under her knees. Flipping open the metal button of his jeans, she unzipped them, loving the way he tilted his head back and parted his lips in pleasure. She felt powerful, yet fragile. She tugged his trousers and boxer shorts over his hips to his knees. He was very hard and very big and right in front of her face. Closing her eyes, she kissed him, reverently, delicately. Lola was so right, but for different reasons. He really *was* beautiful.

'Stop,' he groaned.

'Don't you like it?'

He shook his head, seemed unable to find the words, then said, 'Too much. Way too much.'

Reaching down, he helped her to her feet and kicked off his trousers and underwear. He pulled off her T-shirt, his hands warm as they explored the bare skin of her back. He unhooked the front fastening of her bra, freeing

254

her breasts before slipping the bra off her shoulders. He dealt with her shorts and knickers just as swiftly and they fell on to the bed. If their first time was too eager and hurried, she didn't care. They had plenty of time for slow and delicious, for exploring and discovering, and a whole big bed to do it in.

# Chapter Thirty-nine

The next morning, Matt was sprawled on the chesterfield stark naked save for the hotel guide covering his lap. He was reading it out in a voice like an old-fashioned TV announcer.

' "Hartland Manor offers discerning visitors an exclusive experience in stunning surroundings." Well, that one's true. I've definitely had an exclusive experience.'

Carrie was rubbing her hair dry with a fluffy towel. She'd hardly had much sleep, but she felt cleaner and more refreshed than she had done for months. She scrunched up her toes around the thick pile of the carpet. After living in a camper van for almost a month, she knew she could easily develop a fetish for soft furnishings.

Matt flipped over a page dramatically. 'Ah. Here's the menu. Would madam prefer the Traditional English or the Continental? And do you want your eggs poached, fried or boiled?'

'Do we have to have anything at all?' she said, unable to take her eyes off his body. Even though she'd seen him in shorts, the sight of him completely naked was driving her wild with lust.

He gave her a disapproving look. 'I hope that's not a hint that madam would like to corrupt me again.'

Kneeling between his thighs, she relieved him of the guidebook. 'You seem beyond redemption already.'

Sex for breakfast was all very well, but eventually you needed real food too, so they decided to take Morning Coffee in the Grounds. They chose a table perched on a small terrace overlooking the sea, which this morning was indigo and topped with white caps.

A waiter bearing a tray laden with silverware approached them across a sloping lawn. It seemed churlish to giggle, so they waited with equal solemnity to be served.

'Room number?' he asked, after unloading the contents of the tray with great ceremony.

'Not sure,' said Matt.

'The Bridal Suite,' said Carrie.

The waiter's lips twitched imperceptibly. 'Congratulations.'

'Thank you,' said Matt, in an exaggerated public school accent. When the waiter had gone, he turned to Carrie and said, 'Shall I pour? Would madam care for a ginger nut?'

'Gav the fireman was right. You really are a posh git,' she laughed, as coffee dribbled on to the tabletop.

'I'll overlook that. Cream?'

'Lashings, please. I have to get my strength up.'

She watched him swirl the thick cream into her coffee. 'You know, I could almost get used to this,' she said.

Matt was experimenting to see if he could get a whole ginger nut in his mouth at once, so he took a while to reply. 'It is addictive.'

'That's because you know it's going to end,' she said. She gazed out at the view. Sooner or later they would both have to go back to reality. She'd be in Packley, and Matt would be working on the other side of the world, but at the moment, contemplating the future was like trying to see what lay over the horizon: she knew it was there, but couldn't quite see it.

Matt wrinkled his nose at the remaining biscuits before choosing a shortcake ring iced in lurid pink. 'Bloody hell. I haven't had these for years. We both loved them when we were kids but Mum wouldn't have them in the house. She said it was all the E numbers, but I think it's because you could only get them in Tesco, not Waitrose. When we were young, Rob swore that when he left home he'd live on the things.'

'And did he?'

'Of course not. He lived on beer, kebabs and whatever his current girlfriend could be persuaded to cook for him. My brother may be a brilliant surgeon but he's a stranger to a kitchen knife.'

'Do you think he has a real drink problem?' asked Carrie, wanting to encourage him to talk about Rob.

'I don't think. I *know* he has a problem.'

'And you've asked him to get some help?'

'No way. He'd love that. He tries to provoke me into it all the time so he can call me a sanctimonious, do-gooding twat.'

'Maybe he's just worried about you,' she said limply. And you're desperately worried about him, she might have added, but guessed it was pointless to voice her opinion out loud.

'Robert will sort himself out when he wants to. He'll

just decide one day and swan off and get some help. I've given up trying to understand him. We're totally different people. Sometimes I wonder if Mum wasn't having it off with the milkman instead of Dad. We can't both be his.'

Carrie thought that actually they were more like two halves of the same person, but she said nothing. His voice cut through her thoughts. 'Are you still hungry?'

'No,' said Carrie, hastily swallowing the remains of a custard cream.

'Then let's go back to bed and get our money's worth out of the Bridal Suite.'

They stayed in their room until it was time, according to the hotel guide, for Manager's Cocktails to be served on the terrace. After more sex, Carrie emerged from the bathroom for the second time that day. A cloud of scented steam trailed after her; she'd used all of the complimentary Molton Brown toiletries, just because she could. Later, after a very nice dinner overlooking the sea, she lay awake listening to the sound of the sea. Dawn was stealing in through the windows. Matt had insisted on leaving the curtains open and making love to her on the sofa in the moonlight. She'd teased him about being an exhibitionist, but in truth, she'd loved being naked in full view of the windows and had secretly imagined that someone would wander past (maybe a sleepwalker or a poacher, she'd fantasised) and catch them shagging. She was lying on top of Matt, her breasts pressed against his back.

'I love your arse,' she whispered, shifting to sit astride him so she could kiss the small of his back.

His voice was muffled by the pillow. 'Yours is quite nice too.'

'Only *quite nice*?' She slapped his bottom playfully but a little too enthusiastically.

'It's a *very* nice arse,' he said loudly.

'Not good enough!' she laughed, whacking him again.

'Okay. It's the best arse in the world. I should write a bloody poem to it. Ow! I surrender!'

'Better.' Dipping her head, she kissed her way down his spine, then moved up his back, tracing the patterns with her tongue, leaving moisture glistening on his skin.

When Matt woke, Carrie's rhythmic breathing, the fluttering of her lashes on her cheek, told him she was sound asleep. Her wild hair rippled over the pillow. Her cheek was pressed against the sheet, and he knew that if he touched it, her skin would be deliciously soft and warm. Then she turned away from him with a soft moan and curled up, the curve of her spine and buttocks shimmering in the heat. He got out of bed and padded to the window to look out over the gardens to the sea. But this time, he wrapped a towel around his waist first. In the light of day, he wasn't as bold as he had been the night before.

He turned back to the bed and slipped under the sheets again, knowing he'd never get another chance to tell her how he felt. He said the words quietly, over the top of her head, as if that way it didn't really count.

'You must know I'm in love with you.'

She didn't move, but briefly he couldn't feel her breath on his chest. She didn't say anything, but he was already fiercely regretting his words. He wondered if he could laugh, say something like 'You know I adore you, darling' in a clipped voice like the actors in those black-and-white movies his mother loved so much. 'Are you happy, Caroline?' he could ask, and pretend he'd been acting, living out the outdated romantic fantasy of the Manor and its chintzy, cheesy Bridal Suite.

But he couldn't do that because he knew she'd realise. He was a crap actor, just like she'd told him.

'Matt . . .' she said softly.

It struck him how different she was now to the woman he'd sparred with at Huw's wedding. Then she'd been hurt and desperately trying to gain some control over what had happened to her. Now she was the one in control. 'Do you remember the freshers' disco when you started uni?' he said.

'Yes, I do. You and Huw were there, watching Rowena and me dancing. You do know we'd been warned about predatory men by the SU women's group?' she said.

'They were right to warn you. Huw and I were on the pull, checking out the new talent, and we saw you,' he said.

'Ah, but we were checking you out too.'

'And you decided on Huw?'

Matt knew she couldn't say anything to that because it was true, but he'd started now, so he was going to finish.

'I'm not that proud of this next bit,' he said, stroking her hair. 'But we both fancied you.'

'What about Rowena?'

'Rowena was . . . cute, but I'm afraid on this occasion it was you that we were both after. Huw just thought it was me being bloody minded. He swore that I didn't really want you; I just had to win because he wanted you too. Things got a bit heated and neither of us would back down, so . . .'

She propped herself up on one elbow. 'Don't stop now,' she said.

It was too late to stop anything now, he thought ruefully, so he carried on. 'We went to the gents' and decided to toss a coin to see who would have the privilege of trying to get you into bed.'

'You sexist buggers!' she said, sitting up and glaring at him. But it was a nice glare, he thought, because she didn't feel the same way and was going to let him down gently.

'Well, as you may have guessed, Huw won, but it should have been me, of course, and then . . .'

'Everything would have been different?' she said softly.

'No. I don't think so. I think everything would have been exactly the same. You'd have said no, Huw would have pulled you anyway, you'd still have lived with him and you'd still have split up. I'm not that deluded, Carrie.' Reaching up, he touched her cheek with his fingers. 'And I can see that even now, though we might have had some good times, had some amazing sex, you haven't changed your mind about me.'

She was silent, and he thought her body had stiffened slightly with tension. He could almost hear her mind whirring, wondering how to reply.

'You don't have to say anything. I'm not expecting you to explain or apologise for not feeling the same. But Carrie, I'm going away again soon, and let's be honest, I might not have had the chance to tell you this again. I suppose it was selfish, knowing how you must still feel about Huw, but I feel like being selfish,' he said.

*

Carrie lay with her head on Matt's chest, her heart thumping away, not knowing what to say. The past few months had been the scariest of her life and she'd survived – but this new twist was more than she could take. She'd loved Huw for ten whole years, and look where it had got her. She didn't know how to cope with Matt's feelings, so sudden and so strong. She'd wanted to make love to him and get closer to him; to know more about the real Matt, but hearing that he loved her was so much more than she'd ever expected, and she was overwhelmed.

'It's not selfish,' she whispered eventually. 'I'd have done the same, and you're wrong. I don't feel the same way about Huw, and I feel very differently about you from when we were at uni; differently from when we set off on this trip.'

She propped herself up to see his face and almost wished she hadn't. He was so gorgeous, his eyes full of tenderness.

'Matt, right now, the idea of getting into another relationship scares the hell out of me, especially one where we'd be separated by half the world. It's just not possible. Even you can see that.'

He said nothing, and then threw back his head and laughed.

'What's so funny? Why are you laughing?'

'It's the irony of the whole situation. You being all sensible and stoic, telling *me* so politely not to be so bloody stupid. Who would have thought it back then at the church, when I practically had to drag you away?'

*

After they'd made love, Carrie tried to remember the exact moment when she'd fallen so hard for him. Just like Elizabeth Bennet and Mr Darcy, she couldn't name the first hour or day when it had happened, it had been coming on so gradually. Maybe it had started when he'd kissed her in the alley, or when he'd taken her away from Spike to the theatre; maybe before then ... when he'd told her off on the motorway, she thought with a smile, or even when he'd berated her at the church and tried to stop her wrecking the flowers. He did it because he cared for me, she whispered, then held her breath.

'What ...' murmured Matt, still recovering from his climax.

'Nothing. It doesn't matter.'

She could never tell him. It was impossible. He was going half a world away, but it might as well have been to the moon. She was going to start a new life. She wasn't prepared to give up her new-found freedom for a man; he would certainly never give up being a doctor for her. It was so much easier if she didn't tell him she loved him so much there was a physical pain in her chest. That just seeing him lying beside her, unshaven, sleepy and naked, made her ache in every bone. It was so much easier for both of them if they just went their separate ways.

# *Chapter Forty*

Carrie took a deep breath before she punched Rowena's number into her phone. She was sitting on the bench in the hotel grounds while Matt finished packing their things away in the camper van. Harvey had delivered Dolly that morning, pristine and perfect again.

'Hello. Rowena Kincaid speaking.'

'It's me.'

'Hi, hon. What can I do for you?'

'I was just calling to tell you I'll be home later today. The weather's turned pants and I need to get ready for my course and Matt has some stuff he needs to do and I've run out of clean knickers and—'

'What's happened?' said Rowena suspiciously.

'Nothing. I told you. I've just had enough.'

'What about Matt?'

'He's fine about it. He wants to spend a few days in London with some of his colleagues. Then he's got some sort of medical and a meeting.'

Rowena went quiet, so Carrie filled the gap before she got the third degree. 'How's the glamorous world of the soap star?'

'Bloody hard work. Fourteen-hour days, most of it

sitting around, then there's the lines to learn. My face has erupted because of all the bloody make-up and I'm terrified of putting on weight. The Bitchy Hospital Administrator said I was looking buxom yesterday, the cow! And we're not even on the air yet. God knows what will happen when the series starts being broadcast. I'll be a nervous wreck.'

'Why don't you pack it in, then?' said Carrie mischievously.

'Pack it in? Are you mad? I love it!'

There was a sudden clatter down the phone, followed by gasping sounds.

'Rowena?'

'Oh. My. God.'

'What's going on?'

'I just died and went to heaven, that's what. You are not going to believe this. It's surreal. It's incredible. It's—'

'Just tell me!'

'The love god himself, David Tennant, just came on to the set. On a trolley! Hon, I have to go. They might want me to cut his clothes off or give him a bed bath. Phone me later when you get back.'

Carrie clicked off the phone and laid it on the stone bench. Rowena wouldn't understand why she had turned down the chance to be loved by Matt. Rowena didn't make life complicated; she knew what she wanted and she went for it.

Carrie and Matt managed the journey home to Oxfordshire in a civilised fashion by Carrie pretending to be asleep and Matt paying close attention to a football match on Radio Five Live. For Carrie, telling Nelson about the accident was nothing compared to the misery of parting from Matt, but the time had come to face both.

'Do you think he'll notice?' she asked as Dolly came to a halt, almost with a sigh of relief, at Nelson's lock-up garage.

Matt turned off Dolly's engine, staring out of the split screen. 'There's no need to say what happened. I'll tell him I did it.'

Carrie shook her head. 'No you won't. I'll face the music.'

He held out his hand to her and she wanted to die with longing right there and then. 'We'll do it together.'

# Chapter Forty-one

A week after Matt had flown back to Tuman, Carrie found herself knocking on the door of Packley farmhouse. It was October now, and she'd started her teaching course at the local college a few weeks before, with a mix of terror and excitement she hadn't experienced since leaving home for university.

She'd also decided to sort things out with Huw.

She tried hard to ignore the tub of wilting geraniums by the farmhouse door that looked as though they hadn't been watered for ages. She knew the door wasn't locked, but she was no longer in a position to walk straight in. It wasn't her home.

It was Fenella who opened the door. In fact, she didn't so much open it as almost wrench it off its hinges. She didn't even glance up as she tried to manoeuvre a trolley case out of the door. The wheel had got caught between an old wellington boot and the head of a broom.

'Fucking hell. This place is worse than a midden. Here, take this,' said Fenella. 'And I've got another bag here. Hold on. Bugger, the strap's snapped. Jesus, I've only got half an hour to get my train to Heathrow. My God. It's *you*.'

'Yes.'

Fenella gaped at Carrie as if she was an alien with purple tentacles. Carrie glared back at Fenella as if she was a scorpion she'd found in her wellies. So much for Huw's promise that Fenella would be out when she called, she thought.

'I thought you were the cab driver,' said Fenella.

Carrie was determined to rein in her temper and show Fenella that she at least had some dignity. 'No. But there's one just turning into the drive.'

'Thank God for that! He'd better get me to the station on time or I want my fare back. I suppose you've come to see Huw about the money.'

'Do you want a hand?' Carrie said icily. Offering help to the woman who'd taken Huw from her would once have been unthinkable but now was nothing more than politeness. Besides, Fenella was on her way *out* of the farmhouse.

'No, thank you very much. Huw should have been here to see me off but he's in the bloody milking parlour again. One of his precious cows is ill or mad or something. You'll have to find him yourself if you can track him down.' Fenella tossed her head and her glossy black ponytail quivered. 'You can do one thing for me. Tell him I'll be back in three weeks' time and to get that bloody cleaning woman from the village in by the time I get home, or there'll be hell to pay.'

Carrie had no intention of doing Fenella's dirty work. An answer didn't seem to be required, as Fenella was already teetering her way across the yard, tugging her trolley case and cursing at the various kinds of muck littering the ground. A blob of manure and straw was stuck to one heel, there was a ladder in her tights and the hem of her suit was coming down at the back. She was also slim as a rail, and certainly didn't look pregnant.

The cab drew up and the driver opened the door.

'About bloody time!' Fenella exclaimed, but the driver just shrugged in a world-weary fashion, as if he'd seen and heard it all before. He heaved himself out of the door and sauntered over to collect her trolley case and laptop. As he loaded them into the car, Fenella turned suddenly and said unexpectedly, 'We didn't mean for this to happen, you know.'

Carrie bit back an expletive. She knew that any overreaction would give Fenella a satisfaction she didn't deserve. 'Neither did I,' she said neutrally, 'but it has happened and I've moved on.'

Fenella shrugged and stepped into the car, but as the engine started, the electric window slid down and she called, 'You must hate my guts.'

'What guts?' said Carrie as the taxi pulled away. Fenella hadn't heard her, but she didn't care. She carried on walking across the yard, knowing exactly where to find Huw. Sure enough, he was in the loose yard with Sam the cowman and Trish Harrington the vet. Carrie even recognised the cow, standing with its head hung, lowing miserably. 'Bluebell?'

Huw glanced up in surprise.

She patted Bluebell on the rump. 'Milk fever?' she asked.

'Yes, poor old girl, but she'll soon be back on her feet now Trish has given her some calcium.'

'I'll be going then,' said the vet, picking up her bag.

'Thanks, Trish,' said Huw.

'No problem. Call us if she doesn't improve.' She smiled broadly at Carrie, her eyes telegraphing so much with one expression: sympathy, anger at what had happened, pleasure at seeing her. 'Hello, Carrie. Nice to see you.'

'Hello, Trish. How's business?'

'Always good at Packley Farm.'

Sam only managed a grunted hello but then surprised Carrie with a wink, which almost made her breath catch in her throat. She suddenly wondered if she'd missed the farm, its people and even the cows as much as she'd missed Huw. The end of their relationship had shattered so much of her life beyond just the two of them. All of it had had to be rebuilt and Matt had helped her do it, but she still felt she could never stake all she had on one person again.

'I'll look after Bluebell now, boss,' said Sam.

Huw wiped his forehead with a mucky hand. 'Thanks. You can get off home afterwards. You've been here long enough today.'

After Trish had loaded her kit into her Volvo and driven away, Carrie followed Huw out of the sheds and back into the yard. The fields were shining in the late afternoon sun, light reflecting off the wet grass and puddles.

'Can we talk out here for a bit? I'd like to see the girls again,' she said.

Pleasure filled Huw's eyes. He looked tired and harassed, but then he often had. The farm was a big responsibility; Carrie didn't want to kid herself he'd been ground down by Fenella. That would have been too neat, and she wasn't sure she really cared any more. As they stood by the gate to the field, she remembered Fenella's message. 'I just caught Fenella on her way out . . .'

'Shit.'

'Huw. It's okay. We didn't start rolling around in the farmyard, scratching each other's eyes out.'

'I wouldn't blame you if you did. She should have left half an hour ago. I expect she'll be hopping mad. Carrie, I'm really sorry about the way things happened.'

'You've apologised before and it didn't work. It doesn't matter any more. I came here to talk about the future like you asked me to. That's what I want to focus on now.'

The cows began to plod towards the gate, seeing familiar faces. 'They're as nosy as ever,' said Carrie.

'That's because they know you.'

'Maybe.'

They leaned on the gate, watching the herd in silence for a time, before Huw said, 'Fenella's gone to New York for a couple of weeks.'

'She told me three,' said Carrie.

He frowned. 'Oh. Yes, three. She's got some important meetings out there. Her business is doing well.'

Reaching over the bars of the gate, Carrie stroked Millicent's rough muzzle and was rewarded with a wet tongue around her fingers. She laughed. 'Thanks a lot, Millie.'

'You'd better come into the house and wash your hands,' said Huw. 'Fen would be screaming for the disinfectant by now. Not that she doesn't like the cows; it's just not what she's been brought up with.'

'You can hardly blame her, Huw. A farmer's life isn't for everyone.' Carrie couldn't believe she was defending Fenella, but she didn't want Huw to think she was implying he'd made the wrong choice. Which he had, of course, but . . .

'It's certainly not Fen's cup of tea, but she's got her own plans. I don't expect I'll be seeing much of her over the next year, she's so busy.'

Carrie was desperate to ask if Fenella was pregnant, but she thought she had her answer already. And while Fenella had been harassed, she didn't look like a woman suffering from morning sickness.

'Come up to the house. I need a drink,' said Huw.

He ushered her into the kitchen. The grate was empty even though it was a cool October evening. The kitchen table was almost invisible beneath piles of crockery, newspapers, letters, cat food tins and Macavity himself, who was staring with interest at Carrie but couldn't be arsed to move.

'Mac's put on weight,' she said.

'He's an idle sod. The barns are overrun with bloody mice and Fen feeds him too many treats. Probably why he worships her.'

You traitor, she said silently to the cat. 'Can we get this business sorted out?'

'Of course. Mind if I have a beer?'

Reaching into the fridge, Huw took out a can of Guinness and one of 7 Up.

She smiled as he handed it to her, but he pulled an awkward face.

'Sorry, I should have asked you what you wanted. We've got some Coke too, and some of that fancy herbal tea.'

'I still like 7 Up. I haven't had a complete makeover,' she said. 'I'm still the same person.'

'Not quite, I think,' he said softly.

'Cheers,' said Carrie, raising the can and smiling far more brightly than she felt.

For the next hour, the talk was of practicalities. The situation was complicated because Carrie's name wasn't on the deeds to the farm or the house – they'd never got round to it, one of the many assumptions they'd made about their relationship. Huw had spoken to the family solicitor, and they'd agreed that Carrie would have an equitable interest in the house and that Huw would buy her out. Packley Farm was worth a substantial sum, and her share, though not great, would be enough to put down a decent deposit on a flat or buy into the cottage with Rowena, who was now living in London most of the time.

'What will Fenella think?' Carrie asked Huw, more curious than actually caring.

'She'll do as I say,' said Huw grimly. 'We'll arrange to see the solicitor together next week and get everything drawn up and finalised. Shall we have a proper drink on it?'

He fetched a bottle of malt, poured her a small one and a large one for himself, and clinked her glass.

'To the future.'

'Yes. The future,' said Carrie.

Was it the evening light in the farmhouse, or was his face a little redder?

'Carrie. This is none of my business and you can tell me to piss off if you want, but I heard that you and Matt Landor had been off together in a caravan.'

Carrie smiled. 'It wasn't a caravan. It was a VW camper van. A 1967 splitty with a Canterbury Pitt conversion, to be precise. She's called Dolly.'

His face was a picture of confusion. 'It sounded like a

caravan to me. Whatever, you and Matt together, for a month . . .'

'Just over a month,' she said wickedly.

'So are you two an item?' said Huw.

His face was hard to read. Was he asking out of curiosity, or was he jealous?

'We're just friends,' she said, and it was true. They'd agreed to email each other, when Matt got the chance. It seemed so little after they'd shared so much. She dug her nails into her palm, steeling herself to get back to the business in hand. 'Huw, don't think I'm being rude, but can we get this finished? I've got an essay to write on Learning and Assessments.'

'Oh, right. Your course. I never thought of you as a teacher – not that I don't think you can do it. I'm sure you'll be great . . .'

She enjoyed seeing him squirm. 'Thanks.'

Later, they made their way through the discarded boots and farming journals to the door. As Carrie curled her fingers round the handle, Huw unexpectedly closed his hand around hers. His eyes were suspiciously bright, and for a moment she had a horrible feeling he was going to burst into tears. She had a lump in her throat, but she'd prepared herself for anything, especially to harden her heart in case he showed a glimmer of regret. How she'd longed for that at one time. How she'd dreamed of him asking her to come back to him. Yet now, as they stood together on the threshold of the farm, she felt only numb.

'Carrie. If things had been different . . .'

'But they *are* different. You chose a different person to share your life with and I've chosen a different way to live mine.'

275

'Well, I'm still cut up about the way things turned out. I never meant to hurt you, and I'm so sorry.'

She removed his hand gently and opened the door.

'Huw. Don't take this the wrong way, but I'm not sorry. And by the way, while I remember, Fenella wanted me to tell you to hire that bloody cleaning woman from the village or she'll give you hell when she gets back.'

# *Chapter Forty-two*

Carrie took a deep breath as she walked out of the washrooms of the village hall. Packley Drama Society was doing a production of *Oliver!* and this time she was in charge as director. It had been over a year since she'd said goodbye to Matt. Her life had changed beyond recognition in that year, but as Rowena would have said, the show had to go on.

A little boy tugged at her sleeve. 'Miss Brownhill! Miss Brownhill!'

'Daniel. Calm down. And you can call me Carrie out of school if you like. Everyone else does.' Daniel was one of the lads from her Year Seven class at the local high school, where she'd started her job as a teacher a few weeks before. He was also a talented little actor, which was why Carrie had given him the role of Oliver. Daniel was twisting his baker boy cap in his hands.

'But Miss Brownhill. When I run away from the workhouse, should I actually kick Mr Bumble in the shin or just pretend to?' he said.

'Well, you could do a bit of both,' said Carrie. She didn't like Mr Bumble very much and thought a small boy couldn't do him *too* much damage. Besides, she was the show's director; she could do what she liked.

As Daniel skipped off happily, Hayley popped up. 'Carrie, we've got a problem with the costumes. The serving wenches' outfits are here but they're too small,' she wailed.

'Boss, what do you want us to do with the scenery?'

'Hold on, hold on, one person at a time! I'm a director, not a miracle worker. Let's take five and you can ask me anything you want to. But one at a time!' she shouted as the questions started again.

Later, after the dress rehearsal had finished, Carrie sat on the steps at the back of the hall, taking in deep breaths of chilly autumn air. She remembered the February night she'd stood outside the Starlight Theatre with Rowena. This time, the Starlight had been booked by another theatre company and they'd had to settle for the village hall, but that was the least of the contrasts between then and now. Back then, the rest of Carrie's life had been mapped out as Huw's wife and business partner. Now she was a newly qualified teacher. With her share of the farm business, she'd bought a stake in the cottage and was paying part of the mortgage. With Rowena away so much, it was as good as owning her own place.

She could hardly believe how far she'd come since the day she'd tried to crash Huw's wedding, but if she'd thought that letting Matt go would sort out her feelings for him, she'd been wrong. Every time she logged into her Facebook account, she couldn't help her stomach fluttering with anticipation, and she'd caught herself fantasising about him more than once, even during a lesson.

She'd built up a picture of his life in Tuman from his

emails and photos. She knew the names of some of his patients and colleagues from his messages and pictures. She'd seen pictures of the villagers in their canoes and outside their huts. Earlier that evening she'd had another email. One that had sent her pulse sky-rocketing. She pulled it out of her jeans pocket and read it by the light of the hall windows, unable to believe what it said.

*Hi Carrie,*

*Sorry I've not emailed for weeks. I caught some-thing harmless (but not much fun) and this bloody internet connection is hopeless a lot of the time.*

*How are you? You must have started school by now and I wanted to wish you luck. Or should that be the kids? Poor little buggers – having Miss Brownhill as a teacher. Only joking. I know you'll make one hell of a teacher. I only wish I could be in your class. I'd love to see you frowning at me disapprovingly over a pair of half-moon specs, preferably wearing a mortar board and a very short skirt. Oops. Don't know what got into me there. Must be the heat.*

*I'm going to be out of touch for a while because a few of us are going off to one of the outlying villages to set up an outreach clinic. It's a bit of a hike – well, a bit of a flight; the only way to get out there is by Cessna – but it will be worth it. The last time loads of villagers turned out to welcome us and I had to shake every single person's hand and stayed with a local family in their wooden house. They made me feel so welcome – even shot a wild pig in my honour. You never did that for me.*

*Sorry. Must go. Someone says the generator
might pack up again and we've got more surgery to
fit in before sundown.*

*Btw, I've got some leave so I might be home for
a week or two at the end of this month.*

*Love*

*Matt x*

Carefully she folded up the email and replaced it in her
jeans pocket. Home. Matt was coming home. Only for a
week, but . . . She couldn't believe she was going to see
him again. She recalled the photo he'd attached to the
message, showing him in scrubs with a stethoscope round
his neck, just to prove he was a real doctor, he said. It was
no good, she thought; when he came home, she'd have to
tell him, no matter what the consequences. A year after
she'd last seen him, she was no closer to being cured of
loving him than she had been then.

A few days later, Carrie bounced into the village hall as if
she was on springs. It was the final dress rehearsal for
*Oliver!* and everyone in the cast was walking on hot coals,
but Carrie felt high as a kite.

'Evening, everyone!' she called.

'You look happy,' said Hayley.

Carrie unwound her scarf with a flourish. 'That's
because this show is going to be a huge success.'

'Do you really think so? Mr Bumble has a bruised
metatarsal and is refusing to work with young Daniel.
The costumes still don't fit properly, and the man who
lives next to the hall says can we keep the noise down or
he's going to complain to the council,' said Hayley.

'I'll talk to Mr Bumble, we can manage with the costumes, and as for the neighbour, if he wants to complain, tell him he can answer to me.'

Hayley's eyes widened. 'Wow. What's got into you?'

*A tall, dark, handsome doctor.* No, she couldn't say that. 'Nothing. I'm just being assertive,' she said, then clapped her hands loudly. 'Okay, guys. Let's go for it. Give me everything you've got. This *Oliver!* is going to be the best show we have ever done.'

She'd tried desperately hard not to get too excited by Matt's email – and failed miserably. Tonight, with the added adrenaline of the show pumping through her veins, she was fizzing like a shaken-up bottle of lemonade. The sparkle spilled over into the rest of the cast, and for once, everything ran like clockwork. In the interval, she was having a discussion with the musical director when Hayley bustled over, her bosom almost spilling out of her serving wench's bodice. Carrie made a mental note to ask the costume department to alter it before she had someone's eye out.

'There's a guy in the kitchen. Says his name is Dr Lancer or something,' Hayley said, jiggling about in an alarming way.

'What?'

It was only the end of October. It couldn't possibly be Matt.

'What does he look like?' Carrie asked, her mind whirling like a fairground waltzer.

Hayley shrugged. 'Tall, dark hair, a bit scary I suppose, like a very good-looking Bill Sykes, if you know what I mean. I almost asked him if he'd take part in our model contest. We're looking for guys for next year's Sweet Nothings calendar, though to be honest, it's not really his face we're interested in. Carrie?'

Carrie flew into the kitchen to find Rob Landor standing by the tea urn; a strange combination if ever she'd seen one. He looked so out of place in his sober suit, surrounded by people in top hats, crinolines and urchin outfits. She tried not to look as devastated as she felt; after all, Rob had only made the mistake of not being Matt.

'Hello. What brings you here? Are you that desperate for a ticket?' she asked cheerfully as he kissed her.

'Come over here and sit down,' he said, taking her arm. As soon as he touched her, she felt cold, as though someone had opened all the doors into the cold night.

'It's Matt, isn't it?'

Rob nodded. 'I'm afraid so. He's gone missing.'

# Chapter Forty-three

Carrie's stomach was swirling, her mouth tasted metallic, her legs were weak as water.

'How long ago?' she stammered.

'Over forty-eight hours. I got a call last night but I waited for an update from the medical charity before telling you. Apparently he set off in a light aircraft for some outpost,' said Rob.

'In the Cessna. He said in his last email.'

'Well, it seems the plane never arrived and no one could contact them on the radio, so the alarm was raised. The military have sent out a search-and-rescue aircraft from the capital but they've seen nothing so far.'

'But they'll keep looking, surely?'

'Oh yes. They'll keep looking,' said Rob, proceeding to tell her everything he knew, which was frustratingly little. Matt and the pilot had set off, they'd checked in halfway through the flight, and then – nothing. 'The rescue team will carry on searching while there's a chance.'

She saw his Adam's apple bob and knew he was lying. 'What about your mum?' she asked, thinking of what Mrs Landor was going through. If it was anything like how Carrie herself felt, she must be suffering.

'I don't think she believes it's really happened. She keeps asking me if the staff at the medical base are sure he got on the plane. I had to show her a photo of him boarding it before she'd believe me.'

'But we have to keep hoping,' Carrie said, horrified at the desperation in her voice.

He smiled softly. 'Yes. I suppose we do.'

She was vaguely aware of the cast and crew whispering round the tea urn.

'Let me get you a cup of tea,' said Rob.

She shook her head. 'No thanks, I need to get on with the show. Everyone's depending on me.'

'Yes. Of course. Maybe you should keep busy.'

You're the doctor, she thought, shouldn't you be telling me what to do? Then she realised that he didn't know.

'There'll probably be something on the news about it. It can't be long before the networks pick up the story, but I shouldn't take too much notice of what they say. I'll call you if I hear anything from the charity or the consulate out there.'

'Is that a promise?'

'Carrie. Whatever I hear, I promise I'll tell you. I'll wake you up in the middle of the night if I have to.'

'You won't have to wake me,' she said firmly.

'You can't stay awake for ever.'

Carrie was sure she could. 'Thanks for coming and telling me yourself. It would have been even worse if I'd heard it on the TV,' she said.

She walked with Rob to the back door of the village hall and saw him to his car, hardly knowing how she was going to carry on with the second half of the show. Or the rest of the night, the next few days . . . and beyond. She

284

shuddered with cold and fear as she watched his car turn into the street, the powerful engine shattering the quiet of the village. Frost was sparkling on the pavement, the sky was peppered with stars and she felt very very alone. She was so close to giving in, letting the catch in her throat turn into a sob that would open the floodgates, but there were dozens of people waiting for her to go back in and tell them what to do, where to stand, when to move.

In the hall, one or two people asked her if she was okay, but she shrugged off the sympathy and just said she'd had some bad news about an old friend but she'd be fine. But Hayley was hovering so anxiously that Carrie decided to tell her that Matt was missing and that Rob had come to give her the news.

'You should go home. You look awful. I could take over for tonight. I know it's not the same, but you don't have to do that stupid "the show must go on" thing. The cast wouldn't expect you to stay for them after what you've just heard,' said Hayley, showing a surprisingly practical side.

'I'm not staying for them. I'm staying for me,' said Carrie, touched.

'Well, do you want me to call Rowena?'

She lifted her chin. 'Rob already has, thanks. Now come on. Let's get through this second half. I'm seriously thinking of sacking Bill Sykes and giving the role to his bulldog.'

Rowena was getting out of a taxi at the cottage as Carrie arrived home, well after midnight.

'Is there any news?' she asked through a bear hug.

'No more than you already know,' said Carrie, hoping

she wouldn't blub on Rowena's new jacket.

Rowena pulled a bottle of brandy from her bag. 'I bought this for medicinal purposes. Got it from the Bargain Booze store opposite the station,' she said proudly.

At three a.m. they were both still wide awake, flicking between the news channels.

'You'll have to go to sleep sometime, Carrie. You've got school in the morning.'

'I'm not going to school.'

Rowena turned bolshie. 'Yes you are, madam.'

'No. I'm not. It's an INSET day.'

'What the hell's that?'

'A training day, except we do the training in the evenings so we get the day off with the kids.'

'You part-timers make me sick. I pay your salary, you know, and you just keep having time off. All those holidays . . .' said Rowena, attempting a joke.

Carrie hardly heard her. She was on Planet Worst-Case Scenario, imagining Matt lying in the wreckage of the plane, in pain, unconscious or worse. She thought back to the first of their many rows in the camper van and longed to be able to have a row with him now. She'd walk over hot coals to see him again, even at his patronising and infuriating best. Her voice came out as a whisper.

'Rowena . . .'

'Yes?'

'I love Matt.'

Putting down her brandy glass, Rowena crossed to Carrie's chair and held out her arms. 'Honey, I think I've worked that one out.'

*

It was almost light when she woke, cold and stiff on the tiny sofa, covered with a coat. Rowena was sitting watching TV with the sound turned down, halfway through a packet of chocolate digestives. After a few bleary moments, Carrie realised where she was.

'Has Rob phoned? Is there any more news? Why did you let me fall asleep?' she asked.

Rowena was channel-surfing. 'First, I didn't let you fall asleep. You were knackered. And no, there haven't been any calls. I'd have woken you up if there had been. There's been a report on Sky saying that a British doctor and a French pilot are missing, but they didn't give any names. I suppose there's a protocol about these things.'

Carrie sank back on the sofa. Surely the old proverb was true? No news had to be good news. 'I suppose you're right. Of course. Shouldn't you be back at the studio, Rowena?'

Rowena brushed crumbs off her lap. 'I have to be in make-up by twelve, so I'll leave for the station soon, but I'll make you some breakfast first.'

'I don't think I can eat anything.'

'Honey. Calm down. When Matt gets back he won't want to come home and find you've wasted away, will he?'

Rowena left, promising to come home again as soon as she could get away from the studio. Carrie's imagination was in overdrive, veering between desperation for the phone to ring and dread that it might. The only thing she could bear to do, bizarrely, was the laundry. By mid-morning, the once-overflowing basket was empty and the tumble dryer was ready to explode. The monotony of the whole process gave her a feeling of comfort and control and she began to feel almost optimistic. Even now, she thought, Matt might be in some military base, bruised and battered but safe, joking about having used up the last of his nine lives, smiling and picking up the phone to her . . .

She nearly dropped the iron when the doorbell rang, and flew into the hall, her heart hammering away like a road drill.

# Chapter Forty-four

A figure was half slumped in the porch and Carrie realised it was Natasha. She had dark circles under her eyes and her nose was puffy and raw, from crying presumably.

Aghast, Carrie helped her up. 'Are you all right?'

'Do I look all right, darling? I've been ringing this bell for about ten minutes but no one answered.'

'Sorry, I've had the washing machine on.'

'How terribly domestic. Are you going to let me in?' She wrinkled her nose. 'What's that terrible burning smell?'

Carrie let out a shriek. 'Oh bugger! It must be the iron!'

Her favourite T-shirt had a neat iron-shaped burn on the front. She threw it in the basket and went back into the sitting room.

'Distraction technique?' said Natasha, eyeing the piles of neatly folded clothes on the sofa and chairs.

'Something like that,' said Carrie.

'And is it working, darling?'

'Not really.'

Natasha perched on the sofa with a sigh. 'I should be

at work but I threw a sickie. I expect Fenella will think I've got a hangover or something, but I don't give a toss. Bryony can cover for me.'

'Do you want some coffee?' asked Carrie, not knowing what else to say.

Natasha pulled a face. 'Yuck. No. I've had gallons of the stuff. Have you heard any more news?'

Carrie shook her head. 'Not since Rob phoned me yesterday. Have you?'

Natasha kicked off her shoes, tucked her knees up and started hugging a cushion. Carrie's heart sank. She wasn't sure she could cope with Natasha's anxiety on top of her own. She wished she could get back to the ironing, then realised there was nothing left in the basket. 'Are you sure you don't want something to drink or eat?' she tried again.

'Absolutely. Do you mind very much if I stay for a while? I was going mad in my flat and I tried going shopping but didn't want to be away from the TV in case something happened. I can't stop thinking about him, dear Matt.' Natasha gave a huge sniff and Carrie handed over a box of tissues, pulling one out for herself just in case.

'Me neither,' admitted Carrie. 'I keep thinking that he'll walk in through the door, wondering why we're sitting here together like this.'

'I keep thinking of him lying mangled in the wreckage of the plane in that awful jungle,' wailed Natasha.

'Don't say that. You don't know he's dead or even hurt,' said Carrie, knowing it was the exact thing that filled her own mind.

'Oh, be realistic. Of course he's dead. Planes go down

over there all the time. Apparently, Rob said, there have been six accidents in the past eighteen months. The airstrips are just dirt tracks or mud baths and those light aircraft look totally decrepit.'

'Natasha. Stop it. Please.'

'Darling, I'm only preparing myself for the worst. I warned you not to get involved with Matt. I said you'd get hurt, but you wouldn't listen. You said you didn't care about him but I saw how you were together. No one could spend all their time with Matt and not fall in love with him.'

'But *you* haven't. You said so,' said Carrie, feeling angry.

'Haven't I? You're wrong, darling. Of course I'm in love with him. I have been since we were at school.'

After the past year, Carrie didn't think that anything could take her by surprise any more, but Natasha had just managed it. Even though she'd suspected that Natasha's feelings ran deeper, had almost sensed her desperation on the yacht, she hadn't expected this. Not the L word. Not so bluntly. She hadn't been able to disguise her shock and now Natasha was shaking her head.

'Don't look so amazed! You must have realised,' said Natasha, bright but very brittle. 'I could see how Matt felt about you, darling. Do you remember last summer when we all bumped into each other at the Trout?'

Carrie thought back to the sunlit evening when they'd shared a drink in the pub garden. It seemed like a scene from a movie, it was so long ago and far away, but seeing Natasha brought it to life again in vivid colour and detail.

'I remember.'

'Of course you do. How could you not? Matt couldn't

keep his eyes off you. He kept staring at you when he thought no one was looking. My God, he even ran after you with a handbag.' Carrie thought back to Matt, tall, dark, gorgeous and mortified at holding out her tiny bag. Her heart lurched with a maelstrom of emotions: longing, lust, agony, love.

Natasha laughed bitterly. 'He defended you all through dinner that night, you know, when we were talking about Huw marrying Fenella. He wouldn't hear a word against you, darling.'

There was no point denying her feelings now. 'I never asked for it to happen. I really didn't. I was horrified when I found out he was coming on holiday with me,' she said in a voice she thought was calm, but just came out small.

Natasha smiled. 'The gods love to throw their little obstacles in our way, don't they? Just to keep us on our toes. It was obvious to me that he was mad about you, darling, and . . .' She paused. 'You were in an absolute puddle of drool for him.'

'But I didn't know how you felt. I really thought you'd met someone else. Matt said you'd started seeing a guy from work,' said Carrie, thinking back to her conversation with Matt outside Hartland Manor and the look of relief on his face as he'd told her he'd ended things with Natasha. She closed her eyes briefly, feeling guilty and terribly sad for Natasha.

'I told him that story,' said Natasha. 'There *is* a guy at work. Several, in fact. You see, Carrie, I'll never be on my own, but as for leaving Matt for one of them . . .' She gave a little laugh that left Carrie feeling weighed down with despair; hers and Natasha's. 'No one will ever come close.

I tried on the yacht, you know. One last-ditch attempt to keep him with me . . .'

This was horrible. Carrie couldn't hold out any longer as Natasha ploughed on with her confession. She didn't want to hear it yet she owed it to Natasha to listen, now more than ever.

'On the *Prospero*, I knew that it was all over between us – not that there ever had been anything on Matt's side. You see, I don't think he suspected how I really felt about him. He'd have run a mile if he'd thought I wanted more; he'd never lead a woman on, not intentionally.'

'I know. I'm the last person on earth I thought he'd . . . he'd be interested in,' said Carrie, stopping just in time, a whisper from revealing Matt's true feelings for her.

'How ironic that I knew before you, darling. I could see that he was in love with you, and yet with me he was so nice, so polite, and so . . . so bloody far away. Disappearing off over the horizon, even then. So I decided to just let go. Give up.'

Horrified, Carrie saw the tears sliding down Natasha's face. Her mascara was running. She couldn't bear it.

'Please, Natasha, don't. If I start crying, I'll never stop,' she said quietly, feeling helpless to comfort her. Anyone else – Rowena, Hayley, even Nelson – she might have hugged, but she knew that Natasha would have shrunk away.

Natasha dug a tiny hanky out of her bag and dabbed her eyes. 'I warned you not to fall in love with him. I learned long ago that you rarely get what you want – and who you want – in life. You have to settle for what you can,' she said.

'I don't know what I'll do if he's dead,' said Carrie quietly.

'I know, darling, but you'll have to get over it, the way you have over Huw. We'll both survive somehow.' She stopped and patted Carrie's arm. 'What else can we do?'

# Chapter Forty-five

Natasha left mid-afternoon. Carrie felt as if she was going stir-crazy. She'd cleaned the bathroom, stripped the beds and washed and dried all the linen. The kitchen sink was sparkling and she'd even de-gunged the microwave, the most hated job in the cottage. *If only Matt would be safe*, she bargained, *I'll lick the floors clean with my tongue and I'll never complain.*

Rowena's eyes were like saucers when she saw the sitting room. 'My God. Is this the same house?'

'I had to do something,' said Carrie.

'You must have been feeling suicidal to do all this. Any news?'

Carrie shook her head and, glasses of brandy in hand, they sat down with the TV on silent. Rowena pulled a sheaf of papers from her bag.

'Do you mind reading through this script with me? I need to learn my lines by tomorrow.'

Carrie nodded. 'No. It will give me something to do.'

Acting helped for a while, but halfway through a crucial scene between Rowena and the Cocky Hospital Porter, the doorbell rang again, setting Carrie's heart clanging. Rowena answered, and she heard Rob's voice in the hall.

'It's bad news, isn't it?' she said as he walked in, grim faced.

'It's not good. They've called off the search.'

The realisation made her dizzy. 'They can't . . .'

Rob held her in his arms. 'Their resources are limited and I expect they've done their best. They can't keep looking for ever. It's such a vast area and difficult terrain, thousands of square miles of jungle and mountains. Planes have been lost and never found. There was an accident a few months ago and a couple of the passengers survived, but that was an exception.'

'You think he's dead, don't you?' she said, teary eyed, pushing him away.

He glanced at the screen, his lips pressed together.

'Say something. Anything. Just don't tell me you think that.'

'I don't know!' he shouted.

'I'll make a drink,' said Rowena, edging out of the room.

'Look, Carrie. I know you care about Matt, but I don't have all the answers,' Rob said, sitting next to her with his arm around her shoulders.

'I know,' she said, more calmly, realising there was no point in shouting at him. 'I'm grateful for you being honest, but I – I guess I just don't want to hear the truth.'

Rob drummed his fingers on the arm of the sofa. 'My God, I hope some woman weeps over me if I ever get lost in the bloody jungle,' he said bitterly. 'Typical Matt. Doesn't know how bloody lucky he is. I'm envious of him, you know. Have been since we were little. He always knows what he wants and he gets it. I still don't know what I really want.' He smiled gently at her expression. 'Carrie, you look amazed that I've made an admission like that.'

Carrie hesitated, then almost laughed at herself. What was the point in keeping Matt's secrets now he was gone? She smiled back and said, 'No, I'm not shocked. You see, the thing is, if Matt was here – if he ever comes back – he'd kill me for telling you this, but he's envious of you.'

'What? Of the money I earn, I expect?'

She shook her head. 'Not the money. It was while we were away together, he said something about how, though he hated to admit it, you were brilliant at what you do.'

He stared at her. 'And?'

'And?'

'Don't stop now, Carrie. I know Matt. He must have said more than that. God knows, he's got enough opinions for the rest of us put together. His view of me can't have been entirely rosy.'

She half wished she hadn't started. It wasn't her business, not even now that it didn't matter. She felt she was rushing in where angels feared to tread.

'I suppose he thinks I drink too much,' said Rob.

She decided to rush in whatever the consequences. 'Yes, he does, but he also said he'd never confront you about it because you'd love that and it would give you an excuse to call him a sanctimonious do-gooding twat.'

His face registered shock and disbelief, but almost immediately he started laughing. Big, loud belly-laughs that echoed round the cottage.

'He's right,' said Carrie boldly. 'You *do* drink too much, and he worries about you.'

He pulled his jacket from the chair. 'Correction. He *worried* about me, and you're both absolutely right, of course. I do drink far too much and that's what I'm going to go home and do now. Drink myself into total oblivion, if at all possible. Good night. If I ever wake up and do hear anything, I'll phone you.'

'That went well,' said Rowena, creeping into the lounge as Rob let himself out. Carrie was too shell-shocked to reply. She heard the roar of Rob's Porsche as he left. She didn't care that she'd upset him. She'd said what she thought was right and it hardly mattered now if she'd betrayed Matt's confidence. There was no point now in keeping secrets.

It was the middle of the night before she finally got out of bed and turned on her computer. Her Facebook page was waiting as usual, her inbox empty, even of junk mail. She started typing.

*Dear Matt,*
*I don't know if you'll ever get to read this message. Probably not. If you do see it I'll regret it and if you don't . . . well, I can't even bear to think about that right now. So I'm going to pretend, for my sake, that you will read it and you'll laugh or be embarrassed or send me a jokey email back. Something really insulting, patronising and rude would do. Anything would do.*

*Remember what you said to me in bed at cheesy Hartland Manor? That stuff about me knowing how you felt about me. Well, I thought I knew how I felt about you back then. You see, Matt, I really liked you – that's wrong: I really wanted to have sex with you and I really liked you too. I don't like you any more. Even fond is the wrong word. It's a horrible, meaningless word like you'd use to a pet or some- one who has a crush on you but you don't really want to ever see again. Fond sounds old fashioned, like something from the past that's dead and gone.*

*So if you still feel the same as you did a year ago, I want you to know that I can't bear to lose you. If you don't, I still can't bear to lose you.*

*Carrie x*

*PS I forgot to say it, didn't I? I love you, Matt.*

She didn't remember falling asleep. She only remembered curling up into a ball as the pain of losing Matt tore through her. She remembered crying until her eyes were raw and making extravagant promises to herself or any force that might exist on earth or elsewhere. She'd never be selfish again if Matt would come back; she'd happily dance at his wedding to Natasha or anyone on the planet if only he could be okay.

When she finally dozed, her dreams were violent and surreal. She dreamt she was falling out of a helicopter into the sea, where everyone could swim except her. Huw, Spike and Fenella were floating serenely as she went under.

'For God's sake, wake up. WAKE UP!'

Rowena was shaking her violently.

'They've found Matt. He's on the news now! Quick.'

Half falling down the cottage stairs, Carrie raced into the sitting room and sank to her knees in front of the TV. Matt's face was on the screen. It was an old picture, one she'd seen on Facebook, showing him sitting in a canoe with a friend. The reporter was talking over some aerial shots of the jungle and mountains in Tuman.

'British doctor Matt Landor and French pilot Tomas Montand arrived back at their medical base this morning after three days missing in the jungle of Tuman. An extensive search had only just been called off, but the authorities received a radio message from a remote village saying that the two men were safe. Their plane had suddenly lost power and hit trees as the pilot tried to land at a disused airstrip about forty kilometres from their destination. The director of the medical charity MF said it was miraculous that they survived the crash. The pilot is still in hospital at the base, but Dr Landor, who walked away with only minor injuries, spoke to us about his ordeal earlier this morning.'

'It's him!' shrieked Rowena.

'Shhh!' Carrie didn't want to miss a single second. Then he was there in the flesh, sitting at a table flanked by officials. His arm was in a sling and his face was cut and he had days' worth of beard, but he looked *wonderful*.

'If it wasn't for the villagers who found our plane and led us to their village, I almost certainly wouldn't be talking to you now,' he was saying. 'It was pure chance that they came across us and took us back to their homes. Then they had a two-day walk to the nearest village with radio communications. We can't thank them enough.'

Flashes started going off. Matt blinked.

'Dr Landor? Will you be staying in Tuman?' asked a reporter.

Matt frowned. 'Why wouldn't I be?'

'You haven't been put off your work here by this ordeal?'

'Of course not,' he said gruffly.

'Idiot,' hissed Rowena.

'How do your family feel?' another journalist was asking.

'I should imagine they're very relieved – and thoroughly pissed off with me too,' he said drily.

There was laughter from the press corps, but one of the officials frowned.

'Will there be an investigation into the crash? There seems to have been a spate of them in the past two years. Seven, isn't it?' a journalist asked.

'That's it, I'm afraid,' an official interrupted. 'If you want any further information . . .'

The screen cut back to the studio presenters and Carrie groaned. 'Bugger! Is that all we're going to get?'

'There'll probably be more later,' said Rowena. Her eyes were shining. 'I have never been so happy in my entire life. I told you they'd find him. I knew they would.'

Carrie was still kneeling on the floor, unable to stand up. 'But I didn't, and I never want to go through that again. Oh, there is some more.'

The screen showed Matt surrounded by people. One of them was a red-haired girl, who was kissing him.

'There was great relief and joy among staff at the medical base as they welcomed home Dr Matt Landor and pilot Tomas Montand, who have been missing in the jungle of Tuman for three days. One of Dr Landor's colleagues, Dr Shelly Cabot, said she was ecstatic to have him back safely,' said the reporter's voice. The screen showed Matt embracing the redhead, his hand stroking her hair tenderly.

The breath caught in Carrie's throat. She'd made a pact. She would never complain, never moan. She'd dance at his wedding – to *anyone*. She'd do anything if only he was found safe. She'd lied.

'She's probably just a friend,' said Rowena helpfully.

'I sent him an email . . .' said Carrie, as if she hadn't heard Rowena at all.

'What email? When, hon?'

She put her head in her hands and groaned. 'Last night. I told him how I felt. Everything. Now he'll know and it will all be for nothing.'

Rowena snorted. 'Crap. What you need is—'

'A good night's sleep?'

'I was thinking of a bottle of bubbly. Then you can tell me exactly what you wrote to Matt.'

Carrie lay back on the sofa and closed her eyes, feeling like a steamroller had run over her. There was a pop from the kitchen. Rowena was chattering excitedly. 'You know, I think I might suggest this story line to *HeartAche*. Only set in Scotland or somewhere closer with mountains and lots of trees. Maybe Epping Forest would do. Our budget's not that big.'

# Chapter Forty-six

Carrie heaved a huge sigh of relief as the curtain dropped on the final performance of *Oliver!*. Over the past five nights, lines had been forgotten, scenery had fallen over and Bill Sykes's dog had flopped down and licked his balls just when he should have been savaging his owner. But on the whole, the show had been, if not a triumph, really very good indeed.

'Miss Brownhill! Miss Brownhill!'

A small urchin was tugging her sleeve. 'Yes, Daniel.'

'Did you hear them clapping and cheering for me? And they booed Mr Bumble. They were standing up. Did you see them?'

'Yes. I saw them. You were brilliant, Daniel,' she said, but the Artful Dodger had already hauled him off to the dressing rooms.

Hayley, who had been playing the doomed Nancy, popped up beside her. 'Was I okay? I didn't think I died very well tonight,' she said anxiously.

'Dying's not easy, but you were brilliant. There wasn't a dry eye in the house,' Carrie reassured her.

'See you in the bar then?'

'You bet,' said Carrie, secretly longing to go home and

collapse with a whisky. Her nerves were in shreds after the drama of the past week, real and made up. Rowena, who had made it to the last night, dashed across the stage and threw her arms around Carrie.

'Hon! It was amazing. Well done!'

'Was it really okay? You're not just saying that to be kind?'

'Would I?'

'Yes, you would,' said Carrie.

Rowena laughed. 'I don't think you'll get nominated for an Olivier award, but I don't think you'll be slated by the *Oxford Mail* either. You all did brilliantly. Now relax and enjoy it.'

They made their way towards the bar. Kids were racing about, ripping off costumes and screaming at the tops of their voices. Add dozens of gushing mums and dads and the noise was deafening.

'I'm glad you could make it. I wasn't sure you'd be able to get out of London,' Carrie said to Rowena.

'I wouldn't have missed this for the world. I don't suppose Huw and Fenella are here?'

'You must be joking! But Lola showed up for the first night with a few friends. She's just started her course at one of the colleges in Oxford.'

They grabbed paper cups of white wine from a table. 'I had a good-luck card from Natasha, you know.'

Rowena blew out a breath. 'Bloody hell. Not laced with arsenic, was it?'

Carrie gave a shrug. She would never share Natasha's confession with Rowena or anyone. Certainly not Matt, if she ever saw him again. She and Natasha were never going to be friends, but she had a new respect for her; a bond that only the two of them shared.

'No arsenic. Just a message telling me to break a leg. She couldn't come to the play. She's on holiday in St Lucia with Bryony,' she told Rowena.

Rowena sipped her wine, pulled a face and then said, 'And have you heard from *him*?'

Carrie paused, her after-show euphoria gone. 'I got an email,' she said.

'And?'

She hesitated, her mouthful of wine tasting even worse than she'd expected. She could remember Matt's email word for word, mainly because it was so short. She was afraid she might burst into tears just repeating what he had said.

*Carrie,*
*You might have heard all the fuss on the telly.*
*Everyone was worrying for nothing – we were in*
*safe hands with the villagers. Sorry, I have to go*
*and do a debrief but I'll be in touch soon.*
*M x*

'He just said he'd contact me soon,' she said.

'Well, that sounds . . . promising.'

'Now you *are* being kind, Rowena.'

She didn't deny it this time. 'Didn't he say anything else at all?'

Carrie shook her head, knowing that even in her most deluded moments she couldn't construe Matt's email as anything other than a polite dismissal. 'Nothing. But there was enough between the lines to let me know I've made a fool of myself.'

'Oh Carrie. Sometimes I hate blokes. I really do.'

'But I thought you were happy with that ensemble guy from *Grease*?'

Rowena pulled a face. 'He's great in bed, but out of it, he's obsessed with himself. We're not going to end up selling our wedding photos to *OK!*. You know, sometimes I even miss Nelson.'

'But not enough to get back with him.'

'No. Nelson wants the whole commitment thing. Someone to trundle off into the sunset with, and he's found her, by the looks of it. He called me to say he's met someone else. I'm fine, Carrie. I'm not ready to settle down yet.'

'Me neither,' Carrie said, pasting on a grin. 'There's a whole world out there and it's full of men just waiting to be used and abused.'

'You should definitely stick to directing, hon. That was so unconvincing you wouldn't even get a walk-on part in *HeartAche*.'

An hour later, the after-show party was winding down. People were shrugging into their coats and carrying home bunches of flowers and mementoes of the show. A few stalwarts were gathering rubbish into bin bags. There was crashing and banging as scenery and props were packed away.

'We'd better get our sleeves rolled up or we'll be here for hours,' said Rowena.

It was after midnight by the time everything and almost everyone had made their way out of the village hall. Rowena roared off towards the cottage, her little sports car groaning with leftover food and booze. Only a couple of the older members of the cast remained. The man who'd played Fagin – a postman called Garth – was checking all the windows were closed.

Carrie was ready to drop with exhaustion but she pasted on a smile. 'Shall I stay and lock up?' she offered.

'No. You get on home. You look done in,' said Garth.

'I really ought to be last out,' she said, gritting her teeth.

'Like Captain Smith going down with the *Titanic*? Get off with you,' laughed Hilary, the props mistress, jangling the hall keys. 'Or we'll send Bill Sykes round to get you.'

Carrie nodded gratefully, hoisted her bag on to her shoulder and picked up a box of scripts. Rowena would be waiting at home with a fire, a glass of whisky and plenty of scurrilous gossip. The kind of evening they used to enjoy. It would be normal and ordinary and completely lacking in drama of any kind. It was, she told herself sternly, exactly the kind of evening she wanted and needed. Her arms full, she pushed open the outside door with her bottom and found herself falling headlong into the darkness.

# Chapter Forty-seven

'Carrie? Are you all right? Carrie, speak to me, for God's sake.'

She was lying in a puddle in the car park, sheets of paper fluttering down around her ears. She couldn't speak, mainly because she couldn't breathe. Crazy things were happening to her insides. Kneeling above her was Matt. She turned her head to look at him, wondering if she'd knocked herself out falling down the steps or was having a feverish hallucination that she'd banged right into him as she'd backed out of the hall door.

'Are you really here?' she said.

He smiled down at her. 'I may look like the Phantom of the Opera in this coat, but yes, I am here. Are you okay? Can you get up?'

His breath misted the frosty air and evaporated, but as she reached out and touched his arm and felt the rough wool of his overcoat, the hard muscle underneath, she knew she wasn't dreaming.

'You scared me to death. I thought you were a mugger,' she said as he helped her to sit up.

'No. Not a mugger. Hey. Slowly now. Do you want me to check you over?'

Carrie swallowed hard. Did she want Matt to check her over? Did the sun rise every morning?

'I–I think I'll be all right,' she said bravely. 'But can you ask me again in a minute?'

Matt laughed as he helped her up. 'Don't worry. I'll keep a close eye on you.'

On her feet, with his arm to steady her, she blinked at him. Over his T-shirt and jeans he was wearing a long black overcoat with a purple silk lining. His arm was still in a sling.

'You look . . . different,' she said, when what she really meant was heart-stoppingly gorgeous.

He frowned down at himself. 'This coat is a bit sinister. I borrowed it from the taxi driver who met me at the airport. Some guy had left it in his cab months ago and it was still in the boot. I think it's an old evening coat, but I was grateful. It's freezing here.'

She was dying to slip inside it and hold him. Then she remembered the TV picture of him tenderly embracing Dr Shelly. She still wasn't sure. She had to be sure before she let go, finally, and gave him everything.

'I heard you fractured your wrist. Does it hurt much?' she said, keeping a safe distance from the tempting shelter of his coat and all that lay underneath.

'Not much,' he said, then glanced at the papers on the tarmac. 'I guess I've missed the show, haven't I? I would have made it but my plane was delayed for three hours. I wanted to surprise you. Carrie . . .'

'Yes?'

'I got your email.'

Her heart looped the loop. 'Oh.'

'I presume you wrote it when you thought there was no danger of me seeing it?'

She nodded mutely, a whisper away from flinging herself into his arms.

'Well, as things turned out, I did read it, and I thought to myself: would she still write an email like that if there *was* a danger of me seeing it? If I were suddenly to be resurrected, shall we say, would she change her mind about what she said and run a million miles?' He looked at her tenderly, reaching out his fingers to touch her face. 'Carrie. Why do you think I'm here? I've come straight from Heathrow. I haven't even been to see my family. I wanted to see for myself how you feel about me. The last time we were together . . .'

She covered her face with her hands. 'I was still raw. I still needed to find out what I wanted in life. Well, now I know what I'm missing. I know how much I've already missed and what I might have lost. Last year, it wouldn't have been fair to you – or me – to start another relationship, and you were going away for so long, maybe for good.'

'What else was there to stay for?' he said gently.

'Oh Matt. I should have told you how I felt – how *much* I felt for you – but I was terrified. I'd only just split from Huw, and the thought of getting involved with you so soon after . . . I'd been so hurt, I couldn't risk it again. I saw you on that news report with one of the other doctors, snogging her,' she added quietly.

'Which doctor was that? I've snogged a lot of people lately. You should try being given up for dead. It's really great when you come back.'

'But not much fun for those of us who are left behind!' she burst out.

Matt shook his head gently. 'Carrie, if you mean Shelly, she's Tomas's fiancée. He's the pilot of the plane. I won't say I've been a monk while I've been away, but there's no one serious. Funnily enough, I didn't feel ready for settling down either.'

With his good arm, he pulled her towards him. She pushed her hands under his arms and around his back, hugging him as if she was never going to let him go.

'How long are you here for?' she asked after he'd kissed her so hard, her lips were tingling.

'A few weeks.'

She shook her head. He couldn't come back after all that had happened only to be snatched away again. 'I don't think I can do this, Matt. All this meeting and saying goodbye again. I thought I was strong now, but I feel battered and bruised.'

'Me too, my love. In every way. I've got to go back to Tuman to set up a training facility, but only for a month. After that, I'll be home again.'

'For how long?' asked Carrie, unable to keep the anguish out of her voice any longer. She couldn't *possibly* lose him again.

'For good.'

'Really?'

'Yes, Carrie. *Really*.'

She almost melted at the way he was looking at her; tenderly but slightly annoyed and so sexy she wanted to drag him off behind the bushes there and then. 'I've been offered a job based at the charity's London HQ. I'll still have to do quite a bit of travelling – I'd be away sometimes – but maybe that's good. Maybe we shouldn't spend so much time together. Not for the first year anyway,' he said with a definite twinkle.

'But will you be happy here?' she couldn't help asking, as he held her as tightly as a man could do with just one arm.

'With you, you mean? Oh, I think I can manage as long as you keep persuading me.'

She shut her eyes as she kissed him again, wondering if, when she opened them, she'd be back in the real world. But no. He was still holding her, looking tall and gorgeous and smelling faintly – yes – of mothballs.

'Can we get out of the cold? I'm freezing my nuts off,' he said.

Half-heartedly she gathered up the scattered papers and put the box in her car, while Matt called his mother and Rob to tell them he was safely home. When he'd finished, he turned to Carrie, staring at his phone.

'Well, bugger me.'

'What's the matter? It's not your mum, is it?' she said, wondering what had made him look so stunned.

'No. It's Rob. He's not at home. He's taken himself off to a rehab clinic in Switzerland and says he'll see me when he sees me.'

She thought back to her conversation with Rob, wondering whether to tell Matt about it.

'Well, that's good, isn't it?' she said, taking his hand.

'It's a start. I just never thought he would do it, but I'm glad he has.'

'You said you were cold. Shall I take you home?'

His face broke into a smile. 'Later, but for now I've had a better idea.'

'What?'

'Wait and see.'

A few minutes later, he was standing behind her with his hand over her eyes as she jigged impatiently. In the distance she heard the rumble of an ancient diesel engine. She didn't even have to look to know what the sound was. Sure enough, there was Dolly in all her tangerine glory, turning into the car park. Nelson jumped down from the driver's seat as a vintage VW Beetle arrived close behind and parked next to the van.

'You are joking,' Carrie said, starting to laugh.

Matt frowned. 'No.'

Nelson handed him the keys. 'Right. I want her back tomorrow night, and make sure you mind how you go on these roads. She's crap in the ice,' he warned. He got into the Beetle, his new girlfriend grinning behind the wheel.

Carrie stared at the van in disbelief. 'But it's practically the middle of the night! It's November. It's freezing. We can't just go off in a camper van.'

Matt treated her to his best disapproving frown. 'Why not? You love me, don't you?'

She wanted to cry again, but instead she told him face to face what she'd known for such a long time. 'Yes, I love you.'

He held the keys out to her. 'Then get in. I can't bloody drive, can I?'

She kissed his mouth softly and said, 'Matt. What on earth made you think I would ever have let you?'